Coming Home

Rebecca Caffery

SRL Publishing Ltd

www.srlpublishing.co.uk

SRL Publishing Ltd
Office 47396
PO Box 6945
London, W1A 6US

First published worldwide by SRL Publishing in 2021

ISBN: 978-191633739-8

1 3 5 7 9 10 8 6 4 2

For anyone who needs a redemption arc in their life

~ Chapter One ~
Isaac

It was nothing like Cherrington Academy. As I stepped into the tiny dorm room I'd be sharing with Ben Sharpe, there was a mere metre and a half that separated the two single beds. It wasn't the huge double room with large double beds I'd become accommodated to. I really should have listened to Logan when he said I should be doing all the research I could into life at University. Instead, I'd been more focused on the fact I wanted to move to Quebec and see a different side to Canada, as well as the fact I really liked the English Program they had to offer.

Not that that was a bad thing, I'd found the perfect course for me and I wasn't sure the University should actually matter. Maybe I'd been stupid in regard to that, but at least I could guarantee I was going to enjoy all the classes that were about to start. Whilst I hadn't researched the accommodation, I *had* researched the journalism club they had here and it was one of the best in Canada. As soon as I was settled into my dorm room I would try and get involved with the Bull and Bear as much as possible. Plus soccer team try-outs were right round the corner so that was something for me to look forward to. There had to be something.

"When do you think you're going to have your side of the room tidy?" Ben asked as I sat at the foot of my bed and researched try out dates and times. I surveyed my side and came to the conclusion I had absolutely no idea what he was talking about. I'd opened every box and unpacked all my suitcases. Yes, I hadn't figured out where it was all going to go yet, but I'd made a start. It was only the first day after all, I'd literally only been there a few hours.

"Soon." I tried to resist throwing the empty boxes at him, as I tucked my cases under my bed and placed the folded clothes in my chest of drawers. I was sure when we were both settled in we'd be able to get on a lot better than this.

"If you need any help, just let me know. I am actually considered a bit of an expert in tidying. I can have that desk looking like a great workspace before you know it."

My desk currently harboured one pot of pens, my laptop and a stack of notebooks I had ready to take to classes. How did he actually want me to organise them?

"Don't worry about it. I have it all under control," I replied as I rearranged the pens in the pot and straightened up my laptop. That was all I could do, right? How much more organised could this practically empty desk get?

"Well, I'll be here. Just ask." He had pinned some kind of note pad to his wall. Like ones you'd write on, but this was open faced. *Chess Club try-outs* was already scrawled across the blank pad. So not exactly someone I could see myself being friends with, but it was only one thing. There had to be more to him.

"Good to know. So, what do you study here?" Time to get those typical 'get to know you' questions out the way. Hopefully, it would break the ice between us.

"Biology. What about you?"

"English, thinking about maybe a minor in Cultural Studies or French, but let's see how my major goes first."

2

I chuckled, self-consciously. I'd earned my spot at this University, but that spot still felt a little inferior to a Science student. Even though my parents were proud that I'd gotten into McGill, especially with an academic scholarship, I knew they were worried about what I'd be doing with my degree after I graduated.

Me too, Mom and Dad, me too. That's why I was going to spread my craft out whilst I was here, still taking a poetry module, but also journalism and creative writing. I had to be able to make something out of that in the future.

"Awesome, so do you write like stories?" he asked, like that's all there was to an English degree.

"Something like that, yeah." This room wasn't big enough for me escape his judgmental eyes if I ever planned to write poetry in here. That was one of the best parts about my single room in twelfth grade at Cherrington Academy. Whilst my love for poetry was still hidden back then, I could write away till my heart was content in that room.

"I'm sure there will be a book club or something here, if you're looking for something to join," he said as he finished lining up his brand-new printer with the edge of his desk, before he turned to me and smiled. "Or if you're looking for work the library are probably hiring." He moved over to his closet and started to line up his colour coordinated clothes.

The conversation died and a thick air descended on the room like a fog that slit down the middle of our desks. Would it be rude of me to buy a partition to hang in between our sides of the room?

I silently unpacked the rest of my stuff and prayed that the other guys on our floor would be somewhat nicer. "I'm going to mingle." I'd spotted an open door just across from us, this was my chance.

3

Ben didn't reply. So I left and headed to the open door just two rooms down. "Hey," I grinned, as I looked over the muscular guy who'd pinned a basketball poster behind his bed. We could get on. "I'm Isaac, I live in room six."

"Nice to meet you." He smiled and sat up from where he'd been laid on his bed. "I'm Jack and apparently I'm quite lucky because this seems to be the only room on our floor that isn't shared. Not sure how I managed that," he shrugged. Literally, lucky him. He wouldn't have to suffer through all the awkward conversations and encounters I was about to undergo whilst I shared with Ben.

"I'm already regretting not paying that bit extra for the single," I replied. The rest of his room was pretty bare, very minimal, except his desk, it was littered with crap already. Biology textbooks and a huge PC, desktop and hard drive - not a laptop. He'd already gotten his course reading list and been to the bookstore. Wow.

He noticed me as I stared at the textbooks. "I'm a bit OCD. I like to be organised way before time, I bought those before I'd even unpacked a suitcase out of my car." He rubbed at his neck like that was something to be ashamed about. I half smiled at him, that was definitely something I could imagine Logan doing when he moved to University next year. He'd had more textbooks stacked up on his desk in first semester, than I'd seen in all of my four years at Cherrington Academy. I shook my head, not now.

"Hey, you do you, man. So, Raptors fan?" I gestured to the poster behind him.

"I guess, my dad's been taking me to games since I was a little, I don't really follow it. Still go to the games to fulfil the father/son time quota, keeps him happy and stops him thinking I'm not much of a man just because I'm gay." I let out the shakiest of breaths, that made me feel a lot more relaxed about this dorm thing.

With everything that had happened between me and Logan, I'd had to spend some time working out what that meant for me. I couldn't be gay, I still found girls attractive, I never had any problem being with October, I loved her. So, where did that leave me? Bisexual? I'd never had feelings about another boy other than Logan and I had had feelings for him no matter what anyone wanted to say about it. It definitely hadn't helped that our argument at Graduation had been so public, literally the whole graduating class, friends and family watched as I couldn't bring myself to tell him I loved him and how he'd erupted about it afterward. I hadn't come to a conclusion about who I was, but I had accepted I should be open to just going with the flow. Boys. Girls. Both. It didn't really matter.

"Well that sucks. What do you actually like that isn't basketball?" At Cherrington everyone saw me as the star soccer player, the trouble maker. Nobody saw past that and I think because of that I'd been pushed to keep being that soccer player who only caused trouble. It wasn't until Logan started bugging me about what was in the notebook that I kept tucked in my pocket at all times that I felt like I was comfortable enough to share. I didn't want anyone to feel that caged into one type of personality, having to do things they didn't want to do just to prove a certain picture of them to be correct.

"I like coding. It's what I do in my spare time, literally every moment." That hadn't been the answer I expected. Although, what did I actually want to hear?

"That's really cool. Why are you here for bio if you like computers? Couldn't you do like Computer Science or something?" I was sure something like that would be offered at a school this big. You could literally study anything here, there was like ten different course that revolved around English for me to choose from.

"I love Science as well. I guess I'm a bit of a nerd, you could say. Definitely not the sporty guy my father wants me to be." He laughed, bitterly, it made me want to cringe, that self-deprecation hurt. It wasn't healthy, I'd learned that being surrounded by it at Cherrington.

"You've gotta do what you love, innit? No point being something else if you aren't going to enjoy it," I replied, and I meant it. It's what I had to do for myself as well.

"You got that right." He smiled, as he sat himself down at his computer. I took that as my cue to leave. Not that I was sure where I was headed, I didn't exactly want to go and sit back in the atmosphere in my room. There were four other people still in the dorm I guess I could go and talk to one of them, but I'd felt a little defeated with how the first two had gone.

At Cherrington it had been easy, me and Charlie had bonded from the moment we'd first walked into that double room. It had been so chill, we'd talked for hours about all sorts of crap; soccer, being away from home for the first time, the pranks. I hadn't been worried about getting settled there, because from the first moment I'd had Charlie and then we added Joshua to that as quickly as Charlie had come along.

It didn't feel like it was going to be that easy here. That was a scary thought. I'd isolated myself so much over the last year, left myself with literally no friends when I walked away from the situation at Cherrington. Joshua stuck around, but part of me thought that was only because he knew I'd be completely on my own if he stopped talking to me.

6

I wanted to change that here. Build some new friendships, hopefully salvage a few of my old ones along the way. I hoped the distance between us all would heal the problems that had separated us.

Maybe I needed to rethink my approach to both of these situations. Up my game. I could bond with chess nerds or coders if it came down to it. I just needed classes to start and definitely a night out to feel a little bit more relaxed.

~ Chapter Two ~
Logan

"Brave face, here we go," I said to myself as I pulled into the Cherrington Academy driveway. Thank god I'd learned to drive over the summer and my parents had bought me a nice car, it made being on my own all summer so much easier. They'd labelled it a late birthday gift, but I knew it was out of guilt for the fact they wouldn't see me all summer, as they were away working in Thailand on a legal case. However, for some completely mad reason I'd then chosen to drive from Calgary to Cherrington at the end of the summer break. I'd crossed in and out of 5 different provinces just to get here, but with the money I'd saved from working at camp all summer and the savings I had from when my parents constantly topped up my bank account with guilt money, I'd turned it into a bit of a road trip. I'd stopped off in so many places to break up the thirty-six-hour drive, giving myself a night in every province I passed through. The detour I'd taken through Quebec had been hard. I wanted to see Montreal so badly, but I couldn't take the risk of bumping into *him*. Knowing my luck I'd probably have bumped into him enjoying Fresh week or hanging out with new friends, potential new partners. I wasn't ready to see that.

I'd stopped in Ottawa for a couple of days, Noah had shockingly offered to put me up and show me the capital. Although part of me definitely thought he was looking forward to the lift back to St-Catharine's, as his parents had told him he was now an adult and he'd have to take the bus back to school. I definitely couldn't imagine Noah getting on the bus.

"You really need to stop talking to yourself. You're going to freak all the freshmen out before they've even had a chance to get to know you," Noah drawled out as the car came to a halt outside our dorm and he checked himself out in my overhead mirror. He'd gotten a crazy tan from being in Cancun with his brother for two weeks before I'd met him and now it was this beautiful sun-kissed glow.

"Hardly ha. I'll have you know we still have two days before the new students move in. The only people here right now are me you and Julian."

"Wow, with you two as options to hang out with I have no idea how I will be spending my time." Like he was such a joy to spend time with.

I was ready to throw him out of my car at that point. "Well you can rule me out of that. The list of prefect duties I must do today is as long as my arm and I'm determined not to fuck up. I'm already stressed that I'm going to have Charlie watching over my every move as prefect, I can't mess this up."

"Charlie wasn't perfect, you know that you're going to mess up every now and then that's just life."

"Thanks for the reassurance," I laughed as I stood up out of the car and stretched. "I just don't want to let anyone down, you know?" After everything I'd done last year, I knew people would be watching me like a hawk. They had believed I could be a good prefect and now I had to prove it to them.

"You're going to be fine, Shields. Stop stressing," he replied as he grabbed his case from the trunk.

"How are you feeling?" I asked. Coming back here

9

for Noah must have been tough, throughout his three years of living here he'd been with Jessie, and now she was gone. Whilst he'd come back to live at Cherrington for the final semester of grade eleven, he'd been absent from a lot of classes and the school had given him extenuating circumstances so he still passed all of his classes and could move up to grade twelve.

"Good. Spending that week with Jessie's mom this summer was cathartic. Part of me still misses her every day, but she wouldn't want me to be miserable. She made that very clear to me before she passed that I should move on with my life when she was gone. I plan to honour that this year. Especially when you make me deputy prefect."

"Wishful thinking right there." I still hadn't made that decision. There were a couple of choices I needed to consider, the other being Charlie. I just wasn't sure how he'd react if I made him the Deputy to a position he'd served in for the last three years. "But, I'm glad you found a little bit of peace this summer." He'd done better than me at finding closure. After going to NYC I'd spent the whole summer working my ass into the ground to keep busy. An occupied mind meant no time to think about him.

"Still not spoken to Isaac?" he asked. I shook my head. I hadn't even managed to send him a text all summer. What would I say? *I forgive you for letting me fall for you, even though you didn't feel the same and then broke my heart the second after I told you I loved you.* Not exactly something you should say in a text. Although, it wasn't exactly something I wanted to ever have to say in person either.

"It's his loss, Lo. You know that right? You can do better than, Wells. Think I made that clear from the very beginning, when he was sneaking in and out of your bed whilst still with that poor girl."

"No need to say I told you so," I laughed, bitterly. "Although, no time for all this Isaac talk. I have a speech to write, a dorm to prepare and if you're serious about being my deputy I'm going to be putting you to work as soon as we are both unpacked." He laughed like it was a joke, but he was yet to see all my plans for the year.

I had not been kidding. We'd worked until the late hours of the night. I'd had this crazy idea of making *Welcome to Cherrington Academy* gift bags for all the new freshers who'd be joining us this year. Turned out Cherrington had admitted one hundred more ninth grade students this year, over fifty extra in our dorm than last year.

"I've put one in every room, literally on the pillow. You've already gone over the top and this is only your first proper day in charge," Noah said, as he stood and looked over the banister as the new ninth graders moved into their rooms.

"I think we did good, deputy," I said with a smile. Noah had worked hard over the last couple of days, proved he could be a good second in command. Not that that had been the only reason I'd made the choice. Noah needed to be occupied by something good, just as much as I did. It would be good to have him focused on doing good for others. It was a win-win for both of us.

"As did you, Cap'n." I laughed at him as he saluted at me. He'd been doing this Iron Man impression a lot since I'd been nominated as prefect, most people hadn't gotten it, but it turned out Noah liked Marvel/DC just as much as I did. We'd watched all the films over the summer and then watched Endgame together as the big finale. It had been all kinds of awesome.

"We should actually be down there right now helping them, before all the rest of the students rock up tomorrow." I pushed his shoulder from where he was lent on the banister. "Come on lazy, can't be slacking on the first day of the job."

"Charlie's down there though." He protested as he shrugged my hand off his shoulder and laughed as he caught how I glared at him. "Fine, I'll go help them carry some boxes, put the eight weeks I spent in the gym this summer to work."

"I best go break the news to Charlie that he isn't going to be deputy, I feel a bit bad that he's rocked up to help for nothing," I sighed as I followed him down the stairs.

"You know Charlie, he'll be fine about it. He'd have been here helping regardless of who was prefect, its built into him now." That was what worried me, I didn't want to be that guy who commanded that he was prefect now, but I didn't want Charlie trying to take over or have him interfere in what I was doing as prefect.

"Well it's now or never," I said as we approached him. "Go help the kids, I'll be back." He nodded at me and ventured off outside to where all the parents cars had pulled up to drop off their kids. "Hey, Charlie," I called, and he jogged over to me.

"What's up, Lo?" he said as he pulled me into a hug, this was the first time we'd seen each other since New York. We'd face-timed all summer, but after New York and saving for the road trip I'd been too broke to even consider a visit to Mississauga to see him.

"I just wanted to let you know, I've made Noah my deputy this year. It'll be easier for us to do it together as we share a room and can talk about it whenever, plus he needs something to fill his time now he doesn't have Jessie to go and see." All of that spilled out of me so fast I thought I was about to pass out. I tried to look at him

12

with reassuring eyes, I'd find something for him to do, he just wasn't going to be deputy, it wasn't like we hadn't already discussed some roles he could take on.

"You don't need to justify anything to me, Lo. I nominated you, because I knew you'd do a good job, including picking the best deputy for you and that's Noah. He's changed, we both know it. He's still Noah, just less defensive, less angry. He'll make a great deputy." He grinned at me, eyes soft with pride. "I'm going to finish helping this lot move in." He started to walk away, but before I knew he turned back. "You know Rafael Danetele?" I nodded. "He's just moved in next door to you, he's going to need a lot of your support."

I'd seen a couple of the local papers since I'd been back, he was top of my check list of people I was going to be looking in on over the next few days.

"Got it, don't worry. All under control," I replied, before I headed down the hall to start the check in process for the new students. I wanted every ninth-grade student settled in today so tomorrow, chaos day, would run smoother when every other grade student showed up. Plus, I had a welcome speech to write for the welcome back house meeting tomorrow evening.

The next day, Noah nodded at me as I stood in front of the hundreds of students that filled Edwards dormitory. He'd stayed up almost all night with me to help me write this speech. Even when I'd stuck the whole notebook in the bin, he'd retrieved it for me, yes he'd thrown it at my head, but it meant the speech was finished.

"It's good to be back at Cherrington Academy," I started and there was a chorus of cheers and whoops. "For the ninth graders who don't know, I transferred here part of the way through eleventh grade after being bullied at my old school in Calgary. This was my fresh start, a place to find myself and figure out what the future looked like for me. I hope for everyone who is new here this place becomes that kind of haven for you as well." I grinned out at the crowd of boys, I'd come up with so many ideas over the summer as to how this could be achieved. Starting with employability workshops, there needed to be more options for students and more resources to help us go to university. To other more personal things.

"Cherrington Academy and Edwards dormitory will be a safe space, for anyone in the LGBTQ+ community, for people of different racial, ethnic or religious backgrounds. If you're experiencing any problems in relation to this, my door is always open. If you don't feel comfortable talking to me, Julian Smythe our house head is also here to help. I can also vouch for how incredible the mental health team and wellbeing counsellors are here at Cherrington Academy. If you are struggling with anything from anxiety to depression or stress, speak to them, I promise it'll be the best thing you ever do."

My heart warmed a bit to see relief on some of the ninth graders faces. That was the goal here, I didn't want anybody to be scared when they came to reside in Edwards dormitory or feel they had to worry about anything, especially in regards to things that made them different. I said I wanted to do some good as prefect, to try and right all the wrongs I made last year, this was just the start of that.

"This year we are also introducing bystander training that will be led by three-time prefect Charlie Montgomery, as we are lucky enough to have him here with us for another year." Everyone clapped and even the new students, who looked a little confused about this, cheered for him, the atmosphere towards him was undeniable, he was loved here. I had a lot to live up to.

"For anyone who's interested about learning more about this, there will be a sign-up sheet on the common room notice board, a long side try out sheets for all the many clubs we have here. Not that I'm biased at all, but I'd definitely recommend joining the choir, it's an awesome club."

"And the soccer team," Noah called out.

"Well whilst we have his attention, that's your deputy prefect, Noah Castle, my roommate, he'll also be around if anyone needs to chat if I'm not here or I'm busy. Don't be afraid to pick his brain, he can't wait to get to know all the new students." A smug smile grazed my lips as he shook his head at me and laughed before he rolled his eyes.

"I'm not going to keep you all much longer, as I know there's still a tonne of unpacking to do. Just want to remind everyone of the code of conduct, there's one in your welcome pack to read, they need to be signed and handed in to Julian by the end of the day. Plus don't forget I'll be checking everyone's rooms tomorrow to make sure you are all unpacked and it's tidy - schools rules, not mine." I held my hands up in defence as people around me groaned, but it had to be done. It was all very well being Mr nice guy, but I saw the trouble Charlie got when he was firm, I couldn't imagine the amount I'd have if I didn't follow in his shoes.

"That's all, enjoy the weekend before classes start again on Monday. Oh and for those who haven't been made aware, I'm not going to be residing in the prefects room, I'm in room eight on the second floor with Noah, that's where you'll find me if you need me." I finished to a huge round of applause. It was wildly appreciated, this was a big role from me and I needed to make a good first impression as prefect, not only just to the ninth-grade kids, but to everyone who had heard the stories of what happened last year.

This was my chance to be redeemed here at Cherrington Academy. Noah hollered amongst the crowd and Charlie gleamed up at me from where he was sat at the front. I could do this.

~ Chapter Three ~
Isaac

I'd been here two weeks and I had already realised I was in the wrong dorm. Wrong for so many reasons. Wrong for the fact I definitely wasn't smart enough to be in this dorm. Yes I'd been offered an academic scholarship to come here, I wasn't ashamed of that, but the people in this dorm didn't want to do anything but study. I couldn't do that. As I walked past the other dorms closer to campus I could hear music blaring from the rooms, parties clearly went on there almost nightly, that hadn't happened here at all, not even in Frosh week. I didn't hate the kind of people who lived here, I just didn't want to be with them every moment of the day.

They also reminded me of Logan. Ben and his friends had been sat in our common room colour coding their schedules for hours the other day and damn I missed his stupid walls covered in timetables and to do lists. I just didn't want to make them myself.

Being in class had been better and with try-outs for soccer right around the corner I hoped that's where I'd potentially make some friends. It was weird without everyone around me. Even when the gang had fallen out towards the end of senior year at Cherrington, I still felt like I wasn't alone. I had so many friends back there, even acquaintances that I felt like I could talk to more than some people here. It wasn't that me and Ben didn't get on, we were civil in the room, it was hard not to be when we were just metres away from each other at all times in there. It just wasn't like how it had been when me and Charlie shared a room in our first year at Cherrington, or when me and Joshua had shared a room during our second and third years. There had hardly ever been a moment of silence, even when we were studying. In mine and Ben's room silence had almost become the norm. We'd have the typical conversation about our days and classes, but it wouldn't progress past that. We didn't hang out outside the dorm and after the first day we hadn't eaten many meals together in the canteen.

That had sealed it for me. I'd gone down to the residence life building and asked to move dorms. I'd heard it was an easy process and that most of the time you got moved to where you wanted to be and it really had been *that* easy. I'd walked in, asked to be moved to McConnell Hall, filled out a few forms and with a little bit of charm and persuasion I'd had it approved on the spot. Thankfully one of the guys in my poetics class that lived there had offered to help me move my stuff and between his car and mine we'd done it all in one fell swoop.

I now had a single room, with no colour coded walls or books organised in alphabetical order on a bookshelf that was definitely too big to fit in a tiny double dorm. It was small, but I'd take it.

"So you're the guy who's taking Aaron's room? Poor guy. Think we scared him off."

I turned around to see a girl standing in my door tugging her long, caramel hair up into a messy bun on the top of her head, blue eyes that flitted over me like she was trying to analyse me.

"I guess I am," I replied. "Scared him off how?" I asked, how could that have possibly happened in just the first two weeks of the semester. Although I guess I was a prime example of that, all the academics had scared me straight out of their dorm.

"Think he was looking for a quiet dorm, somewhere he could study 24/7. He already submitted two noise complaints to res life about us," she cackled. Like actually witch cackled. I could see why he was scared. Although, I couldn't complain. I wanted a louder, party dorm and that's what I was going to get from this place.

"Well, you don't have to worry about me complaining about the noise, trust me it'll be a blessing for me right now. I didn't go to any of the Frosh week parties, so I could do with a night out."

The way I'd envisioned life at University would be going out to the clubs and bars, actually not having to use a fake ID anymore now I was nineteen. Not having to worry about sneaking back in through a locked gate or being caught by my best friend. *Ex* best friend. I'd tried not to think about him over the summer, even as the pics from their trip to NYC went up all over Instagram, just the three of them. It sucked when we once were a four.

"That's good to know," she said with a wink, before she made herself comfortable on my half-made bed. "We are having a house party tonight, get a couple of drinks in before sports try-outs tomorrow. A couple of us girls are trying to get on the cheer-leading squad. Do you play?"

"Soccer," I nodded. "Try outs are 1PM, so at least I'll get some time to recover in the morning." I grinned, this is what I'd been looking for, what I'd yearned for when coming to college.

"You need to meet Alex, he's actually your next-door neighbour. He's trying out for the soccer team too. You'd get on well." She was now sprawled out on my bed, her head rested on my pillow as she played with the loose strands of hair that had fallen from her bun. How, when I'd just moved in here a few hours ago, did I already have some hot chick led on my bed?

It was then I realised I hadn't even gotten her name. "Sorry, I'm Isaac," I said as I folded a couple of shirts into my dresser, I hoped she'd catch on and give me her name too.

"Cassidy Roland." She smiled a beautiful pearly smile at me. She was gorgeous, incredibly full lips, beautiful blue eyes that when they shone they caught me off guard, images of Logan looking up at me with those baby blues fleeted through my head.

"Nice to meet you." She stood up from my bed and headed for the door. "So, you going to come and help us set up for this party?"

I nodded in reply. "I have a car, and I'm nineteen, I'll drive us to LCBO."

"Lead the way." She gestured for us to head out of the dorm and right now this was the best chance I was going to have at being involved. I'd take it.

"So, where are you from?" she asked as we pulled out of the dorm's car park and onto the road that led into the town centre.

"Originally from Hamilton but went to boarding school in St-Catharines for high school. What about you?"

"Ottawa, no fancy boarding school for me though, just a simple state school. Why boarding school?" she asked as she turned up the air con.

"Parents idea, thought I'd be more civilised or something? In reality I think they just sent me there because it had like an elite status and they were preppy about things like that. Don't get me wrong though, it was the best four years."

"Oh I can imagine, living permanently with all those girls must have made your dating life so much easier."

"Had a girlfriend for two and a half of those years, so I guess you could say that," I shrugged as I turned into the town and searched for a parking spot.

"You guys break up to go to Uni?"

"Not really, plus she was the year below me, so she still has another year there." I turned the music up in the hopes that she'd get the message and leave this conversation alone. Every car park I saw was rammed, at this rate we were going to end up parked outside of town.

"So what happened?" she pushed.

I sighed, but luckily then I spotted a parking space just metres from the liquor store and swung the car into the space. "I feel like I'm gonna get fined if I park here too long, so we should probably just grab some crates and leave," I answered as we both exited the car and headed for the store. "Are we doing beer or wine? Or mixture of both?"

"Was it that bad?" she asked as she stood in front of me blocking the path towards the aisles. We'd literally met less than an hour ago, why did I need to be spilling my tragic love life to her? Who gave her the confidence to ask all these questions?

"It was messy, that's all," I replied as I side stepped around her and into the store, I quickly grabbed a cart and headed for stacks of beer crates. "I think we just get a mixture, grab some cans and then we'll pick up a few bottles of wine. I'm sure everyone has their own spirits with them, I still have the litre of vodka I bought for Frosh week." That was never going to get drank when the only orientation activity Ben had been excited about was the 6AM lawn yoga.

"That's fine, we have a house shared payment thing, I'll add you to it and we'll pay on there." She stacked a few crates of beer into the cart and moved towards the wine isle. "Look, I know you're probably thinking I'm being nosy, but you seem like a really great guy and I wanna get to know you. That's not a crime, right?"

She was right and it as all I'd been looking for during the first couple of weeks at McGill. It was why I moved dorms in the first place because I wasn't getting it from Ben or any of the other guys on the floor. "Look, I don't want you to judge me within the first few hours of knowing me. I ain't a bad guy, I just fucked up a bit, I hurt her and I'm ashamed of that, but it's just more complicated than that."

"Did you cheat?" she asked as she plonked several bottles of white and rose into our cart.

"Yeah," I replied simply, not that it was that simple at all, but it was the truth.

"Like a fling or what?" She surveyed the contents of our cart, before she grabbed another bottle of white and looked at me intently.

"It wasn't just a fling, it was way more than that." I knew I'd messed up. I'd known it from the very start, almost the moment we'd locked eyes. It had disturbed me to my core, to be able to look into someone's eyes and have that direct connection with them. I saw things I'd never seen before in those baby blues; future, love, belief, faith. That should have been my cue to back away from him a bit, but I didn't. I'd pushed to help him unpack that first evening, I'd worked so hard to convince Joshua to no end a week later to allow Lo to come out with us to the club, because I'd literally have done anything to spend time with him. I'd paid an obscene amount of money that day to get that fake ID so quickly, it had been worth it.

"So the girl you had the affair with, is she still on the scene?"

This was where my sexuality completely conflicted me. There was nothing stopping me here from just saying no and not even acknowledging the fact that said person wasn't a *she*. If I wasn't sure where I laid on my sexuality, do I really need to discuss it with others? However, if I'd learned anything in the past year or so it was that honesty was the best policy. "It was actually a guy I cheated on her with."

"Oh," she said, and I froze on the spot. Stories that Logan had told me about the homophobic bullies at his old school flashed through my head, I wasn't even really out or even sure about my sexuality, I didn't have the energy to handle what he did. "So we can look at guys together then? Because I never say no to another wingman in the club." She giggled and internally I exhaled.

"I mean, you know what yeah, sure, why not." If University wasn't the time to explore these things, then when was?

"Awesome, because there is this guy I've had my eye on for the last few nights, we keep seeing him in every club or bar we go in. I'll point him out the next time I see him. Although, knowing my luck with men that'll probably be never again." She laughed at herself and I couldn't help but laugh with her, my love life sucked pretty hard right now, too.

"Got it, I wing man my friends for girls at home all the time, how hard can it be with boys?" I asked, rhetorically.

"So this guy? Where is he now?" she quizzed as she pushed the cart to the check out and pulled out the app on her phone she'd mentioned earlier so we could all joint pay for the alcohol.

"Back at my old school, he's in 12th grade now, so he will graduate this year," I replied as I packed the bottles into a wine carrier and the crates back into the cart so we could push them to my car.

"But things are also over between him?"

I nodded.

"Christ you really did have a busy final year at high school." We both chuckled, her more amused, me more bitter. She didn't know the half of it.

As we pulled back up to the dorm she'd already called a couple of our other housemates down to help us. "Alex." The tall blonde guy introduced himself to me as he took a crate of beer out of my hands. "Nice to meet you, Cassidy has been blowing up our group chat about you since you got here. She said you play soccer? Trials are tomorrow, you gonna come?" he asked, as we emptied out my trunk.

"I'll be there man," I grinned before I turned away from him to grab another crate of wine to hide how elated I was about this. This felt good, it had made the stress of the move just two weeks into school so worth it.

"Awesome, well we need to get all of this inside, people are coming over for pre's at 7. Plus Lizzy has bought this crazy shot game and I think I'm going to need someone with an actual brain to help me set it up." He grabbed at the game as we brought all the alcohol inside, it was like some weird version of shot roulette but a lot bigger and the parts all needed to be put together,

"I think we can manage that," I replied as I set the wine down on the table.

"Thank god, because this guy is an absolute idiot." A girl with crazy purple hair said as she pulled me into a hug. "Welcome to the mad house, Isaac," she chuckled. "I'm Lizzy, give me your number and I'll add you to mine, Cassidy's and Alex's group chat." My eyes went wide and I looked over her shoulder to see Alex giving me a thumbs up, so I tapped my number into her phone. "Perfect, stick with us and you'll be fine, the rest of the flat are great too, but we are the best."

I'd take that, I'd take anything over being sat alone in my dorm whilst everyone partied and my flat just studied. Alex handed me a beer and I sank into the couch. This was where I belonged.

~ Chapter Four ~
Logan

"If it isn't our wonderful leader," he started as I turned up to class two minutes late, not even turning to look at me as I perched on the stool beside him. He didn't for one second take his eyes of the lab equipment we needed for the next experiment. I'd done something a little crazy and asked to transfer to this Chemistry class and to be partnered with him for the year, so I'd finally have a chance to talk to him. It'd only taken a couple of weeks for it to be approved.

"Rafael," I smiled. He'd moved into the room next door to mine and Noah's at the start of this academic year, yet every time I'd gone to knock he hadn't been there. I worried this might be the start of another Noah situation. "How are you?"

"Sorry, do you not live in this Province? I'm sure you've seen the news and know exactly how I am right now." He gripped the test tube so hard that I thought the glass was about to implode and my blood phobia could not cope with that.

I pried the tube out of his hand and rested it back down on the rack. He finally looked at me and I the bags under his eyes shocked me, they were a shade of dark purple that even I hadn't rocked before, even during the dark times last year. His red rimmed eyes scared me more than his clear lack of sleep, I could understand why he'd been crying so much. He'd dealt with a lot over the last few weeks.

"Actually, I'm from Calgary, so I only live here when I'm at school." He shot a daggered glare into my soul. "Okay that's beside the point but yes, I saw the papers, plus Charlie told me about everything that happened." I didn't want him to see the pity that I hated to see from others, but it wasn't like this situation was something to smile about. Instead I kept tight lipped and hoped he could hear that I sympathised with him.

When I'd read the headlines, it was like something had just wrenched at my heart. He was in line to be one of Cherrington's biggest success stories. He was on track to get a huge sports scholarship for basketball, so big there were talks that some US colleges, that had great connections with the NBA, had been in contact with him. Then he did one small, local interview about playing basketball at Cherrington and their huge championship win last year and without thinking slipped out that he was gay and that was it. The colleges that had been knocking at his door disappeared, the scholarships ripped away and a lot of the players on the team had been hesitant about him coming back to basketball, never mind being captain like he was last year.

"So I'm sure you can understand I'm not great right now. Quite hard to be great when I don't even have a future to look forward to anymore." His position was like being a twelfth grader but excelled by a thousand. We all had the worries about applying to universities, what we'd do when we got there and how we'd cope after with whatever job we could get from it or how we could even afford to pay tuition fees. He'd been lucky, he'd had that cemented for him, he'd had Universities begging for him to go there, and now nothing. It was hard to even think about, never mind live that reality.

"I'm sorry." It was my first failure as a prefect.

27

Charlie would have approached this much differently.

"Join the queue of people who feel sorry. The lines probably somewhere around Schmon Parkway right now." He pulled at the strings of his hoodie, the hood curled up around his face before he planted his face on to his bag that sat on top of the bench.

"Hey," I placed my hand on his shoulder before I pulled at his hood. "You know, more than anything, you can talk to me about this. Can we grab lunch after this? We are going to be lab partners for the rest of the year so you may as well concede now, than be subjected to my nagging for the rest of the year." He offered me a small smile in reply. I banked that as some kind of a win as his prefect. It wasn't just that though, I also needed to be his friend right now.

"I don't know what you think you can do to help, but if you're paying for my pancakes at Denny's, I'm not going to say no." I could still see that smile on his face as he turned away from me to focus on Mrs Green as she started the lesson. Denny's pancakes were incredible, but he wouldn't actually agree to come with me if he wasn't at least a little interested in what I had to say.

The class flew by in a blur of chemicals and I was actually thankful that I'd ended up paired with Rafael, as I watched Noah shatter two different test tubes whilst he tried to work with Ameliah. That was an interesting duo, Noah's snark and her witty responses did not bode well for the rest of the year.

"You *are* paying right?" Rafael said as he slid off his lab stool and packed his notebook into his backpack.

"Fine. Just this once though." I smiled as I slung my messenger bag over my shoulder and gestured for him to lead the way. "I actually have a free period after lunch for prefect duties so getting away from the school for an hour will be nice before I have to deal with the crazy amount of shit that's been piled on me this week." Three boys were already really homesick, understandable, but why all at the same time? I had to chase up their situation in that hour, whilst I filled in five incident reports after the Carson brothers had booby trapped several doors. They were mini Isaacs, but double the trouble, tenth and eleventh grade nightmares.

"Lucky you, I have physics with Dr Bernard and he has it out for me, funnily enough I was one of his favourite students last year and now, well I'm sure you can figure out what has changed there."

"He's a dick," I replied bluntly as we trekked off down the driveway, him with his ridiculously long legs strides in front of me. At six foot four he towered over me.

"Tell me about it, hang on you aren't in that class." He span around on spot to look at me with confused eyes and I almost crashed into his broad chest, stopping myself at exactly the right moment before a collision. That could have been awfully awkward.

"I did that senior class last year, that and biology. I originally thought if I did some twelfth-grade level classes last year I'd be able to graduate early. Turns out that's not how it works here in Ontario," I replied as we stepped into Denny's. I smiled warmly at Melissa as she showed me to my favourite booth and said she'd be back shortly to take our order. I loved this place, it always felt so homely here, plus we'd shared so many good memories here. I'd basically had my coming out party in this booth.

"Well at least it's two credits less you have to get this year." His eyes scanned the menu in front of him, I didn't even pick mine up, Melissa had probably already gotten my order written down.

"True, but prefect business takes up those two free

slots now, I can't even imagine how I'd fit it all in if I still had to take those classes this year, how Charlie did it for three years I have no idea."

"Well he didn't. He failed last year," Rafael said bluntly. Whilst he was correct, I didn't like the tone he'd taken about my friend. I shot a glare at him and he waved me off.

"Charlie was a very good prefect, last year was rough."

"Because you were shagging his best friend and said best friend caused nothing but trouble for him?" he remarked as he slid the menu back into its stand and signalled for the waitress to come back over.

Again, he wasn't wrong. Me and Isaac had played a large part in his year completely tanking how it did. "Pretty much, yeah," I said honestly as I met his eye, I wasn't going to back down.

"Was Isaac really worth all the trouble that came with him? The fights, the arguments, didn't you have a breakdown at one point?" Christ, I knew my business had spread like wildfire across the school, especially in Edwards, but my neck creased as I heard him recall everything that had happened. Even more so from someone outside of our friendship group that hadn't lived through it.

"At the time, yes," I replied. If I wanted to get him to open up I guess I had to open up too. "I mean, maybe even now it still is. Without everything that had happened I wouldn't have grown, I probably wouldn't have been prefect, I don't know if me and Noah would be as close as we are now."

"But you two broke up." He turned to the waitress and ordered the cinnamon roll pancakes. Melissa just smiled at me and asked if I wanted the usual and I

30

nodded. Rafael tilted his head at me like I was crazy, but I just smiled harder.

"We did, but unfortunately that's life. He didn't love me, not like I loved him." I had said it like they were the easiest words in the world to say, but my throat tightened painfully as I spoke them, as if it had constrained all the air I tried to breathe in.

My knuckles went white as I gripped at the edge of the table, desperately trying to keep myself upright and strong. I hadn't had an outright conversation like this about him since the start of the summer. Everyone skirted around the topic, except Noah, but he was an exception from the rule. His humour and snark around Isaac meant no harm to me anymore. I wasn't sure I could do it, talk to Rafael about this, about anything. Maybe I just wasn't cut out to be a prefect if I couldn't even discuss him, even when it could help out another student.

"Are you okay?" Rafael asked from where he was now sat beside me. When had he moved to my side of the booth? He placed a careful hand down on my arm and I gasped as I tried to regain control of my breath, at least with his touch I was pulled back into reality and out of the reel of clips of me and Isaac that flashed before my eyes every time I thought about him or heard his name.

"Fine," I panted out as I pushed away what felt like an ocean resting on my lungs with every breath I inhaled and exhaled in a more controlled manner. I looked up at his chocolate brown eyes and they warm, rather than bloodshot like they had been just before class. There was so much reassurance that came with the warmth of his eyes, it was silent, but it was there. Gratefully I squeezed at the hand that had once rested on my arm and he took it as his cue to slide back into the booth opposite me.

"My team are so worried about what's been written

about me that they took away my captaincy," he confessed as he sank back into the letterbox red, plastic booth, his arms crossed in front of his chest as he spoke. "I think some of them would even prefer me to leave the team. I'm their best player, how could they think that would be for the best?" His voice was cocky, but he didn't smirk and there were still red blotches on his face from where he'd cried just a few hours ago.

"I'm so confused, I know some of the guys on the team, they've never had a problem with me being gay or with Charlie being bi, so why is it such a big deal that you are?" I asked as Melissa placed our pancakes on the table in front of us. We both thanked her as she walked off and he started to prod at the plate with his fork. He didn't look impressed, I wasn't sure if it was because of the food or my questions. The smell of the strawberry butter cream and those beautifully syruped pancakes wafted in front of me and whilst I wanted nothing more to dive in and munch them down, I knew I had to wait considerately for him to answer my question before I moaned at the taste.

He stabbed at the pancakes in front of him. "I don't know, maybe it's because I'm their leader or maybe they are just so worried about their image and other college scouts looking at them, they just don't care how much they are hurting me." He forked a chunk of them into his mouth, before he stabbed again at the stack, this time the fork went straight through the food and clashed into the plate with a sharp crash. "Fuck." The fork flew out of his hand and across the booth, it barely missed my head. "I'm so sorry." His bottom lip trembled and as his chin wobbled the tears began to fall, his glossy eyes not able to meet mine.

I shifted quickly round to the other side. "Hey, it's okay," I reassured as the floodgates open. I wrapped my arm around his shoulder and pulled him into my chest just in case anyone we knew walked past. I knew he wouldn't want anyone to see him like this, it would only make things so much worse.

"It's my final year of high school," he croaked out, between choked sobs and salty tears that leaked past the corners of his mouth. "I just want to it enjoy it, not be stressed that my teammates don't have my back or that my mom might end up having a break down if there's another article printed about the taboo of my sexuality." I stroked my hands on his soft black hair, it was the best way I knew how to comfort someone.

"Everything okay?" Charlie asked as he entered Denny's, he ate here more than I did at that point. He was addicted to their pancake brunch.

I nodded at him as Rafael sniffled into my shirt and reached for a napkin to wipe at his eyes and blow his nose. "All good, man," he said, but he sounded congested from how much he'd cried and his snotty nose.

"We sure?" Charlie asked as he looked at me for a little more reassurance.

"Very. Don't you worry, it's not your job anymore," Rafael said as he looked up at Charlie with the saddest of eyes, but this time he smiled at him almost to confirm his words with actions.

As Rafael smiled up at him, I noticed his cheeks stretch and his eyes dip up and down Charlie's body. Wow, that went from one end of extreme to the other very quickly. It wasn't just him though. I thought I was going to have to tell Charlie to stop staring, as he practically drank in the red-eyed boy. I tilted my head at him and narrowed my eyes just to get his attention, when he finally locked eyes with me I shook my head, this was not the time. He shrugged my glare off and began to look elsewhere before he slipped into the booth next to Rafael.

"Look. We are going to fix this, okay?" I nodded at him and he nodded back, his bloodshot eyes looking that little bit brighter. I wasn't sure if that were because I was about to try and help him or because he was sat next to a cute guy he'd just blatantly checked out in front of me. Whichever, I didn't really care, I just knew that from now I was going to make it part of my personal and my prefect mission to help him. I wanted to get him back on the team properly and figure out how we could make our school's sports teams more accepting and diverse.

~ Chapter Five ~
Isaac

"Class?" Lizzy, Cassidy's roommate, suggested to the three of us as we lazed around on the couch. In the intervals of lazing around Cassidy had puked her brain up, Alex moved only to turn the TV back on after it went into standby mode and I'd only peeled myself from the couch once to collect the Domino's we'd ordered from downstairs.

It was as if she hadn't even spoken because we all just continued to stare at the TV, entranced by Netflix. We'd all became engrossed in the series *Lucifer* whilst in our hungover state and at the rate today was going we'd probably breeze through season one in no time.

"Isaac? We have intro to Canadian Lit," she said as she moved to stand in front of the TV, only to be met by a chorus of groans.

"Hey," Alex moaned. "We're trying to watch this," he said as he shuffled the cushions behind his head and got his feet comfy again in Cassidy's lap. I was sure that before we all knew it, there would be something going on there. If Cassidy weren't so caught up in the nameless, almost faceless guy she would not shut up about.

"You guys haven't moved in eight hours. It's starting to smell in here." She shifted herself from in front of our viewing pleasure and stood directly in front of me. "Please come, if you don't I'm gonna have Connor hitting on me relentlessly and you and me both know he isn't going to be tapping this any time soon," she grinned as she shook her hips in front of me.

"Fine, fine, fine. I'll go grab a change of clothes and then we can leave." As I stood up the stench hit me, the left-over pizza and the fact that we hadn't cleared up from pre-drinks last night was now clogging my airways. I surveyed the damage we'd done after we'd tried to bring a keg into our kitchen last night, there was no way in hell we were going to be getting our housing deposits back after that.

I scurried off to my room and grabbed a plain t-shirt and some sweats before a waft of my armpits caught me off guard. I probably should have showered before I left for class. Instead I just grabbed my deodorant can and sprayed a spritz - that would have to do for now.

"Right, let's get out of here," I bellowed. My phone screen told me we had less than 5 minutes to trek up the hill to main campus for our class, so if we didn't get a wriggle on we were 100% going to be late.

I waited a few beats and heard no movement, so I walked back down the hallway to the living room to find Lizzy now curled up in my spot on the couch, eyes adversely glued to the screen. "Are you kidding me?" I shook my head as she didn't even look up when I entered the room, none of them did. "You remember that class you just begged me to come with you to? It starts in three minutes," I said with a roll of my eyes as I plonked myself next to her.

"Probably a good call if we don't go now. Beckett hates late comers and I don't think my headache could handle her yelling at us right now," she said as she rested her head on my shoulder, but I pushed her forward so I could grab my laptop that I'd slid under the sofa earlier today and then allowed her to fall back on to my side so she could lean against me.

"Woah, woah. Bright light, bad head, churning stomach," Cassidy said from the couch behind us.

"Sorry, sorry," I replied as I dulled the brightness of my screen. "I'm gonna finish writing the paper for the class that we are currently missing so I don't feel as guilty for missing it," I said as I opened up the word document that contained the two-thousand-word paper I'd started a few days ago. I glared at the word count and sighed as it currently stood at two thousand eight hundred words. So many words to cut. Turns out Canadian Literature was a lot more exciting than I thought it was going to be, the paper we'd been set to write on Canadian Nationalism in literature had really interested me as soon as I'd started the research and reading for it.

"You're almost finished?" Lizzy asked, as she sat up and grabbed at my laptop to get a better look. "It's not due till the start of October," she said as she scanned the words on my screen with wide eyes.

"Yeah, October first. Four days away," I replied and pulled my laptop back off of her.

"Why have you written so many words? It's only a two-thousand-word paper?" she asked as she curled her feet up underneath her and nestled her head back on my shoulder. She did this a lot and part of me worried that she'd maybe got the wrong impression of us and our friendship because we spent a lot of time together between our shared classes and the fact we both lived together.

"The books we had to read were actually pretty good and the topic, you'll see when you start the research, is actually quite controversial on how Canadian novelists portray our love for the country and everything associated with the patriotism of Canada," I said as I skim read my words on the page. I had no idea which bit of this I was going to cut to fall back under the word limit.

"You're nuts. What University student has started, finished and basically excelled in writing a paper days before the deadline, you do know it's our job to actually write these things the night before?" She giggled and I felt the laugh vibrate through my chest. I had to find some way to push her away, not just physically, but to shut down whatever emotional connection beyond friendship she thought this could be. I wasn't interested.

"Hey, you do you, this way I can enjoy that party on Friday, when you'll be sat in the library panic writing the paper and I'll have already submitted it." I stuck my tongue out at her and cut out a whole paragraph which was just full of background knowledge that probably wasn't necessary, the analysis and comparisons of books was what the Professor was looking for. It got rid of five hundred words at least. This paper had a lot riding on it as it was twenty five percent of my overall grade for this class. I was determined to keep my academic scholarship and that meant I had to maintain above seventy five percent across all my classes. My brain ached at the thought of that. I ran a quick spelling and grammar check and deleted any extra words in sentences that I didn't see the point of and I settled on submitting the paper at two thousand two hundred words.

"What are we going to do about dinner?" Alex looked up and realised that Cassidy was asleep underneath him, so turned to me and asked a little bit quieter. "I want to get out the house, ten hours on this couch was enough for me. Shall we sneak out and leave the two sleeping ladies here?" he suggested and I peered down and realised that Lizzy had actually fallen asleep as well whilst I'd finished up my paper, her head now rested on the back of the couch.

I nodded and tucked my laptop under my arm as I shifted carefully off the couch, making sure not to wake Lizzy. "Where shall we go?" I asked as we walked down the corridor and out of the dorm. "We could go to the food court?"

"Sounds good to me man, so many options down there. I regret not eating more than one slice of that pizza we got earlier, but my stomach was feeling so ropey." Most of the pizza still lay untouched in the box on the common room floor, between Cassidy constantly back and forth from being sick and how grim I felt after one too many drinks the night before, none of us had really felt up to eating.

"The amount of shots we consumed last night I'm surprised we all made it out alive, those Dollar tequila shots were absolutely lethal. Pure paint stripper." The bright light of the outside burned my eyes as we exited the building and I deeply regretted not bringing my sunglasses with me.

"I feel like we may have to take a couple of days off before that big blow out party in town on Friday, I think the lining of my stomach has gone," he chuckled as we walked down the hill that led to the main campus.

"I agree, plus I'm in the process of writing this article for the journalism club, they've agreed to let me be a part of their main writing team for the year if I can prove that I can actually write. That's due at the end of the week so it'll give me some time to work on it." When I said in the process, I mean I'd made a work document for the article, but I had absolutely no idea what I'd actually write about. I'd contemplated a couple of topics, but what I wrote about for this piece would probably be the topic or issue I'd be asked to write about all the time. I'd contemplated writing about sports, but they already had a huge sports editorial team here. I'd also thought about suggesting a campus life section, reviews of bars, clubs, places to eat, good places study. Maybe that's what I should go with, I'd seen a lot of the town in the four weeks I'd been here.

"You'll kill it, that lit review you helped me write for history got me a seventy-five, I've never seen such a high mark in my whole life." When I'd told them my major was in English they decided that I was now their own personal work editor, they all sent me their essays for me to proofread, edit grammar and spelling, and sentence structure. If it wasn't academic plagiarism, I'd probably set up a business in it and make a killing. Just in the first few weeks of introductory projects the three of them had hit the ground running with great grades.

"Thanks man," I said as we approached the Eaton centre. "I'm craving Chinese right now." We headed towards the escalators to the ground floor and my stomach grumbled loudly, at least it no longer churned with alcohol acid.

"I could definitely go for Chinese," he replied as his phone beeped in his hand, "and that's Cassidy, her and Lizzy woke up and realised we were gone and wanna know where we are." He sighed as he began to type out a reply. "Look, I really like Cassidy, but she's literally been glued to my side for the last month almost, she put off some cheer leading thing to come out last night, even after I told her that it was important to bond with your sports team. I said me and you wouldn't skip out on the soccer team to hang with the girls."

"Think how I feel, not only do I live with Lizzy, but we have two classes together this term and four next term, I'll never be able to shake her." I grabbed a tray from the side of the queue for the Chinese buffet and laughed at the fact that my only escape was the poetry class I'd decided to take, thank god for poetry.

"She fancies you so hard, she was all over you last night," he replied as he scooped some chow mein onto his plate.

"Tell me about it, I was trying so hard to make it obvious I wasn't in to her, I just don't think she got the message. I think she's great and she's gorgeous, but I'm not into her." We walked towards an empty table and slumped into seats opposite each other. The Friday evening rush hadn't started yet, as work had only just finished for people, so there was hardly anyone around.

"Oh, well me and Cassidy definitely got the message after like the fifth shot you babbled on none stop about Logan, you had your phone out waving round pictures of him, we had to reign you in at one point to stop you pissing people off." His eyes blazed in delight at my expense, I should probably delete those photos to prevent any further humiliation.

"Yeah, someone should really confiscate my phone when I'm in that state." I chuckled as I twisted some noodles around my fork and thought about those photos. It had literally taken me two months to change my lock screen of the two of us kissing on Toronto harbour, how would I actually *delete* those photos? Together or not, they meant a lot and held a lot of memories.

"Are things really over between the two of you?" He pursed his lips as if he were about to ask something else and then decided not to.

"Would it be for you if you confessed your love for someone and then they literally acted like they never heard you and then when you said it again you stumble over your reply and tell them you're leaving without a second glance?" He glared at me like I was crazy, his brow arched like I was messing with him.

"Is that what you did?" he asked, and I nodded. "Wow, that's some cold-hearted shit, can you let Lizzy down a little more gently please, we still have to live with each other for the next nine months."

"I was a mess, I really cared about him, but our relationship hurt so many people and then I got in here and for a month I just panicked. I didn't know how I could be in a long-distance relationship that had already been so hard when we lived in the same house. So rather than just talk about it, I pushed him away. It really was my bad."

"Sounds like you truly fucked up if I'm honest, Isaac." He did not have to tell me that, I had thought that from the moment I'd walked away from him.

"And I don't know how to fix it," I replied as I finished off the plate of chow mein. "Should we go?" I suggested as I stood up and walked towards the trash, Alex followed behind me.

"We should probably get a takeout container for the girls before they kill us for leaving the house without them." He laughed and slid his tray on top of the trash.

"So, you gonna go for it with Cassidy?" There was definitely something there between them and how they'd been all curled up on the sofa all day had actually warmed my heart a little. They were very cute.

"Maybe, but I think she needs to shag that other guy first and get over her fascination with him, because I don't wanna try something with her if she's still into someone else." At least he was honest, I could not help but agree though, she was slightly obsessed with this nameless guy.

I scooped a load of the chow mein noodles and special friend rice into the take-out containers they provided, before I grabbed a bag of prawn crackers for them. "At least this way they won't moan that we went for food without them," I shrugged as I paid for their food.

"She'll still moan, you and I both know it." He quickly added a couple of bottles of Pepsi to our order before the cashier rang it up and I shook my head, but nevertheless tapped my card. They'd do the same for me.

~ Chapter Six ~
Logan

"One double with a shot of vanilla," I said as I sat down at the table in Tim Horton's across from Rafael.

"I'm impressed, you know my coffee order." He took the coffee cup from me and inspected the contents to make sure it was just as he liked it, with a shot of vanilla and a sprinkle of chocolate sugar across the top.

"Oh please it's not like it's the most complex of things. Plus, that's the fifth cup I've bought you this week, by the way." I laughed as I stretched out to put my feet up on his side of the booth.

"So you're counting now?" he asked, as he pulled open the box of Timbits I'd also bought and flashed me a pearly white smile as he parted his almond colour lips to place a glazed Timbit into his mouth.

In moments like this I allowed myself to get caught up in him, if I gave myself the chance I could begin to fancy him. He was strikingly beautiful, amber eyes, rich like honeycomb, sat below a thick fan of dark lashes, the same colour as his hair that was pulled up into a sleek man bun on the top of his head. Any guy would be lucky to have him.

However, my stomach didn't flutter at the thought of him. My heart still belonged to the olive skinned, grey eyed guy who had stolen my heart less than a year ago.

It didn't stop me looking though, I *was* only human.

"So why have you called me here again? We are literally fuelling this places profits right now," he joked, but he didn't laugh, just popped in another Timbit and gulped his coffee.

"Well, not a social call if I'm honest, I'm here as you prefect and your friend. I wanna help you and your situation."

"How?" he asked as he leaned back in the booth, arms placed behind his head like a cradle.

"Well, that's what I wanted to discuss, actually."

"You've invited me here to help me, but you don't actually have a plan. Don't waste my time, Logan," he grunted as he scooped up his travel cup and his jacket and started to slide out of the booth.

"Wait, wait!" I shouted and halted him in his tracks as he went to steal a handful of the Timbits I'd bought. "Just hold up okay, I have ideas, but I want to hear from you how you want to help as well."

"What do you mean?" he asked as he paused by the side of the booth, his nose scrunched up like I was about to ask him to eat something disgusting.

"By helping you there are probably so many others we can help. Think how you've felt like for the last few weeks, do you want other people to have to go through this as well?" I did not want to retort to emotional blackmail, but I felt like we could really do some good here.

He breathed out, exasperated, before he strained his neck side to side to stretch it out. "Okay. So where do we start?" he asked, and that was exactly what I wanted to hear, as I pulled out my notebook and pencil case so we could get started on a plan.

"First of all, there isn't just the two of us. I have your favourite person on the way." He cocked his head at me and I just smirked coyly in return. How they probably wished I hadn't been here when they realised how attractive each of them were, it was like something sparked inside of Charlie and I wasn't sure how to turn it off. Or even if I wanted to, I'd never seen a fire like this in him, not even for Beth. I think I'd even seen it more so when I saw how upset he was when he first found out about me and Isaac.

"Stop it," he sighed.

"Stop what? I'm just trying to help," I smiled widely, like I really meant it and he tried not to smile back. "You think he's cute though, right? I didn't imagine that."

"I think he's great, I just can't go there right now. I'm not in the head space for anything like that, but I don't know," he shrugged. "It was nice to be appreciated like that you know, I haven't had that in ages, never really from another guy." I nodded almost animatedly, I really did know that. I remembered exactly how alive it made me feel when Isaac would eye me up. The first time it had exhilarated me when he watched me on the dance floor. I felt invincible.

"Don't worry, he gets that. I made it very clear now wasn't the time." Not that he needed telling, he knew. Charlie wasn't an idiot, he could see that things were still hard for Raf, especially with his sexuality. "I ship you two, though. Charlie is legit the best person I know, he'd make a great boyfriend."

Rafael pursed his lips and contemplated me for a moment. "So why didn't you go for him?"

"The heart wants what the heart wants, right?" I said sadly, the half-smile there by force and he felt it as he reached out to squeeze my hand across the table.

"The heart also needs to know when it's time to stop beating itself up," he reassured, and I wished then that was possible, but I hadn't quite figured out how to do that. Maybe I actually needed to give myself time first.

"Am I interrupting something?" Charlie asked and I'd never seen a pair of hands that retreated as quickly as ours did, god Charlie must have thought all kinds of things, I'd already dashed his hopes and dreams with Isaac, I would not do that to him again.

"Not at all, he's just being a good friend," I replied, as I gestured for him to sit and offered him one of the ridiculous amount of Timbits I'd bought. He took a handful and slid into the booth next to Rafael, hardly any distance between their knees. I could not help the grin that spread across my face at this, Charlie deserved some happiness and so did Rafael, they could be so good for each other.

"Now we can get started." I started to scribble down on the sheet of paper in front of me, switched between a few colours to make it look presentable.

"What is he doing now?" Rafael muttered to Charlie, like I couldn't hear him.

"Who knows," Charlie chuckled, I wished I hadn't been so caught up in what I'd been writing so I could watch their interactions, it would be good material to have on hand to tease them about later.

"One of the exercises I did with Dr Meredith when I first started going to therapy was write down what I wanted to achieve, in the next month, in the next year and in the next five years. I want you to do that." I slid the paper and pens across to him, the title *Rafael Danatele's five-year plan* across the top and little subheadings for every milestone.

"Didn't realise I was coming here for therapy," he muttered, but picked up the pen anyway and started to fill each segment in. To his left Charlie sat and looked at me, at first I couldn't read him, but then I realised he looked a little teary, his eyes glossed over. I went to ask why, but he shook his head. Instead he reached for a phone and seconds later my phone vibrated in my pocket.

'This is why you're Prefect, I'm so proud of you' - Charlie.

I mouthed a thank you at him and he nodded before he wiped away the tears that had begun to treacle down his face. Rafael still scribbled away furiously and it triggered exactly how cathartic this exercise had been for me in the first place. It was about what I wanted, to put me first, my hopes and dreams, nobody else's. It felt selfish in the most selfless way.

"Okay. I'm done," Rafael announced as he placed the pen down on the table and twisted the notebook so we could see what he'd written.

"You really put lose your virginity at the top of the one-month section?" I chuckled, before I glanced up at a beetroot Charlie. "I'm sure that can be arranged." They exchanged a glance that wasn't meant for my eyes and I dropped them back to the pad of paper to pretend I hadn't seen them.

"You asked me to do this," Rafael gritted his teeth as he went to cross off the top answer. I grabbed at his hand to stop it.

"The honest the better, I'm sorry," I replied as I read on. "*Regain captaincy of the team.*" I said aloud. "Okay, we can do this one? We just have to talk to them, get them to understand, make them that little bit more tolerant."

"I quit the team," he shrugged, as he twiddled the pen in his hand.

"We have to fight this, Raf. Quitting isn't the answer." Not that that wasn't completely hypocritical for me to say, not at all.

"You don't have to go to the practices and not get

passed to or be benched because people are refusing to play with you, it's humiliating." I wanted to tell him that I understood. That I'd been side-lined for the first half of high school in every single capacity, but this wasn't about me.

I wanted to tell him I understood. That I'd been side-lined for the first half of high school in every single capacity, but this wasn't about me.

"Raise more awareness for LGBTQ people in sport and open up teams to being more diverse and accepting." I knew that was it. The big thing. It wasn't just personal to him, but to tonnes of people around the country and around the world. Proof that Rafael had a big heart and he didn't just want change for him, but also for everyone else too. "This is a goal." I circled what I'd just read aloud under the one-year category. "I like this."

"Me too," he nodded. "But it's just a pipe dream."

"Not if you're willing to put in the work it isn't."

"I just don't understand what you think us two could do? We are just two high school kids, no-one is going to take us seriously." His honey eyes were dull and defeated as he popped yet another Timbit into his mouth. With him currently being unwelcome on the team I guess he didn't care anymore about what he ate or its nutritional value, maybe I shouldn't have bought a box of a hundred.

"But, how will we know if we don't even try? Look, it makes me so fucking angry what they have done to you, how they've literally stripped you down to this resigned person, you aren't the Rafael I remembered seeing on all the posters for this place last year. I want to help you get that back. But a better version of that, a version that doesn't have to worry about his sexuality. Don't you want that for yourself? Or for other men and women who are gay and want to play sport, but don't think they can?"

Hesitantly, Charlie covered Rafael's hand with his.

"Logan is right, I wish this wasn't our responsibility, but as members of this community we have a duty to make it a safe place for others, for those who follow after us."

Rafael looked down at his hand and then back up at me, his eyes looked brighter than I'd seem them in weeks. He gave me a proper smile, like an ear-to-ear grin. "I'm in, if you both think we can do this then I'm in. What's first?"

"We start on the ground, right here, with the team, with the school. The only way is up from there." I scribbled out a mind map so we could brainstorm and from there the ideas only continued to flow and just a few hours later we had a plan together and ready to put into action. "What do you think?" I asked as we observed the mind map that now spanned across four sheets of A4.

"I think we might be a little crazy, but if it works the results will be incredible," I nodded and wiped at my brow. Who knew trying to manage such a big project could be such sweaty work?

"I think we can do this," Charlie grinned, and there were smiles all round. All we had to do was start to put it into action.

~ Chapter Seven ~
Isaac

If you'd told me that when I rolled out of bed at 9:20AM this morning for my 9AM class, because my stupid phone charger decided to break in the night, that I'd been ending the day with an eighty percent grade on my first submission to my poetics class and that the soccer team would have just beat one of the best teams in our league 6-1, then I'd have told you that pigs definitely couldn't fly.

Yet here I am, showered and dressed in those ridiculously tight skinny jeans Logan had once forced me to buy and the shirt he'd told me complimented my eyes, ready to go celebrate our teams win tonight, the poetics paper with a big red mark that said *A* on the front pinned to my cork board.

"You ready?" Alex asked as he poked his head round my door, a beer for me in his outstretched hand.

"So ready." I took the shot I'd just poured myself and grabbed the beer from him. I took a long swig, practically downed half the bottle. "So fucking ready, let's go," I hollered as we made our way out to the kitchen.

The four of us had planned our own little pre-drinks, which consisted of a tonne of flipped cups that once upon a time had alcohol in and a game of truth or dare that had gotten significantly out of control, when Cassidy made Alex streak up and down the stairs of our dormitory.

It had done the job though, as the taxi pulled up in front of us, Cassidy almost dropped to the ground in her heels and Lizzy couldn't even figure out how to open the taxi door she was so drunk. Alex was the most sober amongst us as he helped everyone pile into the cab, even me as I struggled to see straight, he even belted us all up to keep us safe.

Me and Alex held the girls by the nook of their arms as we walked into the club, we managed to feign soberness so we could be granted entry.

"Oh my god. That's him!" Cassidy screamed in my ear just as we walked into the club, she grabbed at my arm and swerved me in the direction of the guy in question. God, I wish she hadn't done that as the eighth beer I'd drank swilled around in the pit of my stomach.

The room spun a little, the neon lights around me flashed frantically in my eyes, but amongst that I could see who she was talking about and, even with my beer goggles on, I could see why she'd been searching for him in every room we'd walked into over the last few weeks. He was hot. I could only really see him in side profile, but his jaw line was chiselled and his blonde hair was gelled back into almost a perfect quiff.

"Talk to him." The words stumbled out of my mouth, but she'd already started to guide me in another direction away from him, unfortunately towards the bar.

"Vodka?" she asked as she ordered us several shots of tequila and then a double each of vodka and coke, my previous question went unanswered.

"Sure," I nodded as I passed the shots down the line via Lizzy and to Alex. We clinked the tiny glasses together and cheered loudly as we chucked back the liquid and let it burn the back of our throats. There was a tingle of regret with this shot as it disturbed the beer mixture in my stomach once more. "Gross," I muttered as I sipped on the double vodka and coke, at least the sweetness of the soda would bury the taste of the god-awful black tequila she continued to buy us on every night out.

"Talk to him," I repeated, as I saw him walk closer towards us, headed for the other end of the bar. "He's right there, come on, buy him a shot and go over there." I signalled for the bartender to come back over to us so she could place another order, but she backed away from me and the bar. Chickened out yet again. I refused to hear her moan about it anymore if she wasn't going to seize the day and just go for it with him.

She skirted quickly away from him, dragged me behind her as we headed in the direction of Alex, we'd already lost Lizzy to her book club friends and their posse who were sat in the booths on the other side of the floor. I was sure we'd reunite with them at some point during the night, she never strayed for long. For now I'd stick to Alex like glue so he could look after the both of us.

By the time we reached Alex through the masses of people, both our drinks were empty and Cassidy had already began to beg Alex to go and dance with her, she knew in the state I had been in that there was no way in hell that I would be out on that dance floor. I'd have probably chundered everywhere.

"Please, Alex. One dance, don't be boring," she pleaded as the two of us boys took a seat in the booth. Alex had found a water jug that they left scattered around to prevent people from becoming dehydrated and had poured the three of us glasses, I glugged mine quickly in the hopes that I'd sober up just a tad, the night was still so young.

"Give me a couple of minutes and I'll join you," he compromised and that was enough for a severely drunk Cassidy as she skipped off on to the dance floor but remained within eye sight. She'd find someone else to dance with in the meantime, she always did.

"I'm fucked," I slurred out, as I poured myself another glass of water and whacked my legs up in the booth. "I actually don't think I've ever been this drunk in my life." I tried to keep myself up right on my elbows, but that was not meant to be and I would have ended up being a crumpled heap on the floor under the table if it hadn't of been for Alex.

"Woah there, big guy." He steadied me into an upright position, my head lent back against the plush booth. The music being so loud was the only thing keeping me from letting the luxurious material absorb all of my weight as I was drifting into sleep. "Do you need to go home?" He asked as he waved in front of my face to get me to focus on him.

I shook my head wildly, to the point the room began to spin again. "Nooooo," I protested. "A couple more glasses of h2o and I'll be raring to go again," I replied as I reached out for the cup and sent it flying across the table.

"Uh-huh," he said and pushed his cup into my hand. "Slow sips please." He prescribed like a doctor as he guided my hand to my lips and I managed to swallow some of it, only dribbled a few drops down my chin and on to my shirt.

"You're an absolute mess, thank god you and Cassidy have no interest in each other because together you'd be an absolute nightmare. Literally handling both of you is like trying to fight off World War Three, one big uphill battle." He could have said something really important, but I'd tuned out, now completely focused on the bright lights that flashed around the stage, tempted me to get up on it and shake away my inhibitions.

I pulled away from where Alex literally had me

pinned to the seat and kept my eyes stuck in the direction of the stage, that was my goal. I'd climb whatever mountain that was put in front of me to get there. I wanted to climb that stage, it was made for me, I could do this.

"No, no you don't," he said as he jumped up to pull me back down by my arm. "Sit the fuck down and stay here." He pushed me over to the back of the booth so I was trapped behind the table, it would take a lot of effort for me to try and escape again and I could feel my eyes droop, as I rested against the cushions.

"Okay, you're the boss," I signalled to him like he was the captain.

Suddenly glasses smashed around us and both mine and Alex's heads shot up in the direction of the dance floor, to see Cassidy with a sheepish look on her face as a bartender stood in the middle of a dozen glasses now fragmented across the floor.

"I think someone else needs rescuing." I gestured a floppy arm across the dance floor, I hoped somewhat towards Cassidy, but I really struggled to co-ordinate my body parts as the alcohol rushed through my veins.

"Kill me. I'm not coming out with you two again unless I'm just as smashed. Actually scrap that who the hell would look after you guys if I were screwed too." He sighed as he pushed himself out of the booth and waged his way through the crowd to pull Cassidy away from the situation she'd created.

I took this as my chance to run, I sloped my body onto the floor and crawled under the table until I was certain I wouldn't bang my head on it or in my case till I was at the foot of a crowd of people who looked down at me like I was berserk.

My jeans were now covered in white dust that I brushed away sloppily, before I steadied myself up against the bar and took a few deep breaths. I looked over at the stage again and it seemed way too far in the distance, I'd rest here for a moment.

"What are you drinking?" A guy side-lined up to me and lent against the bar as we both surveyed the club. I watched as Alex spun Cassidy round loosely, his hand lost grip of hers and she crashed into a group of girls that danced beside them.

"Double Disaronno and Coke please." If he were offering, I was not going to say no. Plus, I'd already bought a tonne of drinks this week, being bought *one* would not hurt.

"Coming right up, gorgeous." He'd probably been able to buy a bunch of people drinks tonight if he were that smooth. He placed the orders quickly at the bar before he turned to look out on the club once more. "Are you here with them two?" He pointed to where Alex was trying to peel a drunken Cassidy up off the floor as she kicked her legs around in some weird dance move.

"Unfortunately so," I laughed as I took the drink from him and sipped a long stream of it. It was only when I felt the liquid drip down the side of my mouth I realised just how drunk I was too, it was probably a good thing I wasn't out there on the dance floor with them.

"I think your girlfriend needs to go home." Cassidy attempted to do the worm and only ended up smacking her face on the floor. What a disaster of a night this had been, Alex practically had to restrain her to get her stood upright and as he led her towards the bathrooms I knew that this was only going to end one way. Cassidy with her head in the toilet for the rest of the evening.

"Definitely not my girlfriend," I replied as I downed the rest of the drink, my hand gripped on the underside of the bar as my head went as light as a feather and the room swirled together for a second.

His hand found my arm and steadied me, as I leant against his chest for a second. Turned out he was just as drunk as me, his stability sucked as his back crashed into the bar. I stayed pressed up against his toned chest for a minute, until my eyes could differentiate between the faces that surrounded us.

"Fuck. I'm sorry." I tried to stand up straight without his assistance but my knees wobbled like jelly and I almost clattered to the floor. "Christ, I really should have paced myself," I slurred as his arm slotted around my waist. "Good thing I've got you to hold me up with your big strong arms." I almost purred, as I stroked up his rock-solid bicep, it tensed under my hand and I let my fingers wander down his chest, before they came to rest at the hem of his shirt.

"You're a real tease." His hand trailed down to my waist, and onto my ass, well this was new. But it was all the encouragement I needed to press more up against him, my fingers slipped under his shirt and onto his warm skin. This contact felt so good and I moaned as he began to place sloppy kisses down my neck, before they were on my lips and our teeth clanked together messily, but we just laughed into the kiss, the mixture of his vanilla vodka and my almond amaretto mixed together just nicely.

His arms wrapped around my waist to keep our lips locked together, but a stranger stumbled into us and broke us apart, suddenly the music around us became louder and I realised I'd drowned it out when I'd draped myself all over him. "I live down the road," he suggested and I nodded enthusiastically.

"Lead the way." I'd deal with Cassidy and Alex in the morning, they'd already forgotten I'd existed and Alex would be occupied for the rest of the night having to take care of the other drunken mess.

~ Chapter Eight ~
Logan

"Hey," I said as I bent down beside Oscar where he was sat in the common room. "What's going on?" I'd had my headphones in for hours as I studied away. Turns out not even the two twelfth grade classes I'd taken last year could prepare me for having to do a full course load of them this year, especially combined with my prefect duties and being president of the choir. I'd been so busy I hadn't even noticed Oscar sat in the bay window with tear filled eyes, as he stared out into the empty driveway.

Oscar was the shortest ninth grader I'd ever seen in my life. He was someone I'd noted down on my list of people to keep checking in on from that year, a list of people that I thought may need a little bit more help to settle in and get involved. I just hadn't gotten around to him yet.

He looked up at me with red rimmed eyes. It was the look of how much I'd already failed him. Failed at my role as a prefect. "It's my sisters, they are twins and my aunt is just too ill to look after them anymore, so they are probably going to end up in foster care." He snuffled and wiped at the fresh tears that had fallen. "I was lucky, I got a free ride here on an academic scholarship, but they are only ten, they are too young to come here. If they go into care they could end up anywhere in the province and I might not get too see them much."

58

That was the reminder I'd needed that there was so much going on outside of my own life. That's why I'd been nominated prefect, because people thought I could handle this and I could, I knew I could. I hadn't done a great job so far, but I could fix this. I just had to find a balance. "First of all I'm so sorry, Oscar. That royally sucks. How about we go and see Julian and see if he can help us at all? If he doesn't have any suggestions, he'll be able to point us in the right direction."

Oscar nodded at me and palmed at his eyes to stop the tears completely. "Okay." I wrapped my arm around his shoulder and guided him down to Julian's office. This could be fixed. It could all be fixed.

Julian had been helpful, he had contacts in the foster care system he said he'd get in touch with to try and make sure that Oscar's little sisters would be placed close to St-Catharines so he'd be able to visit. I still felt guilty though. I should have spotted there had been a problem. How did Charlie do this? Keep tabs on everyone, make sure everything was always good?

That's why I found myself headed up to the sixth floor and into the old prefect room. "Let yourself in why don't you?" Charlie laughed from where he was sat at the top of his bed, one of his many books open in front of him.

"You're forgetting this is technically my room," I sighed as I sat myself down at the end of his bed, arms folded tightly in front of me as I rested my chin on my chest.

"What's happened? I know that look, I used to see it in the mirror all the time," he said as pushed a bookmark into his book and placed it on his bedside table.

I rubbed at my temples. A gnawing headache had begun to form behind my eyes. "I already feel like I'm failing. I missed a problem with Oscar because I've been so caught up in my work and the ten thousand other problems I've been trying to get a grip on in this dorm. Turns out the Carson brothers are basically mini Isaacs, I'm literally this close to having them DNA tested to see if there is any relation between them," I said as I held up my fingers up less than an inch apart.

"Yeah I've witnessed a couple of the stunts they've performed, the confetti canons are a new one, I'm quite glad Isaac was never that creative."

All I could see was the rainfall of condoms Isaac had once created, there had been very little clear up for Charlie after the boys had gotten to them. Unlike with the confetti. "Besides the point, you're doing an incredible job, I've literally heard nothing but praise about you. Even from Noah. Actually, even *about* Noah as well. You can only do your best, Lo. Sometimes you miss a couple of people." His face looked pained and I knew he carried so much regret for what happened with Noah and his girlfriend.

"I know. I just wish I could catch them all," I said as I stood up off his bed and surveyed his overflowing bookshelf. I still remembered seeing it the first time I'd come in here, it had relaxed me more than anything I could have asked for. "I've just been focused on what's been going on with Rafael, it's a lot. I can't help but want to devote whatever free time I have to him and helping him get his future back."

"Doesn't help he's easy on the eyes," he nudged my shoulder playfully from where he was now stood next to me.

"I hadn't noticed," I shrugged. Except I kind of had. And I'd tried to not think about him like that, but it wasn't there. "Stop it. If you think he's so cute I'd be happy to pass on your number to him."

"Or maybe I'll just give it him myself," he suggested, an Isaac like smirk pulled at his lips.

"Be my guest," I replied, before a knock at the door pulled me away from having to think about it anymore.

"I'm here to take you out to have some fun," Noah said as he hovered in Charlie's doorway.

"You text him?" I shot a glare at Charlie and rolled my eyes. I loved that we all got on so well now, but now it was so much easier for them to gang up on me when I started to get a little bit stressed.

"He did, but we need to get out of here anyway. I've had two ninth graders at our door this afternoon complaining about Mr Bernard and his workload."

"You know that's part of your job as deputy prefect, right?" Charlie commented with a smug grin.

"You coming, Montgomery? We're going bowling." Noah lent up against the door frame like he was some kind of model.

"Nah, stuff to do. Have fun though," he replied, as he grabbed his book again and reopened it, that was our cue to leave. I smiled as I watched him get lost in his book once more, I was glad that that was his busy now.

"Right, just me and you then, Shields. Let's go." He headed for the stairs, strides in front of me, but I didn't move. I desperately wanted to protest this outing, I knew I had so much to do tonight before the school's council meeting tomorrow.

"Can I get changed first? I don't think these pants are bowling appropriate."

He turned and surveyed my skin tight pants. "Sure thing. Quick detour to our room and then off to the bowling alley."

I sighed in reply. "Noah, I'm kind of knackered to be honest. I dunno if I'm in the mood for bowling." I hadn't been to that alley since last year, with him and the guys.

I'd told him on one of our Facetime calls last summer that I'd felt the beginning of the end with Isaac last night and just hadn't want to believe it. I had no desire to back to that place right now.

"You need to get laid. As much as it pains me to say it, it's time. You have to stop thinking about Wells and move the hell on," Noah grunted impatiently as we arrived back at our room, to the point he opened my wardrobe and chucked me what I'd named my going out sweat pants. They were grey and had tailored cuffs, they could pass as slacks in certain light.

"I have," I said, my arms crossed in front of my stomach. I didn't care how much of a lie it was, I didn't want to have to have another conversation about Isaac.

"Bullshit. Actual bullshit. Look, I didn't want to be the one to have to do this, although if you've moved on it shouldn't be too hard for you to see." Noah replied as he pulled out his phone and thrust it in front of my face. Low and behold it was a picture of Isaac kissing someone else. Another man. You could practically see their tongues rammed down each other's throats in the corner of the club they were kissing in. Damn this *Spotted at McGill* page for contributing to my ongoing heartbreak over Isaac Wells.

I snatched the phone out of his hand, zoomed in on the picture and almost choked. Both of the men were just side profiles, but I could clearly make out that it was Isaac. I could spot him in a crowd of a thousand people, I had that face memorised down to the placement of each individual freckle. The boy he was kissing was your typical Abercrombie guy, his shoulders were broad and the arm muscles that I could see were toned, he had piercing blue eyes and floppy blonde hair that was slicked back with what was probably sweat from dancing in the club. I'd seen Noah's hair get like that when he'd come back from soccer practice, it was gross. The way the blonde locks would matte together made me feel sick, almost as sick as I felt as I looked at the picture. There was too much familiarity that came from the photo. I wasn't sure if it was because it was another guy kissing Isaac or because...

"Oh hold the fuck up. That's your brother! Isaac is kissing your fucking brother!" I almost wanted to throw the phone at him or maybe even the wall, anything to get rid of the sight of that photo.

"I'm sorry man. He's a pig. I've already yelled at him don't you worry." He held his hands up in defence as I crushed his phone in my hands.

If I hadn't been so caught up in how my blood was boiling, I'd have probably felt somewhat proud of how far me and Noah had come for him to be sticking up for me like that, but instead I just wanted to hop on the next flight to Montreal and hunt down his brother. Fucking Wyatt. I would be kidding myself if I said I couldn't see why, Wyatt was gorgeous in every way, if me and Isaac were on good terms I'd have probably congratulated him. *Happy bloody long weekend to me.*

"Are you still going to come back to Ottawa with me this weekend? For some strange reason, my parents are really happy you decided to come," Noah asked, as he snatched the phone back out of my hand before I crushed it under my foot.

"What and have to spend time with the guy who's just slept with my ex? Christ what if it's actually something serious between them and he brings Isaac home for the dinner too? I'd actually *die*, Noah."

Noah just grinned in reply as he shook his head at me before he erupted into laughter. "There's something you need to know about my brother, Logan, he's a man whore. He sleeps with everyone and anyone and he never,

never settles down. You don't have to worry about him bringing Isaac home, that would never happen."

"Well that makes me feel ten times better, Isaac's now just sleeping with random guys? Brilliant. Glad I was that special," I sighed as I flopped on the bed dramatically.

"You're such a drama queen," he replied with a huff and I would bet my life on the fact he'd probably rolled his eyes as well.

I shot up and glared at him. "Why your brother? Why did he need to rub it in my face? Look I've dealt with the fact that he wasn't in love with me, and that maybe I was just some kind of experiment for him? Doesn't mean I want to see him kissing anyone, especially your gorgeous brother. It's not fair."

He gagged, I lobbed a pillow at him. "First of all, please don't say those things about my brother. Secondly, it's exactly what I was just saying to you. You need someone to get over Isaac. Move on. What about Rafael? He's literally just next door, it would be so easy. Plus you *have* been hanging out a lot."

"He's going through too much to date right now. Plus, I'm helping him, you know, like a good prefect should. I'm sure you could be some assistance as deputy in our conversations."

"Oh please, there is no interrupting your conversations with him and Charlie. Plus you know I don't like criers and he's been walking around lately looking like he's either really stoned or that he's just cried out the Niagara Falls. Plus I saw you guys chatting in Times the other day; you, him and Charlie, I didn't want to be the fourth wheel to your third. Seriously you should have just let them get it on in that booth and left them to it."

"Eurgh, why is everyone else coupling up, but me?" I groaned and the vision of Isaac and Wyatt kissing reappeared in my mind. "Could you just ask your brother not to kiss my ex again, please?" I whined.

"You know I'm not going to do that. If we aren't going to go bowling? Can we go do something else?" he asked as he wheeled his desk chair over to the side of my bed, his eyes pleaded with me and that look got to me. Noah had cabin fever. He could not just sit still, he wanted to constantly be on the move. He'd said something to me at the start of the summer that resonated with me - *'life's for the living, Logan.'* It had been what had prompted me to go on the road trip before I came back to school, but for him it was something more. He wanted to live life to the fullest, for her, for Jessie.

"Okay," I grumbled as I peeled my pants, that had practically glued themselves to my legs, off from where I laid on the bed and tugged on the sweats that he'd thrown at me. "Bowling it is," I surrendered as I threw my arms up in the air.

"Perfect, let's go." He raced for the door and I sighed up at the ceiling, one last second of being comfortable before he called out again. "Move your ass." I closed my eyes but pushed myself up off my bed. He had a promise to honour and I was not going to stand in the way of that.

~Chapter Nine~
Isaac

My head splintered as I sat up in the bed that was way too big to be mine. A warm body snored like a helicopter next to me as I tried to unscramble the comforter that had tangled round my body as I slept. What the hell had happened last night?

When I'd finally freed myself from the ridiculous mass of blankets that were harboured on the bed, I realised this wasn't even a dormitory room I was in. It was a proper bedroom in like an apartment or house, with big windows and proper curtains and furniture that didn't all match. It was filled with a huge king size bed that you definitely wouldn't find in a dorm and a walk-in wardrobe with doors that hung wide open. The snores still echoed throughout the room, so it wouldn't hurt for me to just take a peak in there to get some kind of idea about who I'd come home with.

I checked that the body was still slumped up against the wall, a pillow covered their face and was clutched in place by a big pair of hands, so it wasn't like I could just move it to get a better look at them.

With this in mind I took a step into the closet, the rails lined with the same style of shirt, just in different colours. Slacks draped messily over coat hangers, and worn boxers littered the floor. Nestled amongst the rainbow of shirts I spotted the red, white and black jersey I knew so well. Ottawa Fury Soccer Club. I'd seen them play my club in Toronto many times. I fingered the silk of the jersey and frowned, I could have at least slept with someone who supported a decent team.

As I opened the drawer below the shirts, a navy and white tie caught my eye. It was a tie I'd wished I hadn't recognised. It was the tie that represented Edwards Dormitory, white pinstripes and everything. The guy passed out from me just metres away was someone I could have gone to school with. What was that saying about not shitting on your own doorstep?

I gathered up the tie in my hand, that familiar silk slid between my fingers as I crushed it into a ball. Trouble really did follow me everywhere or was it that I'd followed the trouble. Charlie would probably say the latter.

My stomach gargled loudly, a rush of acid sprinted up my oesophagus, why had I chosen to come in here over the bathroom? Everything I had consumed last night was ready to erupt back out of me. I wondered if I cracked open the closet draw and squeezed out, would I be able to round up my clothes and leave without disturbing the sleeping body. I sighed and scrubbed my hand through my sweat drenched hair. I needed a plan, I could not stay in here forever.

A mirror rested on top of his dressing table and I surveyed my appearance in it, my skin was grey as it always looked after I'd had one too many drinks, complimented by purple circles that drooped under my tired eyes, one too many nights out that week. I turned away from the mirror, no longer interested in how rough I look, only to be met with a small corkscrew board, plastered with photos. Photos of him in sports attire with his team. Photos of him on nights out and the photo that stuck out the most. A photo of him with one Noah Castle. They looked almost identical.

Oh shit, that was Wyatt Castle fast asleep in that bed. I surveyed the bruises up and down my neck and chest. He had really done a number on me. I wanted to smack myself, damn the vodka that had allowed me to become just another notch on Wyatt Castle's king-sized bedpost.

As I attempted to pin the photo back on to the board above his dresser, the whole pin board toppled over and landed on the floor with a thud. I rushed to the closet door, trying hard not cause any more noise, but it was too late. As I peered out from behind the door I saw him move.

With a long groan, the body rolled over in his bed, he stretched, before he whined. "Why are the curtains open?" The sun streamed in and from where he lay hit him perfectly, probably blinded him when he opened his eyes.

"We didn't shut them last night, I guess," I shrugged as I emerged fully out of the closet. I tugged the curtain shut and flicked on the desk lamp to stop the room from becoming too dark.

"Thanks," he muttered as he pushed himself up into a sitting up position. "I need about a gallon of water right now, my mouths as dry as the Sahara Desert."

I really hoped he didn't expect me to go and fetch that for him, because there was no way I was going to run around after his hungover ass. "So…" I started, the Edwards tie still gripped in my hands. "Turns out we actually know each other." I dangled the tie in front of him from where I was stood in the middle of his room.

He wiped at his sleep filled eyes and looked, blearily at what I was holding. "What are you talking about?" he asked.

"I also possess one of these," I laughed as I flung it in his face and perched on his desk. I pulled the photo of him and his brother off of the corkboard. "I also know *him*. Very well actually, he's my ex's roommate."

Wyatt looked more confused, until his eyes widened and he realised I had shown him a picture of him and Noah. "Hold up, that Logan guy is your ex? Wow, why didn't Noah tell me he was gay? I would have definitely tapped that," he said, as he chuckled to himself.

I looked at him. Unimpressed. The thought of him and Logan together made my toes curl.

"Wait a second. You *do* look familiar," he said as he stood up out of his bed and got a closer look. "Were you friends with that guy who became prefect when he was in tenth grade? Charlie?"

"Ding, ding, ding, give the boy a prize."

"Isaac Wells. I recognise you now. Don't know how I forgot such a pretty face," he grinned, as he cupped my cheek, thumb swiped over my lips.

I swatted away his hand. "Yeah, yeah, I definitely haven't forgotten about you and the way you try to come onto anyone with a pulse."

"You wound me," he replied, his hand clutched dramatically at his chest. "What are you doing here in Montreal?" he asked.

"I go to McGill, I'm a first-year English major," I replied, as I searched for my jeans. I wrestled them from where they'd become wedged under the corner of the bed and tried my best to put them on effortlessly, but my body was just a floppy hungover mess. I couldn't co-ordinate myself and ended up with one leg thrusted into the jeans whilst they were still half inside out.

"Leaving so soon?" he wrapped his arms around my naked chest and purred into my ear. "I have an en suite just through there, I'm sure we could both do with a shower."

"Nice try. I have to drive back to St-Catharine's. It's

69

reading week, promised I'd go see the parents, as I'm not spending Thanksgiving with them this year." I grabbed my t-shirt and tugged it over my head. "Have you seen my phone?" I asked, it wasn't anywhere to be seen on his desk or chest of drawers.

"My jeans pocket. I remember taking it off you last night as you tried to drunk dial half of your contact list." Well at least he was capable of doing something nice. He'd probably saved me from a lot of embarrassment.

"Thanks," I said as I retrieved it from his jeans and pocketed it. "Well, uh, see you around I guess."

"Of course. Any friend of Noah's is a friend of mine. You're always welcome," he winked as I stepped out of his bedroom door.

"I wouldn't say we were friends," I replied and closed the door behind me and sprinted back to my own dorm as quickly as my legs could carry me, without giving in to the urge to puke with every step I took in the blistering heat of the midday sun.

After I'd showered, downed two litres of water and doused myself in cologne to stop the stench of a brewery that wafted off of me, I was ready to take on the eight hour drive I had ahead of me.

I had to tell someone about the mess I'd found myself in last night. Definitely not Cassidy or Alex, she would kill me that I'd slept with the guy she'd had her eyes on for weeks and Alex, although he knew I was gay, it still felt like a bit of a weird topic to broach with him. I couldn't exactly have rang Charlie to tell him, even though he would be the best person to share this news with right now.

So I settled for Joshua, I loaded up his number on my blue-tooth screen in the car and pressed call as I drove out of the campus car park.

"Speak of the devil and he shall appear," Joshua said into the phone, that little bit too loudly for the sensitive head I currently harboured. I winced audibly in reply. "I was just on a morning run with Callum." So it definitely wasn't good things that were being said about me.

"Delightful," I replied. Callum and Joshua had both ended up at University of Toronto. Joshua doing Biomedical Science and Callum doing sports science. They didn't even live that far away from each other, same dormitory, just different floors.

"Well you sound cheery this morning," he commented.

"Where do I even start," I replied. I'd have rolled my eyes if I didn't think it would have been incredibly painful.

"Hungover?" he asked without a second thought.

"Yep and just about to start the eight-hour drive back to St-Cats," I groaned. The maps currently showed only light traffic and I prayed that it would stay that way the whole way home.

"Yeah I saw your Snapchat celebrations last night. Congrats on your win by the way, I'll have to come up and see a game at some point this season," he replied. I heard a door close behind him and my voice echo back on me.

"Where are you?" I asked, as I realised I was currently on speaker phone. This wasn't a conversation I wanted to be having if Mr Perfect was still around.

"Just left Callum, back in my dorm room now, gonna throw some clothes in a suit case and drive back too. We still good for tomorrow?" he asked. We'd arranged to meet up for coffee and catch up, even though in less than a week we were going to Quebec for a few days to celebrate Thanksgiving and get a few nights out in together before we headed back to classes.

"Sure, we still meeting at Edwards?" I checked. Although for the life of me I couldn't see why we had to get coffee there when we could go to many of the Timmies or Starbucks that filled St-Catharines.

"Yep. I'll be seeing you at 3PM."

I felt as though he was about to end the call, so I quickly blurted out, "I did something really stupid last night, Jay."

"Oh god, what? You didn't try and call Logan again did you?" he laughed. When I'd seen Joshua over the summer just before he'd moved to Toronto and me to Montreal, we'd had one more drunken night out in L3. Being there had brought all of those memories of the first night out with Logan. The night I couldn't take my eyes off of him and realised that I actually fancied him.

"No, much worse," I sighed as I pulled on to the freeway, the traffic ahead did look pretty clear, thankfully everything was on the move and I could see no hold ups.

"Just tell me. The suspense is killing me." He was excited with glee and I was afraid I was just about to crush that.

I took a deep breath and replied. "I slept with Wyatt Castle."

"What the actual fuck, Isaac?" he screeched. "How? Actually no, why?"

I instantly regretted telling him. I didn't need his judgment right now, I already hated myself for going there. "I was drunk, I didn't even know it was him until I woke up this morning, found his old tie and saw a picture of him and Noah. Trust me, I'm already feeling the shame," I deadpanned.

"How was it?" he asked and I cringed because I couldn't even remember. The bruises on my neck and the red, raw scratches on my back told me that it was pretty damn good.

"Who knows. But I'm battered and bruised right now, so you make of it what you want."

He gagged down the phone. "I know we don't ever talk about shit like this, but you slept with another guy? What does that mean?" he asked, he sounded hesitant as if he was about to have to tread all over broken glass.

"I don't know, Jay. It is what it is, I'm just going with the flow. Just doesn't seem like I'm bothered whether it's a girl or a boy. Although, last night it could have been anyone I was so wasted," I replied. When I thought about it, I hadn't even been shocked when I'd woken up in Wyatt's bed. There'd been no rush of panic when I realised it wasn't a girl, it didn't feel wrong at all. It just felt like that's how it was. Maybe that made me bisexual or maybe it just meant that I didn't care what gender they were. I was sure there was probably a word I needed to educate myself on for that.

"Just wondering. Always here if you wanna chat about it. Although, I'm happy if you're happy. Look, my flat mate is banging on my door. I'm driving him to Hamilton on the way back home, so I need to finish this packing and get going. I'll see you tomorrow though and you can give me all the sordid details."

"In your dreams, Jay. See you tomorrow," I replied and hung up. Just those seven and a half hours more to drive on my own.

~Chapter Ten ~
Logan

My palms had clammed up and sweat dripped down the back of my neck, I'd never felt this stressed and worried for another person in my whole life. We'd had this all planned for weeks now though, it was the first step, the first huge step.

It probably didn't help that I felt completely disgusted as I stood in the middle of the empty basketball locker room, the smell of sweat-drenched clothing and grubby boy odour engrossed my nostrils.

Rafael was late and that was understandable, he must have been freaking out, but I really did not want to be stood here, alone, when the team returned from practice, that really would look weird. I'd already dropped him a couple of texts to ask where he was but received no reply. I'd give him one more minute and I was out of here, I did not want to be accused of trying to perv on the basketball guys, even though none of them were my type. Not even Rafael, apparently.

Fortunately, the door pushed open just seconds before the sound of trainers slapping against the plastic floor echoed throughout the changing room. "I'm sorry, I'm sorry," he rasped out as he tried to catch his breath. "Dr Bernard kept me behind after our tutoring session."

It didn't matter, it was too late for it to matter as the team congregated suspiciously in front of us. Not only did that make the stench unbearable, but also my second-hand anxiety so much worse. In that moment I pushed Rafael forward, I was here to support, not lead, it was his battle to fight.

"We are here to talk," he said. I cleared my throat and although he glared at me, his honey eyes dark with fear, he knew I was right. "I'm here to talk to you."

"But you quit." One of the guys, whom I recognised from my English class, called out from the back of the crowd. Jesse his name was, he wasn't a boarder here, so apart from a class together I'd never really seen him around.

"After you took my captaincy from me just for being gay," he said through gritted teeth. I gripped his shoulder and squeezed, being defensive in that moment wasn't going to work, this needed to be a nice, calm discussion if it was going to work. "Eurgh," he groaned. "I didn't *want* to quit, but what did you expect? I've been your captain since tenth grade and all of a sudden I come out and after I lose my whole future, you take the one thing I still had going for me away."

There were some sombre looks around the room, thankfully from the people I hoped were still decent people - Conner from choir, Kelvin who I'd been lab partners with last year. People who I was friends with and hated to think that they were somewhat homophobic.

"I want to be part of the team, but I can't. You guys have no idea how uncomfortable you've made me. We were supposed to be friends, teammates, brothers. Especially you guys," he said as he turned his line of sight to Justin and Bailey, his best friends. "Some of you guys might know Logan for various reasons; you board or you've met him in classes or clubs, but you also probably know he's gay. Yet you and you," he pointed at Kelvin and Connor, "have absolutely no problem with him, you freaking sing with him, Con. So why is there a problem with me?"

Connor went to speak, but Rafael just interrupted once more. "I'll tell you why. Because you're all cowards. You're so scared that what happened to me will happen to you. I can understand why you're scared, trust me the reality of it happening is shit, but being gay isn't contagious." I rubbed at my temples, he needed to get this off his chest, but this wasn't how we planned.

"What he's trying to say is this wasn't the right way to handle everything, stripping him of his captaincy solved nothing, it just produced more bad press and made things ten times worse for him," I interjected, my arm placed in front of Rafael to keep him from kicking off with anyone, violence would solve nothing.

"We know," Bailey finally spoke up as he stepped forward from the pack. "We've all talked about it a lot and we know we fucked up, we just didn't know how to reach out."

"We live in the same dorm, most of you have my number, we all go to the same school." Rafael's voice got louder and louder, there was no point in trying to hold him back at that point, the volcano needed to erupt before the storm could clear.

"It wasn't that, we just didn't know what to say. You're our brother, our friend and our leader and we all feel a bit lost without you on that field. Look, we all panicked, we were worried about our futures as we saw yours get destroyed and that was wrong of us, we should have banded together and rallied around you, not tossed you out. That was our bad and we have to live with that, but we want to make things right. We have your backs, none of us care if you're gay, straight or a dinosaur, just that you come back and be our captain and lead us to a Championship title again this year." The whole team whooped and hollered around him and I pushed Rafael forwards once more into their arms, as they grouped around him and pulled him into a huge team hug. This was progress.

The overhead speaker rang throughout the school as the final period of the day ended and disrupted the touching moment in front of me. "Could every student and teacher please gather in the grand hall." Right on time, thank you very much, Dean Withers.

**

"Ladies and gentlemen. I know it's late and most of you would normally be sitting down for dinner right now, or on the way home to your houses, but I have called this mandatory school meeting for a very important reason. Since the beginning of Cherrington Academy eighty years ago we have been a school of tolerance, a school of loyalty, a school of strength and a school of courage."

Tolerance and loyalty were written on the Cherrington Academy crest on the two shields that crossed over each other. Strength was the motto of Edwards dormitory and courage the motto of Victoria. It had been almost hammered into me during my prefect training. But still, the words that Dean Withers spoke were important for what was about to happen.

"Some of your great grandparents helped to build the school on these grounds, stood strongly together for a boarding school to be here for those who needed to seek strength and courage here on a more permanent basis."

I was one of those people, I'd needed this boarding school for the very reason it was created.

"That's why I was so disappointed when stories came to light of how someone was treated on the of basis of his sexuality. We've all seen the news stories and I hope

Mister Danetele doesn't mind me saying that I was horrified on his behalf, not only about how the press acted, but how his teammates acted. When you become part of a club or a team at this school, you become a little family. I remember that very well when I played on the baseball team here and we would never have treated one of our own like that, you guys are lucky to still have your places on the team. Whether your motives were fuelled by homophobia or not, *this* was an act of discrimination. Today, that ends. I won't tolerate it here, one foot out of line from anyone on any grounds, be that race, religion, gender, sexuality, or disability and you will be gone. This is now an exception to the three strikes policy here."

There were mutters in the crowd, but I shut them out as I stood backstage with Rafael, well I stood and he paced around me.

"That's why I've been asked by the prefect of Edwards, Logan Shields and student here, Rafael Danetele if they could talk in this assembly today. We've discussed a few schemes and initiatives that will be ran throughout the school starting next week and now they'd like to talk to you about them, so please welcome them to the stage." Everyone clapped, as Dean Withers returned to his seat between the house heads Julian and Jessica. That was our cue to walk on stage.

As we appeared from behind the curtains the cheers got louder and I searched the crowd for familiar faces, Noah's, Charlie's, Amelilah's. I needed to know they were out there to be able to talk in front of all these people about such a personal topic.

I grasped the microphone with shaky hands and took a deep breath. "In the middle of the first semester of eleventh grade I decided to switch schools, not only switch schools but move two thousand miles across the country to *this* school. At my old school I was bullied and beaten for being gay." There were gasps in the audience and I'm sure looks of pity, I blocked them out, my eyes tuned on my friends, Charlie nodded at me in support to go on. "I came here for a fresh start, to a place where I could be accepted and I was, no one here judged me for my sexuality, I didn't have any fear here. Yes, last year wasn't great, but it wasn't because you guys were intolerant towards me and you have no idea how thankful for that I am. But that doesn't matter to me when I see things like this happening to somebody else who is gay."

Rafael stepped forward and he took the microphone from me. We'd planned for me to speak most of the time so I my mouth dropped a little as he stepped forward in front of the podium with it. "I was tired of hiding who I am, I've known I was gay since the seventh grade, but I hid it for years and years, terrified that things would end up like this because of it. I came out with the support of my family and I hoped with the support of my friends and teammates, but that didn't happen, until today, until they understood the meaning of acceptance, of loyalty and courage, strength in numbers and that's what me and Logan want to achieve with everyone here, starting today."

My heart swelled with pride, pride at the fact that he'd owned his narrative in front of anyone, even when he didn't have to or maybe didn't even want to. I clapped my hands on his shoulders and smiled. "Me and Rafael want to set up more chances for sports to be inclusive, be that for people from the LGBTQ communities or different genders to what is considered the norm for certain teams, or if you believe your disability might be holding you back from taking part. The sports team coaches at this school will be trained in inclusivity and Charlie Montgomery, ex prefect of Edwards, will be extending the bystander training he is currently offering to boarders, to everyone. This is so you know how to recognise discrimination and bullying and how you can help support the victims and help them report it."

"This is just the start of our battle for inclusivity and no discrimination, but I love this school, I'm proud to be a student so we feel it's the best place to start," Rafael added and the crowd leapt to their feet, an overwhelming amount of applause followed. He clasped my hand and squeezed it, in front of everyone and we reassured each other. Today we'd been bold enough to start something incredible, together. As we bowed off the stage there was none of the anxiety I'd felt beforehand, just a rush of excitement in my blood for what was to come.

**

Noah had just finished lacing up his shoes as I re-entered the room from my shower. He was all dolled up in a crisp white shirt and black jeans that clung to his long, muscular legs in all the right places. This was not an outfit I'd ever seen on him before, I hadn't even thought he'd owned anything so nice. Most of the time I saw him in sweats or his uniform.

"You killed the assembly speech; you and Rafael make quite the team," he smirked as he finished the final buttons on his shirt.

The clock on the wall read nine o'clock. "Where do you think you're going just two hours before curfew?" I reclined on to my bed in just my boxers and a vest and watched as he shoved his wallet and keys into his pocket.

"Just out." He didn't look at me as he replied, just pulled back the comforter on his bed to grab his phone from the charger.

"Anywhere nice?" I pressed as I placed my skincare tray down in front of me in preparation for my night time routine.

"No-where in particular. Just out." He checked himself over once more in the mirror before he made a beeline for the door.

"Noah," I called out, which stopped him right in his tracks. "Have a good night okay? Text me if you aren't going to make curfew and whatever you do be safe." I smiled before I chucked the spare copy of the gate key towards him.

He grinned up at me, his eyes wide in surprise at my reaction, but if I'd learned anything over the last year it was when and where not to pry into what Noah was doing. If he needed me, he knew that I'd be there and that he could talk to me. "I'll see you later." He shut the door behind him and I shook my head. *That boy, so mysterious.*

As much as I was grateful to no longer have to hide all my creams and potions in my bag in the bathroom, it was nice to be able to do this routine alone. Without Noah's curious eyes I could take as long as I wanted, sloughing all the moisturiser I wanted on my face and spraying toners and serums until my heart was content. However, I knew I probably wouldn't sleep until he rolled back in.

Cue 2AM as I struggled to stay awake, I blinked my eyes heavy with sleep as the door opened and he stepped in quietly and kept hold of the door till it shut silently behind him. "You're late," I muttered and the dresser beside his bed rattled as I assumed he walked into it.

He flicked on the light that rested on said dresser to see me half sat up in my bed, arms crossed over my chest.

"Christ, Logan. You trying to kill me?" he asked as I eyed up his ruffled state, his once neatly tucked in shirt hung loose from his jeans, a few more buttons of it undone than when he'd left hours ago.

"You said midnight and I text when it got to one AM but got no reply. I was worried," I grumbled out, as my eyes adjusted to the bright light of the lamp.

"I'm sorry," he replied, sincerely as he unbuttoned his shirt and chucked it in the laundry hamper we shared. "We just lost track of time and then my phone died and well, I'm here now," he said as he stripped to just his boxers and perched on the end of my bed. "I really am sorry if I made you worry."

"So it's a *we*?" I smiled, before that turned into a weary yawn. I shuffled my head back on to the pillow as I knew I was about to fall asleep at any minute with how my eye lids kept dropping, but I wanted to hear this.

His cheeks tinged pink and he broke eye contact with me in favour of glancing at my plain, navy comforter. "It's early days okay? Don't get a head of yourself. It was only our first date."

If I hadn't been so truly exhausted I probably would have clapped ridiculously or hugged him tight, because that was such a huge progress for him after Jessie, but sleep was about to take me, so instead I opted for throwing him a nod. That was enough for him right now.

"I want to hear more tomorrow," I said as he retired to his bed.

"Good night, Lo," he shot back.

~ Chapter Eleven ~
Isaac

"I literally almost broke my wrist the other night. Drinking games at college are lethal I'm telling you," Joshua said as he flicked his wrist as if he was downing a shot. He wasn't half dramatic sometimes.

"You don't have to tell me. Don't get me wrong I'm so glad I moved dorms, but Cassidy and Alex are actually wild. They write papers drunk like it's nothing."

I'd walked in the doors at Edwards and it had been like coming home. That rush of nostalgia that came when you walked into the warmth of all the good memories that had been shared here. Even all the bad things that had happened here. It was good to see Joshua, at least things weren't strained between the two of us anymore.

"To be fair, with the amount of papers I have right now their technique might actually make them a little bit more bearable," he said as he flopped in to the armchair in the bay window of the first floor.

"Remind me again why we chose to go to University?" I laughed, not that I meant it, it had definitely been the best decision for me and in my opinion apart from the obvious, it was going pretty well at that point.

"So we can actually get good jobs and do something with our lives?"

"Why did you want to meet here?" I asked. It had felt a little bit weird when he'd suggested meeting at our old dormitory.

"I'm gonna go see Charlie after this, so just made it easier I guess," he shrugged and took a sip of his coffee.

"Well, I'll make myself scarce before then. He still isn't returning my texts." I must have messaged him at least fifteen times over the summer, at first to just check in, ask about Logan. I'd seen that after Graduation they'd stuck around in St Catharine's for a few weeks so Charlie could put him through training to be the new Edwards prefect. I'd hoped he'd be able to tell me that he was doing better. He just didn't reply. Then I'd asked about a dozen times if we were okay and if we could talk. Again no reply.

"Just give him time. He'll come round. You guys have been friends for too long for him to hold this against you forever." I just hadn't been sure that was enough anymore, that we'd been friends for a long time, it meant nothing really after everything that had happened.

"I know," I replied reluctantly.

"Can I steal him away from you for a minute, Jay?" Charlie asked from behind me. My jaw gaped open at him as I turned around to see him. It had been months since I'd last seen him at Graduation and even longer since we'd last spoken. I definitely hadn't expected him to want to talk to me today.

Joshua didn't protest, so I followed Charlie up to the common room, there were so many memories, good and bad, in here for both of us. A rush of nostalgia hit me and churned my stomach, as everything that happened in here with October and Logan came flooding back.

"Hi," I said with a small smile, biting my lip to keep it from getting any wider. My heart raced a little about having a chance to speak to each other properly, but I had no idea how this conversation was about to go.

"You look well," Charlie said, a smile on his face that matched mine as he led us over to a set of armchairs that sat in the bay window of the common room. "Sit. I have a couple of things I need to talk to you about."

"Still the same bossy prefect I see, even when it's no longer your job." I hadn't been able to stop myself. It came naturally to me when I was around Charlie, it was the only way I'd ever been around him. The banter I hoped would also help fight off the awkward atmosphere that had settled around us as we sat down.

"Isaac," he warned, but the smile was still there, his frame wasn't tense and his eyes were still bright. It reminded me of how he'd used to look at me in our first year here when everything was so much more relaxed, there was no stress of him being our prefect, no strain on our friendship because of the trouble I used to cause.

We settled into the arm chairs in the far corner of the room, nestled in the bay window. For a while he just stared down at the floor and I started to run through all the possibilities of what he was about to say to me. I'd tried a lot with him over the summer and hadn't gotten a single reply.

"So, how's McGill?" he finally asked. He still looked at me with unsure eyes and it put me more on edge than what I felt when he'd first asked me to talk.

"Wow. I thought you were about to end our friendship forever, but all you wanna know his how Uni is going? Christ, Char, you really had me worried." Then I saw how he pulled at the skin around his finger nails, his nails chewed completely. This wasn't about my life at McGill. "But, you wanna tell me what you actually wanted to ask?"

The breath he exhaled only made me even more on edge. I shuffled in my seat, I felt like I was about to be told off for some prank I'd pulled. Such a sense of Deja

Vu.

"Right. Where to even start. When we met in ninth grade I literally felt like I'd landed on my feet. Middle school wasn't exactly a great ride for me, figuring out I was bisexual didn't help my popularity. Especially alongside always wanting to be in the school musicals with all the girls and reading all the romance books."

I smirked at him. He was right, when he'd arrived at this school with his Glee DVDs and his Wicked musical posters, I had worried about him and how the other boys in the dorm would react to him. I'd come from a middle school where there were rankings and being gay or bisexual definitely left you at the bottom of that pile.

"But you weren't like that, you didn't even bat an eyelid when I watched Singing in the Rain three times in one week."

"In my defence, I didn't actually realise they were the same film until Joshua told me that he'd seen you trying to watch it in class," I interjected. He just waved off my comment and continued.

"You helped me put that shelf up in our room to stock my overflowing book collection." His eyes flickered in remembrance, they lit up joyfully like a child on Christmas day.

"I probably should have banned you from Chapters and Inglot at that point, think we broke a lot of house rules nailing that wooden shelf to the wall." I laughed, what he didn't know was I told Julian it had been my idea to put the shelf up for my sports trophies. The two weeks detention was nothing.

"Stop interrupting, I'm trying to say something here." I gestured for him to continue. "That meant a lot to me. Actually everything you did in that first month meant a lot to me, it really helped me settle in here.

Before I knew it, it kind of developed into something more and I should have just told you then, but I just couldn't and then…"

"Oh no," I squawked as I tried to duck in front of Charlie in the hopes as he approached me, he wouldn't have seen me. It was too late for that as his eyes locked on mine.

"I'm sorry," Charlie said as he wrung his hands out in front of him.

"No, shit! Look behind you." I stood up, like the chair had burnt my ass. There was a fire in his eyes as Logan paced towards me, Noah in tow. Charlie swivelled round to figure out why the hell I'd interrupted him.

"Oh shit, what have you done now?" he asked.

"I have no idea," I replied. I'd racked my brain in the five seconds I'd had to think about it. Nothing sprung to mind.

His hands collided with my shoulders and I practically flew across the floor. Damn I forgot how strong he actually was. "What the fuck was that for?" I yelled, as I pushed myself up off the floor.

"Wyatt? Really? You couldn't pick someone a little further away from home?" he screamed back. Noah gripped at his shoulder to keep him from pouncing again.

I'd really screwed up if he knew about what had happened between me and Wyatt. Exactly what I didn't need right now, to have to have a lovers tiff in the middle of the school with my ex, once again.

"Woah, woah. Wait, what are you saying?" Charlie asked, his brows knitted together as he glared expectantly at Logan and Noah for an answer.

"He kissed my brother." At least they didn't know I'd slept with him, it could be worse. Although, that wasn't what the pain that throbbed in my ass said from where it collided with the wooden floor.

"You kissed Wyatt?" Charlie turned to ask me and there was that look of hurt again, his shoulders drooped as he grimaced at me. It was exactly how he'd looked at me when he questioned me about why I'd been seeing Logan.

"How did you even find out?" This literally happened a four hundred miles away from here, there was no-one else from this school that knew us there. Who the hell could have told them?

"Wyatt literally shares everything on line, he reposted a picture of you kissing that the club photographer took," Noah responded. He then pulled up the photo and showed it to Charlie. Because that was *really* going to help my case right now.

I grabbed the phone so I could get a look at the picture, it wasn't like I even remembered what had happened that night in the club. I was literally attacking his face in the photo, although the bruises that followed after that night looked like he'd mauled me, so at least we were somewhat even.

"I obviously didn't mean for you to see this, but what do you want me to say? I'm not going to apologise for kissing someone." I probably should have just apologised and been done with it, but I didn't want it to seem like I was ashamed for what had happened between me and Wyatt, because I wasn't. I wasn't going to bang down his door for a date, but it'd made me feel a little more relaxed about all the thoughts I'd been having about my sexuality. He'd all but confirmed I was probably pansexual. Definitely not something I was going to apologise for.

Logan rubbed at his eyes and he turned vacant as he retreated away from me, Noah's grip on his shoulder softened. If he'd had cried right then, I wouldn't have known what to do. This was the first time I'd seen him since graduation. Those tears had broken my heart, just as I'd stomped all over his. I couldn't see them again. Especially because of something I'd done.

"That's your problem, isn't it, Wells?" Noah growled at me. "You don't care about what you do or who you hurt when you're doing it. You didn't care about October when you cheated on her, or how you hurt Logan when you took off for Montreal without even a second glance after he risked everything to be with you. He's my brother, man. Picture or no picture, we'd have found out, Wyatt unfortunately tells me everything." There was something in me that clicked when he said, "he's my brother," and it was the fact that I wasn't sure if he was referring to Logan or Wyatt. Damm it sucked that Noah was able to be there more than I was for Logan.

I knew that Logan and Noah had become close, but when I thought about everything that had happened between *them* last year, I never once pictured them having each other's backs like this in the near future. If someone had told me that, I'd have laughed in their face. Part of me was glad, though, it was good to know that Logan had someone on his side if anything was to go down whilst I wasn't there.

"Noah's right," Logan agreed. My gut twisted. It was one thing to hear it from Noah. Another to hear it from him. "I'm sure there are a tonne of guys at your University that you could have made out with, it didn't have to be with someone that was going to get rubbed in my face. It was hard to see, Isaac. Just four months ago I told you I loved you and I waited for you to say it back and you didn't." His eyes blazed the more he yelled at me, I was practically rendered speechless by his rage. "You don't understand how much that hurt me and here I am, trying to get on with my life here. Be a good prefect, enjoy my final year, move on, but you're literally everywhere at this school. You've ruined my time enough here, you don't get to keep doing that in another province and then rock up here for me to see you and be reminded of that. Now leave. You aren't a student in this school. You can't be in this dorm." And with that he stormed off, Noah once again hot on his heel.

"I thought I'd seen him angry after you dumped him at graduation. That was next level. You really kissed Wyatt? I'm confused. I honestly thought when everything went down between you and Lo, it was just because it was him. But, if you're kissing other guys, is it more than that?"

"I think I'm pansexual," I shrugged. "I don't even really know myself and I really don't even remember kissing Wyatt, I just woke up in his bed with a dreadful hangover and saw his tie in his wardrobe, that's how I worked out who he was."

"You've *slept* with Wyatt? I'd get checked. You know what that guy is like, he'd hook up with anyone and everyone." Charlie shook his head at me and laughed, there was something about it that was just a little too forced, but I hadn't had time to deal with that right now, no matter how much I wanted to.

"Thanks," I replied. "Do you think I should go after him?" I gestured to where Logan and Noah had just left into the corridors, probably back down to their room.

"Unless you want to be castrated, I'd stay well away. You should probably just take his advice and leave, he is prefect, he will get Julian to chuck you out." He clapped his hands on my shoulder and for a moment, he just stared at me, before he scrubbed his hands over his face and walked away from me.

"I can't work out if that was two steps forward for

you or two steps back," Joshua shrugged from where he was now stood in front of me, his eyes twinkled and if I wasn't concerned with him being potentially my only friend then, I'd have probably slapped him.

~ Chapter Twelve ~
Logan

"Where does he get the nerve?" I yelled, as I sped down the driveway. Amongst all the chaos I'd forgotten I was supposed to be meeting Rafael down town to get dinner.

"You're asking the wrong person, Lo. I don't know what we expected, this is Isaac, he does what he wants." Charlie's voice echoed through my blue tooth speakers in the car. "I know it's hard, but don't let it get to you. You've let Isaac hurt you way too much in the last year."

I knew he was right and that was the hardest pill to swallow. I just couldn't get over him. Did you ever really get over the person who took all your firsts and then threw the three most important words back in your face? "You don't think I know that, Char, I can't help it. He boils my blood and seeing that photo it was like a fire had been lit inside of me. He could literally have chosen any guy, but he chose someone who we both know, who I'm going to have to see next weekend over turkey and green beans."

"You'll be fine. You're the bigger person, Lo. You have to be. Definitely don't let Wyatt Castle get to you, he's the biggest player ever. I should know," Charlie reassured.

"What the hell does that mean?" The way it seemed to me, everybody seemed to be getting with everybody before I'd moved into Edwards. It was like a sexual breeding ground.

"Look, before me and Beth got together in the second term of ninth grade, I did a bit of experimenting, just like every fifteen-year-old boy, you already know I kissed Callum, but I also kissed Wyatt, once. It was the attraction of the older man, what can I say?" he chuckled into the phone. I didn't laugh with him.

Yes, Wyatt *was* gorgeous and he'd been a great brother to Noah in his time of need, but now all I could see was him kissing my ex. And now also my best friend. I sighed loudly in reply and let my head rest against the steering wheel as we stopped at a red light. I never wanted to be this jealous, bitter person. Especially over a guy that had hurt me so bad. I just couldn't stop the burning sensation in my chest every time I thought of Isaac with another man.

"Lo, are you still there?"

"Just trying to bleach my mind of all the awful images I'm envisioning right now," I replied, as the lights turned green and I pulled away from the school.

"You can't say you wouldn't want to kiss him. Even if now I think about it, it is a little bit like kissing Noah. They look scarily like twins."

"I don't wanna think about kissing my roommate, or the guy who's now kissed my ex," I replied with a clenched jaw. "It's gross."

"This isn't about Wyatt, we both know it. You would still care who he was kissing even if it weren't him."

"Ding ding ding, give the boy a prize. What do you want me to say, Char? That I still love him? Because of course I do, you'd know that feeling more than anyone. It's him. He's still under my skin and I miss him. Do you know how hard it is being back and him not being here? That I turn the corner in the school and think of memories that we shared there or that I hate coming up to the top floor because he isn't there. That I haven't been going to places because they were *our* places. I know people think I'm an idiot to still feel like this, but I'm done denying it. Look at the mess it's left me in."

The screen bleeped to notify me that Rafael was calling me, probably because I was half an hour late to our booking at The Works. "Rafael's calling. I'll call you back." I said sharply, before I ended the call to answer Rafael's.

"Look, Raf, I'm on my way, I'm coming past the Pen Centre now. It's been a day and a half, I'll be there in ten," I sighed. What had given him the right to show up in my home? Like it wasn't bad enough having to go back to my house in Calgary, the atmosphere in the house always icy and tense, I spent most of my time there walking on egg shells to stop anything kicking off between me and my parents. I didn't want to have to worry about it being like that in the dormitory, the home I'd made for myself. I didn't want him to be able to just show up whenever he wanted.

"It's fine. I've ordered us a milkshake. Are you okay?"

"No. Isaacs here and I'm just so fucking done, Raf. Why did he have to come back here?" I choked. I always knew he was going to come back eventually, that we'd probably have to see each other or maybe even speak to each other as we still shared friends. I just didn't think it was going to be this soon.

"Hey, hey. Take a breath. He'll be gone soon and you won't have to see him again till at least Christmas."

"That's the problem," I sobbed. The tears streamed down my face and onto the white shirt that I'd thrown on in an angry rush to get ready after the showdown with Isaac. That was a mistake, I'd probably end up spilling burger sauce or chocolate milkshake down it and ruin it forever. It would be just typical of this day. "I don't want to have to see him ever again, why should I? It's just a continuous painful reminder of everything that happened. I know I was in the wrong too, but that doesn't change that I fell in love with him and then he just threw me out like I was some high school trash that he couldn't possibly love now he was off to the wonderful McGill. Can I just ban him from the dorm? I must be able to as prefect?"

"Lo. You need to calm down, I've never heard you so pent up like this. Just get here and we can eat our feelings and it'll all be okay." He tried his best to soothe the situation, but my hands started to tremble and I couldn't catch my breath.

"Raf. I can't," I gasped out. Clouds of grey fog blocked out my vision and I struggled to keep a grip on the wheel with how clammy my hands had become. I swiped them on my pants, but it didn't help, the wheel was greased with sweat.

"You'll be here in a minute, just focus on getting here, not on him Lo, he doesn't deserve your tears."

I didn't catch what he said, the loud screech of my tires ripped through my car and although I'd tried desperately to brake, I couldn't stop the shaking in my legs enough to hit them with full force. I'd only managed to stop the car enough for it to spin out of control on the edge of the highway, the other cars that drove around me turned into metal blurs.

"Lo?" I heard a voice murmur, I tried to hold onto that sound, but it just drifted further away from me, a white noise muffled my ears until I couldn't hear anything at all. Except my heart as it palpitated in my chest. The tears slithered down my face and burnt my cheeks, as I tried to grab at the wheel again, but it wasn't there. I couldn't find anything to grab on to in front of me. Nothing but empty space surrounded me in the darkness that had embraced me.

The darkness felt like forever, but in reality it was seconds until I was thrust forward and the car rampaged into whatever was in front of me, the air bags inflated and I collided with it like it was my pillow after an exhausting day, a rainfall of glass shattered around me, pierced my skin. I yelped in pain as the driver door crumpled on top of me and pushed me into my seat, my ribcage crushed in the brutal force. I tried to cry out again, but there was no air to catch and the world went black once more.

This time, when I woke up Noah wasn't hovering over me like the first extreme panic attack I'd had. I was met with bright walls and frantic voices as I was sped down a corridor, the lights whipped by and caused my eyes to burn. I closed them quickly and let the darkness take me again.

~ Chapter Thirteen ~
Isaac

"Okay, now don't panic," he said down the phone to me, as me and Joshua walked out of Denny's. Why did people always say that when they were about to tell you panic inducing news?

"Charlie, what's going on?" I said as I started to pace up and down the driveway in anticipation of his reply. Joshua tried to get a grip on my arm to find out what was going on, but I just shrugged him off. I'd never heard Charlie sound so worried.

"So, Logan got into a crash, he's on the way to the hospital. I've got Noah with me and we are going to go see him. I just thought you should know before this becomes gossip and you hear it from someone else. As soon as I know anything else I'll let you know, can you tell Joshua too."

"Are you kidding me? Is he okay? You can't just drop a bomb like that and expect me to just wait for news. I'm coming. We both are." I nodded at Joshua, as he looked at me with confused eyes.

"Do you really think that's a good idea? You two just had that explosive row, you're the last person he wants to see. Trust me. Don't come. Just stay close and I'll call you when I'm at the hospital and know more." And with that the line died and he hung up.

"Logan's been in a crash," I said as I pocketed my phone and searched around for my car keys.

"Oh shit. Fuck. Is he okay?" Joshua asked.

"I don't know. Charlie didn't know. He's going there now and we need to go too. Come on," I replied as I strode across the parking lot, frantically searching for my car.

"Charlie just told you not to go, didn't he?" I didn't reply. I didn't care what Charlie had to say. Logan was in the hospital and I needed to be there. "Isaac, I'll go and I'll keep you informed, but if he's been in a crash he's probably already in a lot of pain, you don't need to add to that.

"I don't mean to make this about me right now, but I need to see if he's okay. I don't want you or Charlie or this Rafael guy feeding back to me. I need to see him with my own eyes."

Whatever Joshua said next was white noise over the sound of how my heart pounded in my chest. I rested on the hood of my car to try and collect myself, Joshua's hands clapped on my shoulders.

"What if he dies, Jay? The last time I'd ever have seen him, spoken to him was when he was raging at me, screaming in my face, because I'd screwed up yet again." My hands clenched into fists, to keep them from shaking. "How do I live with that on my conscience?" I screamed, my fists collided with the metal of the hood of my car. There was just no way this could be how it ended, after everything we'd been through together, he couldn't just leave me like this.

"Isaac. You need to get a grip. I ain't taking you to the hospital in this state. Calm down." He pulled me away from the car by my shoulders and forced me to look at him. I couldn't even bring myself to hold his eye line, I held my hands up in defeat and backed away from him.

"I'm calm. Look I'm calm," I insisted, before I

dragged my shaky hands through my hair. "Can we go now please," I muttered.

"Yes, hand me your keys you aren't driving anywhere in your state." So I threw the keys at him, if it meant we'd get to the hospital quicker I'd let him drive my baby.

The drive flew by at a quick, erratic place. I couldn't focus the whole time I sat in the passenger seat, my hands fidgeted restlessly with my shirt, the radio, the seat belt. Anything to stop them from punching something or shaking like I was some raging alcoholic.

"Charlie just text me. They are in the emergency ward; can you just take a couple of breaths before we go in there please. It isn't going to help anyone, especially Lo, if you go in there all guns blazing," Joshua said as he parked up my car as close to the main entrance as he could get.

"Yeah, I get it Joshua. Tone down the anger, so sorry that my, my... my ex has been in a crash and all I can picture is the worst. Don't worry, I'll just be completely calm and collected."

"At least unclench the fists please, we don't need to doctors throwing us out before we even get to see him."

The walk down the corridors lasted forever, why had they situated him at the furthest away ward? "Joshua, where the hell is he?" I bellowed as my feet thudded against the floor with the huge strides I took. "Literally we've been past every ward."

"Charlie said ward eighteen, we are almost there." Joshua sounded calmer than me, but he was hot on my toes behind me as we strode past ward fifteen of the third floor of the hospital.

"I feel like I'm going to pass out," I replied as pure adrenaline carried me as we glided down the corridors and straight through the doors of the ward Logan was in.

"Well, at least if you do we are in the right place," he

tried to say cheerily, but as he sped ahead of me he stopped with almost a crash into chair outside of a single room. "Christ," he cried out as he looked through the window.

"Oh my god," I said as my forehead lent against the window to his room. My hot breath fogged up the glass as I panted after I'd sprinted down the corridors. "Oh my fucking god. Look at him." There was blood everywhere, it covered his face and his arms and soaked what was left of the shirt on his body. Dark aggressive bruises silhouetted his eyes and his nose. He looked so lifeless. "Is he going to die? Am I about to lose him?" I panted up against the glass, his body still didn't move.

Joshua pulled me away and into his arms. It didn't help, I just shrugged him away and gripped to window ledge under the window into his room. I didn't want to take my eyes off him for a moment if this was the last time I'd potentially get to see him. "Don't touch me, Jay. Fuck, fuck this, why is this happening?" I breathed out, my knuckles turned white from my hard grip on the ledge, but if I let go I'd probably pass out. I couldn't let go.

"Stop it," Noah said from behind us, he hadn't been here when we'd arrived, Logan was alone in the room. "He isn't going to die." Noah stood in front of us and blocked the path to Logan's door.

"The doctors have said he's in a bad way, but he's been stable all the way to the hospital, he just passed out because his body went into the shock due to pain. However, he's conscious, there's no head trauma, he's already had a CT scan and there's no internal bleeding or swelling, a slight concussion, but that's it. He's going to have a few x-rays as the doctors think he's broken a lot of bones, but he isn't going to die," Charlie confirmed from beside Noah.

It was exactly like in every film when people collapsed in relief or shock, I slid down the wall of the corridor and onto the ground. I buried my head in my hands and let out the shakiest of breaths. The tears were there, but I wiped away at them viciously, now was not the time. I needed to be here for Logan, to support everyone else in whatever happened here.

He was going to be okay and that was the important thing.

"What happened?" I asked as I looked up at the group from the floor.

The footsteps that pounded down the corridor pulled everyone's attention away from my question. The figure that ran towards them said, "I'm here, I'm here, what the hell happened? Is he okay?" Rafael asked as he stopped next to Charlie and lent his sweaty forehead on his shoulder.

"We don't know, he called me about five minutes before he crashed, but he hung up because you were on the line and he was late for dinner with you," Charlie answered.

"We were on the phone and he was freaking out, then the line just went silent and I heard this big bang and that was it. I tried to call him back but the line just rang out and then I got the call from Noah to say he was on the way to the hospital and I should be too." He panted as he lent up against the wall beside the window frame. Doctors had entered Logan's room amongst the commotion of everybody's arrival. I'd jumped to my feet so I could get a better look at what they were doing, as they checked his vitals.

"This was my fault, wasn't it?" I sighed angry at myself as I watched him sleep, nothing about him looked peaceful like he usually did. "He yelled at me and then he got behind the wheel whilst he was still fuming with me, this is on me." I felt a hand rest on my shoulder and as it squeezed gently I turned around to Charlie and Joshua as they hovered on either side of me, it was Charlie's hand that comforted me.

"You can't think like that," Joshua replied as he too stared through the window of Logan's room. "Accidents happen and this was exactly what this was." Charlie nodded beside me.

The first wet tear dripped down my cheek and my body felt weak under me, my legs trembled and I thought they were going to turn to jelly. Luckily, Charlie and Joshua clung to me, kept me up right and I leaned into Charlie, rested my head on his shoulder and allowed the floodgates to open.

"Hey, hey," Charlie said as he wrapped his arm around my waist to keep us both from ending up in a heap on the floor. "We aren't going to do this, he's the one in the hospital bed not us. We need to be strong, because he's going to need all of our help when he wakes up.

"I've done enough," I snuffled into his shirt. "He isn't going to want to see me, let's be honest." I wouldn't have wanted to see me either after today, especially if I were going to be waking up in as much pain as he would be waking up in.

"That's true, actually." Noah said from behind me. "Look, I'm not going to chuck you out the hospital, this is a free country and you can stick around to make sure he's okay when he wakes up, but you can't go in there. Whenever you leave, me and Charlie will send you updates, but he needs to be calm and comfortable whilst he recovers, that isn't going to be the case with you around," Noah said honestly, before him and Rafael entered Logan's room. When they shut the door behind them, Logan's eyes opened slowly. He stared around the room, blinked repeatedly to readjust to the white light and polished hospital walls, before they landed on me, where I stood still lent up against Charlie like a pillar. For a second he smiled softly at me, but as I went to smile back it was gone and he was distracted by Rafael and Noah's presence in his room.

"He's awake," Joshua gasped, the three of us clung to each other, like we had done for so many years, but this time it was like life depended on it and in some ways it did. If he died, I had no idea what would happen to any of us. Even the two in the room with him, maybe even Noah more so than the rest of us. He'd suffered way too much in this life for an eighteen-year-old.

"He's going to be okay." Charlie's fingers gripped into the back of my shirt and relief washed over me, that he was awake and that the three of us still had each other to hold onto like this when times were hard.

"I need to sit down," I muttered as I pulled away from the pair and dropped into a nearby waiting room chair. I let my head rest between my knees and took deep breaths in and out to overcome waves of guilt and nausea I'd felt as I watched his lifeless state. I dry heaved into the floor below me and the contents of my stomach churned like hot acid.

"Get him a sick bag or something," Charlie said as I gagged in my throat. Joshua flung one of the polystyrene bowls that looked like a hat next to my feet and I emptied everything I'd eaten that day into it until my throat burned like hell.

My head hung between my legs for a good few minutes after that, my eyes rested closed as I regained my composure. I wiped at my mouth before I looked up at Joshua and Charlie in front of me, a doctor not far behind them peered over to check that I was okay and I nodded in his direction to get him to leave.

"You okay?" Charlie asked as he sat down beside me and placed his hand on my knee, his thumb brushed gently up and down in a soothing manner and I breathed in time with the circular motions to bring myself back to reality.

"No," I replied simply, but how I felt was the least of my worries. "Not really, I feel like I've been hit by a truck." I laughed bitterly and sick rose to the back of my throat once more, I spat it into the bucket and sighed heavily. "Was that too soon?"

"If we don't laugh we'll probably all sit and cry." Joshua picked up the full bucket of sick and dropped it into the trash before he fetched me a new one. I did not deserve these people in my life, not after what I'd just done to one of our friends.

"Incoming," Charlie said and I turned my head to where his eyes were locked onto October, Ameliah and Libby as they hurried down the corridor towards Logan's room. I swiftly averted my gaze from my ex, this waiting room was not the time for us to reunite and probably fight. I'd let them go and see Logan and leave them to it in peace.

"I know he probably doesn't want to see me." I said softly, as the girls breezed past us like we weren't even there, "but, I'm not leaving until I know everything, till I know he is going to be okay and there is no permanent damage."

"I think that's fair," Joshua nodded as he took a seat the other side of me. "We'll stay until then."

~ Chapter Fourteen ~
Logan

Between CT scans and X-rays and the shit tonne of painkillers the hospital had given me, I was exhausted. Not that the pain would let me sleep. It didn't help that I was also completely grossed out at the fact I'd been in this shirt and jeans for almost 24 hours now and they clung to me with a mixture of sweat and dried blood. I hoped the hospital knew that I'd be suing for the fact they'd cut the sleeve off one of my favourite shirts.

I must have looked awful, especially if I looked even half as bad as I felt. Although, Noah refused to get me a mirror. He'd just sat vigil at my bedside from almost the moment I'd been admitted to the ER. He'd brought me a variety of clothes that I couldn't move to change into, books I couldn't open because I was in so much pain and grapes that he kept having to feed me. I couldn't complain to him though. I knew how hard it must have been for him to be here. No this hadn't been the hospital that Jessie had been in for months, but a hospital was a hospital for anyone who'd watched a loved one slip away in one.

Plus, I'd rather be in here with him, rather than in the waiting room. I knew Isaac was still out there, even though I'd told him to go home to Montreal, but now he was out there with Charlie, Joshua and Rafael. It all felt just that little bit awkward, a group of people that could be a recipe for disaster. I just couldn't have them all in here right now. The doctors had told Noah that the room should not be overcrowded as I was concussed and just needed to rest, so they'd been shut in the waiting room for over five hours now.

Rafael looked distraught and like he was going to hit Isaac, although Isaac also looked like he was probably going to hit Rafael too. Joshua kept having to pull Isaac by his shirt to keep him under control and Charlie just kept fussing, like the old prefect inside of him. Thankfully, Noah had gotten rid of them all from the window before it had hit breaking point. Again, thank god for Noah.

"I want to go home," I moaned, as I tried to shift in the lumpy hospital bed.

A face appeared at window of the hospital door and if I wasn't in so much pain I probably would have shot up in shock. But my wide-eyed look was probably enough for Noah to see exactly how surprised I was to see her as she peered through the window. She waited for me to beckon her in, but as I couldn't even lift my arm right now I had to sort of crank my head to the side so she'd get the message to enter.

"I did tell you a few other people had turned up, her being one of them. I didn't know if she came in peace or not so I told her to wait until tomorrow. I didn't know she was gonna stay all night," Noah shrugged as October entered the room.

"Hey, Lo. You look like shit," October said, as if her showing up was the most normal thing that could have happened right now. "Can you give us a minute?" she said, her eyes narrowed in on Noah. She'd never gotten the chance to know him like we all had.

"Of course," he nodded, before he looked down at me, his eyes searched mine to check that I was okay with being left alone with her. I couldn't possibly be in any more pain right now, so even if she did punch me or something it wasn't going to make this situation worse. I nodded at him and smiled the tightest smile the pain would allow and he left the room.

Amongst the pain, a pit of dread was disturbed in my stomach. It was the special kind of acid rush that I only ever felt when we had to be in the same room, I got it every time I walked into a prefect meeting or passed her in the corridor. It was dread I'd brought on myself, but still dread none the less.

"What happened?" she finally asked, as she sunk into the chair Noah had been previously sat in. She tucked her curls behind her ear and made herself comfy like she was settling in for the long haul.

"From what we've pieced together from the paramedics and Raf, I was yelling down the phone to him and ended up having a panic attack, that led to me crashing my car into a tree. I don't really know though, I think I blacked out before I even swerved off the road." I shut my eyes tightly, tried to muster up any other memories of the accident, but it was all a bit of a blur after arguing with Isaac. The doctor had also said I'd gained a concussion which probably wasn't helping with the memory loss.

"Christ, Lo. You're lucky to be alive by the sounds of it. I've seen the shows where the car wraps around the tree and normally the people die instantly. Why were you so worked up?"

"You don't want to know," I replied. I really didn't want to end up having another row about everything that happened last year.

"Isaac? I saw him in the waiting room, he's practically frantic. Joshua's going to have to buy a leash to reign in his pacing soon, otherwise he's going to drive everyone nuts out there." She spoke about him with a strained voice, a tone I recognised from my own whenever I had to talk about him. I knew she was trying her best to be light-hearted about this, not that I deserved it, but I didn't want to laugh right now. My ribs would probably shatter if I tried.

"Yeah, I think everyone's told him to leave, but I guess he didn't get the message." I half shrugged, the best I could with one broken arm, a fractured collarbone and two broken ribs that had punctured my lung.

"He cares about you." Oh god. This was not what I wanted to hear from her right now. "He *really* cares about you. I know things didn't end well between you, between us, but even I can see he cares about you, however much I don't want to. You guys broke my heart, but when I saw the look on his face when I arrived, some of that heartbreak felt like it had been worth it. I'm not justifying what you two did at all, but he never looked like that over me. Never."

"We tried, October. Too many times, even when we shouldn't have been trying at all. I loved him, I really did and he just didn't love me back. He probably just feels guilty that I crashed because I was angry about our argument." Not that I blamed him, at all. I shouldn't have gotten behind the wheel in that state, that was on me.

"It's not that I want you to two together. I'd really rather not have to see that, but we were all friends once, we all loved each other, I want at least some of us to end up happy." She smiled wistfully at me and I half smiled back at her. We shared a look at each other for a moment. It was a look of forgiveness. "Look, I just wanted to make sure you were okay. We were all worried." By 'we' she meant Libby and Amelilah as well, I watched as they both hovered outside.

"I'll be okay. Plus, now I'm going to have Noah at my beck and call," I chuckled nervously. I wished I could have reached out and fiddled with literally anything to keep my mind occupied right now, instead of fretting about every word I said to her.

"Yeah, I still can't get over seeing you two be friends. It's weird."

"He's one of my best friends," I admitted out loud for the first time. I'd always considered Charlie to be the sole owner of that spot, but it was more of a co-own now between him and Noah. "Once you get to know him, he's not that bad."

"I'll take your word for it," she agreed, almost a little reluctantly. "Get well soon, okay? I'll see you in the next prefect meeting."

She smiled one last time at me and it put out the final bit of the fire in my stomach, it was a good start to things being okay between us again. She shut the door behind her softly and with all my strength I mustered up a wave at Libby and Amelilah as they walked off.

It was then I heard her yell. It had been the first time since my birthday. This time, it wasn't directed at me. "You need to leave, Isaac. For god sake he's got several broken bones and is feeling rough, at least respect him enough to honour the fact he doesn't want to see your right now."

Noah re-entered the room before I could hear his reply or any of the commotion that probably followed afterwards. "They are all going to get themselves kicked out at this rate, the doctors don't like to have to deal with crazy people in the waiting room."

"I don't even know what just happened, my head hurts too much to comprehend the fact that I think me and October just ended out feud and now she's out there yelling at OUR ex because he's being a douche, yet again."

"Yeah, she was pretty scary, even for me." Well, he had scarpered back in here pretty quickly as soon as the yelling had begun.

"You're going to have to remind me about all of this tomorrow, the pain meds have made me so sleepy I felt like I just hallucinated most of that."

Noah laughed in reply and tucked himself back into the seat next to my bed. "I will, don't you worry, your face was a picture when she walked in, I thought you were going to pass out you looked paler than you normally do."

"You can go home now, you know? I'm fine. They are going to get me all plastered up soon and when my lungs have healed they'll let me go home. If I'm not at school, Edwards needs it's deputy."

"If I leave, I'm going to get Charlie to come in and sit here until you can go home," he said as he stood up and grabbed his jacket from the back of the seat.

I'd grown up an only child, with very few friends in grade and middle school, even for the first two year of high school. I'd never felt loyalty before. But I'd have to say this was it. Me and Noah in the last six months had built some crazy brotherhood. Helped each other grow, him from the pain of losing Jessie, me from the breakdown and the mess I'd caused last year. I held so much pride towards him, as he did towards me.

"Fine. Send him in," I caved. "Can you update Julian on my situation please and take everyone who's still in that waiting room with you."

He nodded. "Sure thing. Anything else, my lord?"

"Well, there are a list of prefect things that need to be done. They are pinned to my wall, if you fancy doing any of them in my absence, feel free."

Noah shook his head and smirked at me. "I'll do my best." Which meant he'd do all of the easier things and leave all the hard ones for when I got home.

"I'll see you later," I smiled. "Send in Charlie."

There were literal seconds between when Noah exited my room and Charlie entered. "Don't look at me like that," I said as he stared at me with sad eyes and a pained smile. "I'm fine, a little bit broken and bruised, but fine." I gestured for him to sit, I'm sure Noah would have given him his orders anyway. "It's just been a bit of a rough 24 hours."

"It really has. I'm sorry I told Isaac. It just felt wrong not alerting him about what happened. Even with everything that went down last year, he still cares and he deserved to know." He perched on the side of my bed and placed his hand on top of mine. "I need to say thank you, for yesterday."

"What do you mean?" I asked with narrowed eyes.

"Well, just before you pushed Isaac on his ass, I was about to tell him that I used to be in love with him," he confessed, before he looked away from me to peer out the window behind my bed, I assumed to make sure Isaac had actually left.

I grimaced at the thought of that conversation, I couldn't even imagine how Isaac would have reacted to that. He had the emotional sensitivity of a fish.

"It was time you know?" He squeezed at my hand. "I'm over him, completely. I needed to do it, for me, but I'm still glad you interrupted. He was so distracted the whole time we were talking. I think he was looking for you, trying to catch a glimpse of you. Don't think he expected to see you in the state you were in though, that was some rage."

If I could have moved my arms to cover my face, I would have. Damn those broken bones. "I'm actually mortified that I did that. So embarrassing. I didn't mean to push him that hard at all, I feel bad that he ended up on the floor."

"Is that why you crashed?" he asked.

I didn't really know. I was so angry, but I think the panic of seeing him had overwhelmed me more than the anger. "I'm not sure. Partly. I had a panic attack just before I crashed, I just remember feeling like I couldn't get control of my breath and my hands wouldn't stop shaking."

"Logan, have they called your parents?" he asked. "Do they know you've been in an accident."

I shook my head. I was seventeen, they weren't legally required to contact my parents. "I got them to call Noah, just made more sense I guess. Although, probably wasn't the smartest ideas. I don't think Noah needs to get any calls from the hospital for the rest of his life."

"He called me straight away and I grabbed him and drove here. Raf arrived just after, he's been in the waiting room all night with us."

"You two got to spend some quality driving time together then?" I chuckled, before I remembered the punctured lung and began to wheeze. I quickly pointed to the water jug and Charlie poured me a glass so I could get a grip on the wheezing cough I'd developed.

"Oh yeah, between Isaac throwing up and walking the length of every corridor to calm down, Joshua being well Joshua and the girls sat the other side of the waiting room glaring at us. It was a complete barrel laughs."

"Hey, don't let me being an absolute idiot stop you doing your thing with him," I croaked out before taking another long glug of water.

"I think we were both just too worried about you, plus me and Joshua had to take turns clearing up Isaac's sick, I actually stink right now, don't think he'd want to kiss me in this state."

"You were really going to tell him?" I asked.

Charlie nodded, all be it a bit reluctantly. His face softened and he pushed himself up against the foot of my bed so he could get comfy. "Like I said, it was time. I want to move on, properly from all of this."

"With Rafael," I muttered under my breath and he grinned at me and shook his head.

"He has enough going on without me lusting after him," he laughed, before he stretched his legs out so we were topping and tailing on the hospital bed.

"I don't care what Noah said to you, you aren't staying here. Who's still out in the waiting room?" I asked.

"No-one. Reluctantly they all left. Jay took Rafael and Isaac with him and October grabbed Libby and left."

"What about Ameliah?"

"She left with Noah, I think." That was weird, why hadn't she just left with the girls?

"Well, soon you need to as well. Someone needs to supervise Noah whilst he's in charge." I yawned as I tried to laugh, the pain meds had really started to kick in.

"Noah wants me to stay. I think he's a bit worried about leaving you on your own."

"I get that, he wasn't there when Jessie died and I know that must be hard, but I'm not going to die. The bones will heal, the concussion will fade. I'll be home in a couple of days." I couldn't be watched 24/7 for the duration of my time in hospital, I still needed my space. "If anything changes, I'll call straight away, Noah's my emergency contact remember?"

"Okay. Fine," he said as he peeled himself up off of the bed, he leant over to half hug me and he messed up my hair even more as he went to leave.

"I need you to do a couple of things for me, if that's okay?" Charlie nodded. "Find out what happened with my car and if you go in my top drawer of my desk my insurance papers are in there, engage in a little fraud and get me a courtesy car for the next couple of weeks whilst I wait for the insurance to get me a new one. Then when Noah undoubtedly comes back tomorrow can you make sure he brings me a couple of changes of comfy clothes and my skincare and maybe a couple of magazines."

"Bed rest is going to turn you into a monster," Charlie commented as he pulled out his phone to make a note of everything I said.

"Hey, you're talking to the sick and wounded here, have a little bit of respect," I joked back, before I began to wheeze again. Yep, laughing was still a big no no.

~ Chapter Fifteen ~
Isaac

I'd escaped back to Montreal at the first opportunity, fortunately with Joshua in tow for our French-Canadian thanksgiving plans. We'd found an Airbnb in Quebec City and planned to do some touristy shit, whilst we laid low away from the chaos we'd left behind in St-Catharine's.

"He's going to be okay, you know?" Joshua said as we unpacked our cases in the Airbnb. We hadn't shared a room like this since junior year. After everything, I was just grateful he still wanted to be in the same room as me. It must have sucked to have been Jay amongst everything that happened last year, he was the middle man between all of us, it really hadn't been fair to him. "Seriously, Isaac, you're going to give yourself worry lines before you are even out of your teens at this rate."

Charlie had stuck to his word, he'd kept us updated. Logan was being allowed to go home three days after his accident. They'd monitored his concussion and were happy with how it was looking, as long as someone stayed with him for a couple of days after, which was easy when he had a roommate. Not so good, his broken arm, collarbone and ribs. "I was terrified, Jay. I don't know how I'd have lived with myself if the last moment we'd shared together was filled with anger and hate. I'd literally never be able to forgive myself if that had been the case," I said as I crumbled on to my bed, my face flopped into the comforter.

"You can't think like that man, he's fine, he's alive, a bit battered, but he's going to be okay," Joshua replied as he kneeled beside my bed. "Noah's gonna take care of him and he'll be on the mend before you know it."

I nodded in reply. I knew that, but it would not stop the worry that was tugging in my chest. "I don't want things to be like this anymore. I don't want him to hate me, I just want things to be fixed between us."

"Man I don't even know what to say, I still don't understand how it got to be like this. What happened that day at graduation? Neither him nor you have ever said a word about it, it was like talking about it became forbidden without either one of you saying anything. I think Noah knows, but that's about it."

What had happened? That was a good question, sometimes I wasn't even sure I knew. Even in the moment it had been a bit of a blur. "After we graduated, Logan told me he loved me."

Joshua's eyes went wide and I wasn't ready for his excitement. Even though our relationship hadn't bloomed in the best of circumstances, I knew he wanted us to be happy. Who wouldn't want their two best friends to be? I knew it had been all he'd wanted for far too long. "You must have been expecting that though, Isaac? We all saw how he looked at you, when we actually realised what was going on between you. Maybe we even saw it beforehand and just thought it was some little crush."

"It doesn't matter now though, does it? I fucked up." I sighed as I rolled over to look at him as he crossed his legs at the end of my bed.

"What did you do?" he asked.

"I didn't say it back, I basically just told him I was leaving and broke things off with him. I didn't even give him a chance to understand. I just walked away without another word."

"Oh shit. Why man?" he questioned.

"Because I was terrified. Absolutely terrified." I admitted. I hated to, but it was true. "He scares me because I feel something for him that I've never ever felt. Man I was thinking about all kinds of shit when we were together and I just felt like I was in way too deep way too quick."

"What kind of shit?" he asked as he got up off the bed and propped open the window, it was ridiculously hot for October in Montreal, to the point I wasn't sure if the sweat beads that dripped down the back of my neck were because of the heat or because for the first time in months I was being forced to talk about all of this.

"Settling down kind of shit," I sighed and ran my fingers through my hair with a grunt.

"Wow," he grinned as he sat himself back down on the other bed next to mine. I still wasn't sure how we'd managed to bag such an amazing apartment in the middle of Quebec City with a room with two double beds. This is why I hadn't said anything to Joshua. He bounced on the bed next to me, unable to keep himself still. The stupidest of grins stretched from ear to ear, it was almost making me nauseous with how much he rocked back and forth.

"Stop it. I don't want you to make a big deal of this because it's already too late. He's gone and he's moved on, you saw how Raf was, they are clearly together." I shook my head at him, I didn't want to get upset about it again. I'd cried as soon as I'd gotten back to my dorm that day of graduation. I'd skipped out on dinner with my parents to pack up my room and take down all the photos and memories. I'd sobbed into my pillow that night, I'd never cried like that before, like real snotty wet tears that I just couldn't get a hold on.

"I'm not going to do that," he said as he forced his hands under his thighs. "I just think we should talk about this, it may be cathartic or something," he shrugged. His emotional range was either ecstatic or easy breezy living, it never went past that into the depths of sad or upset or anything like that.

"I don't know," I replied and flung myself backwards on to my pillows.

"Tell me about what you were thinking back then?" he asked as he turned on his side to face me and pulled one of the way too many pillows out from behind him and clutched it to his chest. "I wanna hear what your thoughts were and then maybe we can work out what to do."

"There was a moment, we were stood on the end of the harbour in Toronto and all I could think about was that this was it. This was forever. I wasn't disappointed that this was how it was always going to be, I was excited, content. It was perfect. I thought we'd go to university, graduate, move in together, start a family. I know that sounds absolutely ridiculous for an eighteen-year-old to be thinking that, but god I was so lucky to have been with him, to have found him so early on in this life. Then I blew it, because the fear kicked in and I thought I needed to go and do some more living before I settled down, but I realised the moment summer started and then I moved to McGill that I could do all that living with him by my side and it would be a hundred times better."

"That's some marriage shit, like that speech could have been part of your vows," he replied and moved to the end of the bed, pulled me out of my foetal position and practically shook me. "Why didn't you just tell him this?"

"I let it go on too long. When I got inside my own head I began to question everything and then it was months too late." I could almost smack myself, I'd literally ruined all of this on my own.

"There's still time though. Like a whole lifetime of time for you guys to make this right. But you have to actually tell him how you feel."

"I don't know how to do that. You saw how he was with me in the hospital, he actually hates me. I broke both of our hearts that day." I could still see his face in my head as I selfishly ruined one of the biggest moments of his life and just stomped the whole moment into the ground. It was gross, I was gross. It literally broke my heart to think about as the tears slid down his face, as the look of hope drained from his eyes, as his body shuddered as he became overcome with emotion. It was only worse when I remembered that I'd just walked off and left him to deal with all of that by himself. I hoped that Charlie or Jay or someone would see him and make sure he was okay. I still didn't know what happened after, I wasn't sure I wanted to, but I knew that what I'd done before I turned and walked away was the worst thing anyone could do.

"We can sort this. We just need to figure this out, if you care about him as much as you say you do, it will work. We just need a plan."

"Like what?" I said, frustratedly, my teeth ground together as I contemplated all the options I'd thought about for the last few months. Running back to St-Catharine's and declaring my feelings, writing him a long old message to tell him everything. I'd thought of endless possibilities. I couldn't see any of them working.

"With an attitude like that, nothing at all. Get your shit together, it's crunch time."

"Well, crunch time is going to have to wait because I

119

need to switch out my shirt and then we needed to go and meet Cassidy and Alex for dinner," I replied as I tugged my top over my head and grabbed a grey button up out of my suitcase. "Just a prewarning they are honestly so excited to meet you, it's actually disgusting. I've told them so many stories about you they are literally in love. They'll probably try and invite you into a threesome, but don't be shocked, it's just how they are." Thank god those two had finally got their shit together over the reading week break and had started to date each other. About flipping time.

"Sucks that she isn't single though, because she is exactly my type," he moaned from where he was still splayed out on the bed. I buttoned up my shirt and threw his jacket at him to prompt him to get up.

"And she's definitely still my flat mate, I don't want you shitting on my doorstep." When he didn't move, I prodded at his shoulder so he'd open his eyes and get a move on as our dinner reservation was in five minutes.

"I can't believe I'm still single. Our whole friendship group has been in and out of relationships for years and I've not had one girlfriend. Nineteen and still single, how tragic."

"Can you brood later, we need to go," I replied as he moved off the bed and we headed for the door.

We practically had to speed walk into the town to make our reservation, luckily Alex and Cassidy had gotten there before us and secured our table.

"So you're the famous Joshua," Cassidy squealed as she jumped up from her seat and wrapped her arms around his shoulders. "Isaac definitely downplayed how cute you were," she said as she pulled away from him and punched me in the arm, hard.

"What the fuck was that for?" I yelped as I stepped away from her to take our seats across from them.

"For abandoning us on that night out before you went home and then legit not even telling us where you were until you got back to your old school. Even then you didn't tell us what happened," Cassidy replied as she sat back down in her seat. I had to avoid the eyes of everyone in the room as they were probably completely disturbed at her high-pitched screeches and her outbursts.

"Oh hang on, I can fill in those gaps," Joshua began. "Isaac hooked up with…" I desperately started to shake my head, but Joshua didn't get the message in time and the name had already slipped out of his mouth. "Wyatt and then he came home and it caused so much trouble, like actually a crazy amount of drama."

"Who's Wyatt?" Cassidy quizzed her eyes wide with a glow of excitement, that girl loved nothing more than a good gossip. Well she wasn't going to love this.

"A tall, blonde Abercrombie guy who literally walks around like he owns the earth, you couldn't miss him if you tried." And Cassidy definitely hadn't missed him. I watched her catch up with what had just been said and as her jaw dropped as she had her lightbulb moment. I collapsed my head into my hands as she turned to yell at me.

"You didn't?" she screeched as I peered from behind the cracks between my fingers, I really didn't want to have to look her in the eye right now. If looks could kill and all that.

"Oh god, what have you done now?" Joshua exasperated. People around us stared as they chewed down their food, why did we end up being entertainment everywhere we went? Alex just looked at us all with narrowed eyes and his head tilted to the side like he had just tried to figure out the meaning of the universe.

"You slept with him?" Her tone was dangerous, the question a lot more serious this time as she glared daggers at me from across the table.

"I'm sorry," I began to grovel. "I was drunk and one thing just led to the other and well, here are. Don't worry, I've already been punished for it; yelled at multiple times and also caused my ex to get into a car crash. So you know, please go easy on me."

"Logan was in a car crash?" Alex interjected his eyes wide and dark with fear. "Is he okay? Are you okay? What the hell has happened over the last few days?" he asked as the waiter came over to take our drink order. At least it would break the tension for a little bit.

"I think I'm gonna need a beer if we are about to rehash the last few days," Joshua laughed and ordered himself a pint of Amstel. Both Alex and Cassidy nodded in agreement, although Cassidy could probably do with some water for the flames that had exploded out of her ears.

"Me too, beers all round please, sir," I requested and the waiter sauntered away, quickly, to fetch our drinks. How I wish I could have followed him.

As Joshua and I recalled the tales of everything that had happened over the last few days and the couple just sat and gawped at us. Cassidy shuffled in her chair as she twitched with her napkin and cutlery, probably about to burst with all the questions she needed to ask. Alex took her hand on the table to stop her from clattering around, but he looked concerned. Yep, me too Alex, me too.

"So you've basically been banished from St-Catharine's by both of your exes," Alex grinned, he was almost overjoyed at the sad state my life was in right now. Me and Joshua just looked at each other and laughed, if he only he knew all of the crazy that went on at Cherrington Academy. But, when he put it like that it was pretty funny, I laughed at the fact I'd been yelled at by both Logan and October in the last forty-eight hours. The prefect power had really gotten to both of their heads.

"You could say that." I took the last swig of my beer and caught the waiters eye to get him to come over so I could order another. I handed everyone out a menu so we could soak up all the alcohol we were about to consume, then I realised Cassidy still had that death stare in her eyes. "Go on, yell at me."

"I literally just can't believe you screwed him. I've been trying to do that for weeks and it only took you a couple of hours? Also, that you knew him and he's your exes roommates brother. Wow," she breathed out heavily with a huff and shook her head. I thought she may have been about to erupt, but then she giggled and I felt even Joshua next to me relax. "Your life is fucking crazy and I'm so glad I get to be a part of it. I love the drama," she clapped. We really all were completely fucked up.

"Right, let's get a couple of pizza and then do some shots. Me and Cass saw a great looking club on the walk from the car we should head there tonight and we'll crash at yours," he suggested and we all grinned like idiots and agreed with him.

"Let's get messy," Cassidy cheered as she downed the rest of the beers and ordered us a round of shots. Tonight was going to be wild.

~ Chapter Sixteen ~
Logan

The whole drive Noah had tried to cheer me up, help me think about anything but having to see Wyatt. He'd let me plug my phone into the aux cable and play the *Dear Evan Hansen* soundtrack. We'd even discussed the latest development that had taken place in the saga of Rafael and Charlie. Rafael had text me just as we'd pulled out of Cherrington.

Charlie asked me out last night. Like out, out. - Rafael.

I'd almost squealed when I'd seen the message, Charlie had made it beyond obvious how he'd felt about the basketball star so it was about time he made a move.

I'd sent back my immediate congratulations, whilst I kept Noah on hold in the seat next to me about what had me so excited. "Charlie asked Rafael out."

"Fucking finally. The sexual tension was too much between them, I have to sit in between them in English Lit and I felt like I was sandwiched in the middle of a threesome," Noah snickered.

"Well, now we are going to hear them going at it with Raf living next door and all that," I chuckled. I had not laughed much after I'd gotten out of hospital, my ribs felt as though they splintered every time I breathed, never mind laughed.

"Wonderful. I can't wait," he drawled out, as he

switched gears to up his speed on the freeway, the trees flew by at what felt like the speed of sound as I rested my head against the window.

The hours had flown by, especially when I'd fallen asleep with just an hour to go to Ottawa. Noah had woken me up just as we'd pulled into his driveway. I still wasn't sure about this, even as we pulled up the long-cobbled drive to his gated house. It was still as stunning as when I'd been here the first time over summer. Turned out Noah came from 'old money' - meaning in basic terms that like every generation that came before him was rich. According to his parents, I was from 'new money,' being that my families fortune only started a couple of generations ago with my Grandparents. You learned something new every day.

This time, it wasn't that I was worried about not knowing which knife or fork to use at each course, I'd seen both Castle brothers eat and they were gross. This time, my hands were clammy at the thought of having to see Wyatt.

I mean, I wasn't happy that he'd slept with Isaac because he was my ex, but mostly I just wasn't happy that he'd slept with Isaac. Fuck, I was so stupid to think I was special. That I'd been the only guy Isaac would ever be interested in. That I'd been his first and stupidly thought I'd be his last. It just wasn't fair that I still wasn't over him and he was just out there getting over me with Noah's gorgeous older brother.

It had been all I could think about, to the point I'd ended up lost in my own worst nightmare of what could go wrong if I had to spend a long weekend with a guy who'd slept with my ex. Not something you should ever really have to do in this life and not something I'd even wish on my worst enemy.

"You need me to help you out?" Noah remarked

sarcastically from where he stood on my side of the car.

"Well, actually yeah. You remember the broken arm, fractured collarbone etc etc," I laughed, as I attempted to cross my arms in protest.

"You're really going to milk this aren't you?" Noah asked as he carefully wrapped his arm around my waist and pulled me out of the car and to my feet. He closed the door behind me and proceeded to empty our luggage out of the trunk, at least there were some bonuses of having been in so much pain.

Before we'd even knocked on the door, Eliza had pulled the door open for us and stood with open arms for our arrival. "Logan, it's so lovely to have you back with us. We were so delighted when Noah said he was bringing you here for a few days. Freddie is currently at the office finishing up some work before the weekend. He'll be home for dinner," she said as she pulled me into the warmest of hugs, still being careful to avoid squashing my broken limbs. Like she was welcoming a third son home for the holidays. "Go get yourself settled into the guest room, dinner won't be till seven."

I beamed at her, even through the pain her motherly warmth made me feel something I hadn't felt since I was little kid. I couldn't even remember how it felt, but I'd seen it in pictures when I was younger, of family vacations to Miami, where we went every year till I was six, there was a delight in my mom's eyes as she cuddled me close in the picture that had once been in a frame upon our mantelpiece. Now, the mantelpiece was bare, saved the clock that ticked over.

As I trekked up the winding staircase, slowly, to allow for the fact my punctured lung still needed time to heel, I could hear Noah hot on my toes behind me. The two suitcases he'd attempted to carry up the stage clashed against the metal edges of each step, yet he still reassured me he could manage when I'd turned back to suggest he did them one at a time. I had brought my whole skincare regime after all.

As I reached almost the top step, movement on the top floor startled me. If Freddie were at work and Eliza was downstairs in the kitchen, it left only one other possibility of who it could have been. The one person whom I had absolutely no desire to see right now.

"Fuck," I swore under my breath, pain splintering up my arm and into my shoulder as I attempted to reach out and grip the hand rail, to keep myself steady as I went a little lightheaded at the thought of having to see Wyatt in that moment. I cried out as I took another step upwards, the twitch of my arm still radiating hot pain that burnt like hell, to the point salty tears had welled in my eyes as the pain became unbearable.

Unfortunately, just to make the situation worse, when I'd yelped I'd attracted the attention of one Wyatt Castle and found myself face to face with him as I reached the top of the stairs, his smug face just metres from mine. God I'd love to punch him.

"You okay?" he asked as I tried my best not to look at him or maintain any kind of eye contact with him, but that was almost impossible as the whole landing wall was littered with Castle family portraits. So I settled my eyes on the real thing and flashed him my best fake smile.

"Fine, thank you, Wyatt. Except for the obvious." I gestured to where my arm was in a cast, that had now been signed by several people, and the cuts and bruises that were splattered across my face. He gave me nothing but an amused smile before he breezed past me to grab my case from Noah who was still struggling behind me with both of them.

"Am I putting this in the guest room or mine?" he

wiggled his eye brows at me suggestively at me and shot me a wink. If that wasn't humiliating enough, he then began to weight lift my case like it was nothing. Jeez, I felt embarrassed for Isaac right now and the fact that he'd fallen for this cocky charm. How on earth had he gone from me to him?

"Can you tell your brother to stop humiliating himself please, Noah," I pleaded, sarcastically, without taking my eyes off of Wyatt himself.

"The first room will be fine, thanks, bro. Back off Logan, I think you've caused enough pain this week to last us a life time or at least until his broken bones heal." Noah replied far more blasé then I'd managed, I guess he'd learned not to give Wyatt the attention he seemed to constantly crave. Maybe that was the key to the defeat of Wyatt Castle.

"Hey, I didn't break his arm," Wyatt protested. "What am I meant to have done?" he asked as he grabbed at Noah's arms to stop him as he walked away.

"You slept with Isaac," I whimpered out from behind the pair of them. This was *my* battle with Wyatt, I did not need to cause him and Noah to fall out right now. Their brotherly bond, despite how much Noah thought he was a man slag, had been really strong since Jessie's death. I would not be the one to ruin that.

"Ohh shit, he told you that?" He scanned behind him for where Noah had disappeared into his bedroom, his cocky facade slipped away as his brows knitted together.

"He didn't have to," I said as I pulled up the photo on Facebook and shoved it in his face with all the might my broken body could give. "Maybe if you posted a little less online?" I suggested as I attempted to skirt around him, but he only moved in front of me to block my path once more.

"Look, I did not mean for you to see that at all, I was so drunk I didn't even realise it was him." He ran his fingers through his floppy hair and I actually thought I was about to get an apology from Wyatt Castle, that maybe he wasn't a jerk. "I mean, if I'd have known *you* were gay, I'd have definitely gone for you over him. You're far more my type."

"I heard that," Noah called as he reappeared after setting down the cases in our rooms.

"What? You can't tell me that if you were gay you wouldn't want to get a piece of that ass?" Wyatt smacked my ass and Noah saw red, as he dove at his brother and tackled him to the floor, I stepped out of the way just in time to avoid any more injuries.

"What's going on boys?" Eliza poked her head around the top of the stairs to survey the tousle that had taken place between the brothers.

"Wyatt is being an imbecile," Noah replied as he pushed the arm Wyatt had wrapped around his shoulder when their mom had appeared.

"What have you done now?" She rolled her eyes at her eldest boy. *I feel you, Eliza.*

"He slept with Logan's ex and now he's trying to hit on Logan, tell him mom." Noah crossed his arms like a spoiled brat. It was one of my favourite things about having gotten to know him and spend time with his family, having now seen him in his natural habitat and how he actually acted. He was a real mommy's boy underneath all of his snark.

"Wyatt," she chastised, as she shook her head. "How could you do that? That's Logan's first love." Not that I needed that reminder.

"It's a free country you know?" He smirked and his mom clipped his ear, before she pulled the boy away.

"Apologise please and stop hitting on Logan. He's family." That should have made me warm and fuzzy inside, but me and Noah cringed in sync after what Wyatt had just said about me, that was not something you'd want to hear from a member of your family.

Wyatt dragged out a groan, but quickly apologised under his mom's fiery gaze. "I'm sorry, I won't sleep with anymore of your exes," he offered up.

"Now you," she pointed at Wyatt in his boxers and tank top. "Go get dressed, dinner is in five and you are not coming downstairs in your pyjamas. You may be off University for the weekend, but you will get dressed in this house to eat, and you two go downstairs and grab yourselves a drink. There's a bottle of white in the fridge, help yourselves."

"Mom, you know Logan is heavily dosed up on painkillers right now?" he reminded her and she chuckled softly. If I weren't going to be eighteen in just a couple of months I would have handed this woman my adoption papers.

"So he is, well one won't hurt." Noah glared at her pointedly and she brushed a greying curl behind her ear. "Fine, fine, there's some lemonade or juice in the fridge help yourself, Logan," she replied as she ruffled my curls, before she walked towards the bathroom, Wyatt traipsed behind her to go and get changed.

"Your mom is right, one wouldn't hurt," I said as we headed down the stairs. It would also make dinner with Wyatt, the smug git, a lot more bearable.

"Eliza is always right," Freddie confirmed as he entered through the front door, placing his briefcase at the side of the door before he engulfed his son into a hug. "Alright son?" he said as he clapped Noah's back, but his eyes looked in my direction.

"As well as I can be," I nodded down at my arm in its cast. "It's good to see you, Mr Castle." A wide grin formed on my face as he patted me on my good shoulder and passed us to go to the kitchen. We followed after him as he popped open the bottle of wine and poured a couple of glasses and handed the other to Noah.

"Sorry, son, not in your condition. Come back at Christmas and you can drink all the eggnog your heart could desire," he said as he clinked his glass with Noah's and they both laughed an identical laugh. *Christmas*. It was an invitation.

Both of the boys got their fathers wit and humour, that's why I was glad it was that Eliza had disturbed our fight upstairs, not Freddie. "How's school?" he asked the both of us as we settled at the breakfast bar. The kitchen smelt incredible, a blissful mixture of spices tingled in my nose as the curry bubbled away on the stove.

"Busy." Noah took as a sip of his wine before he placed it down on the countertop. "Logan has me run wild with prefect duties amongst all my studies for final year."

"Amongst you sneaking out on your little dates that you won't tell anyone about you mean?"

"You seeing someone son?" Freddie asked, his eyes warm as he sipped his drink and smiled over at his son. I'd forgotten how close the Castle family had been with Jessie's family, maybe I should not have said anything.

"As I've told Logan, multiple times. It's early days okay?" Freddie just nodded, before he cast a look at me.

I nodded back at him and he left the topic. "What about you, Logan? Any guys in your orbit right now?" I wanted to throw my head back and moan loudly.

"Well, as he's already turned down me tonight, I'd think not, because if he's stupid enough to say no to me, he would never say yes to anyone else." Wyatt entered the kitchen and swiped the bottle of wine before he poured his very own glass.

"Well, if you married Wyatt, you really would be family," Freddie chuckled heavily, before that turned into a heavy smokers cough. As he regained his composure he cheered glasses with Wyatt and I dropped my head back, they really were three peas in a pod.

"His loss," Wyatt smirked, coyly, as he lent across the breakfast bar directly opposite me trying his hardest to catch my eye.

"This may have worked on Isaac, but it won't work on me. You aren't my type."

"Who's Isaac?" Freddie asked, as he moved to the patio door to light up a cigarette.

"Catch up dad, he's Logan's ex-boyfriend and Wyatt's latest hook up," Noah said from where he stared down at his phone, fingers tapping furiously at the screen. I couldn't help but wonder if he was texting his new girl, I wished he wouldn't keep me in the dark about her.

"Look at my sons, sharing men," Freddie said as he puffed out a ringlet of smoke.

I wrinkled my nose up at him, both at the smell and at how the warped mind of the Castle boys worked. They were lucky, that even with their gross sense of humour and their brutal honesty about absolutely everything, this was where I felt most at home when I was away from Cherrington Academy.

~ Chapter Seventeen ~
Isaac

The email had been open on my screen for almost ten minutes. The grade still the same as it had been the first time I checked. It never changed once, no matter how many times I'd refreshed the page. Forty-two percent. A fail. A big fail.

I felt physically sick. Like I could have actually just vomited all over my laptop right there and then. The grade churned my stomach like a washing machine and I knew, even as I clicked the email link one more time to reopen the grade page, it wouldn't change, which only caused my gut to whirl faster. I tapped relentlessly on the keyboard, but I didn't type anything, I just needed to keep moving otherwise I was worried the whole world was going to stop. Fall apart.

I ran through the grade in my head, tried to put together how much it would dent my average as it made up seventy percent of the final grade for this class, the answer was too much for me to consider. I'd need to get literally one hundred and ninety percent on the next paper to maintain the seventy five percent average I needed to keep my academic scholarship. I let out a deep breath, but the weight of the grade still remained in my chest.

Fuck, I slammed the laptop screen shut and lobbed the stupid book I had only half read for this paper across the room, it collided with the wall with a thud and bounced on to the floor. I had no idea what was even wrong with the paper. I'd been in a worried and drunken haze throughout writing it less than a week after Logan's accident.

Noah had thankfully stuck to his word and kept me up to date with Logan's recovery, he'd even sent a few stupid photos of the two of them as they hung out with Wyatt. That had partly tipped me over the edge the one night I'd wrote most of the paper. In between paragraphs I'd glugged down many beers, Cassidy kept me stocked with an endless supply till I submitted the paper at 4AM.

I'd seen her and Alex for the first two months of term write literally every paper drunk and still get low sixty percent grades, but I'd have happily taken that in contrast to the fail I'd received for this.

I could definitely do with a beer right now. I shot Alex and Cassidy a text to see if they were around and had any alcohol, as they'd bled my stash dry the night before. Even I was shocked when Cassidy messaged back to say *It's only midday? You okay?* The girl never turned down a chance to drink, I just hadn't realised that it was barely noon.

Beer first, talk after, I replied and within minutes both of them had appeared at my door, a six pack of cans in each of their arms.

"You called?" Cassidy half-smiled, as she gestured for me to let them into the room.

I flopped back down on my bed and covered my face with a pillow so at least if I let out the scream I wanted to, it'd be somewhat muffled.

"What the hell has happened?" Alex asked as he perched, cautiously, at the end of my bed and Cassidy hoisted herself up on top of my desk. She cracked me open a beer and I pulled away the cushion and sat up to rest against my headboard to take the beer.

"I'm going to fail Intro to English Literature. That big project I submitted a week ago, yeah, big fat fail. I'm so fucked right now." I took a long gulp of the beer and emptied almost half of the can in that one flick of my wrist.

"It's just one class? You can still pass the year with a fail, trust me I've been calculating my grade for this semester so far and I can easily level it out to a sixty percent pass for the year with a few good grades," Cassidy shrugged, like it was nothing, like it wasn't my whole future here that I'd be losing with this fail. Then I realised where I was, no-one understood that here. That was part of the reason I'd been put into the academic dormitory the first-time round, to be around like-minded people in a scholarly environment.

"You don't understand." I curled my fingers into a fist, my fingers clenched hard as I breathed past the rage.

She hung her head and suddenly I felt a cold sadness that I'd taken my failure out on her, she didn't understand, why should she? I'd never discussed my academic scholarship or my parents with her, we'd breezed past all of that and got straight down to drunken nights and crazy parties, which I guess was exactly what university was supposed to be about for most people, originally it had been what I'd wanted too, but when I'd seen that forty two percent I realised maybe I shouldn't.

"I'm sorry," I said as I placed the unopened can on the floor and grabbed her hand from Alex's protective shield. "I just can't be a fuck up, you know? I don't have it in me to deal with it. It's not your fault."

A smile crept up her face and she pulled me in for a hug and I felt the frost melt. "Don't worry about it. We are gonna talk about this though, but first me and Alex are gonna get some pizza so this doesn't turn into a wild night, we'll walk to Buffalo's and get it, then we can discuss your problems, okay?" I nodded and she squeezed me again, before her and Alex left.

I flopped down in my bed and reached for my phone from the shelf. There was only *one* person who would understand all of this.

I'm such a failure - Isaac

I typed it out quickly and sent to Logan, as my other hand clutched at the can of beer, my finger marks imprinted into the metal.

I could not believe I had allowed myself to get into this mess, that I thought to get drunk and wallow in my worry was a better idea than just having pulled myself together and pushed on. Then I'd have at least written a somewhat decent paper.

My parents literally text me every other day to check in on me and how university was going, but most of me knew it was to keep me on track. How could I tell them about this huge fat fail? They'd kill me. Like actually drive up to Montreal and maim me. They'd ran a small business together since I had been born, they didn't even know how to fail. The business had never took off like they'd intended, but it had worked well enough for us to constantly be able to get by. They only knew how to work hard, they'd be so disappointed to see that I'd let that slip from my very own work ethic. I cracked open another beer at the thought and chugged.

My phone bleeped and pulled me from that thought, I'd became so lost in my parents disappointed faces, I'd almost forgotten I'd sent that text to Logan.

What do you mean? - Logan

Coming Home

I got a 42 on my latest paper - Isaac

Almost as soon as I'd sent that text my phone began to ring, Logan's name flashed up repeatedly on my screen and with every ring my heartbeat raced more and more. I downed the final drop in the can and flung it in the general direction of the trash can, before I clicked accept on the call.

"Hello, Logan," I sang into the phone, before I reached for a can that had rolled down on to the floor. Thank god Alex and Cassidy had gone out to get some food, I really needed it to soak up the amount of alcohol I'd consumed in such a short amount of time.

"Isaac," he replied and his voice, god his voice, produced goose bumps up and down my arm. "You okay over there?" he asked, warmly, his tone a verbal hug around my tipsy body.

"I can't believe I've failed, Logan. What is wrong with me?" I asked as my voice cracked, I was so glad the other two had left, so I could be vulnerable around the one person I trusted enough to allow him to see me like this, to be completely exposed.

"Hey. Don't say that. It's not true, one bad grade doesn't define you. If that were the case I would have failed the whole of the eleventh grade." He laughed and the fact that he could laugh about such a bad time allowed me to relax, my body slumped more into mattress as I turned on to my side so I could get completely comfortable.

"I'm scared," I admitted. "I don't wanna fuck this all up just because of one grade, it could derail everything. If I lose my scholarship I won't be able to afford to go here anymore."

"You listen here, mister. The guy I fell in love with isn't a quitter, he isn't a failure and he definitely would not

137

be sat there moping over one grade. He'd have marched down to that professors office and given them hell and told them exactly what happened, so that he could get a rewrite. Then he'd smash that bloody rewrite. So, stop worrying about me, the doctors said I'm heeling nicely, it'll take time, but I'll be fine. But, for heaven's sake, stop drinking, when has that ever helped either of us?"

I spluttered around the bottle of water I kept on my night shelf that I'd grabbed to do as I was told, he was right. The vision of him being drunk and throwing up on Charlie's slippers flashed through my mind. "Yeah, I remember that night way too well," I grinned, in my tipsy state I could almost feel him as he ground up against me on that sticky floor, he had moves that would put any dancer to shame.

"Don't even remind me, so much humiliation in just one." If I closed my eyes I could picture his flushed skin, how he blushed like a beetroot at the thought of us basically going at it on the dancefloor.

"You were so hot that night," I started, more of a mutter than clear words, but as I went to continue, I heard him clear his throat. "I'm sorry." I said softly, somewhere in my subconscious I could still tell that this was an inappropriate topic between the two of us.

"Don't worry about it. You're drunk. I just don't want you to say anything you'll regret."

"My friends have gone to get us pizza." I quickly changed the topic of conversation, I couldn't ruin all the progress this talk had helped us to make.

"Good. Joshua said that he met both of them and from what he could remember that they seemed really nice. I quote *'Cassidy was hot, but unavailable'* was amongst his compliments for them."

To be fair, I was surprised that Joshua could

remember anything from that night; he'd stumbled down half a flight of stairs on the walk back up to our Airbnb he was so drunk. "Yeah, they are kind of the best," I replied, they'd literally just gone and walked a two-mile round trip to our favourite pizza place that didn't deliver just so I would feel better.

"I'm glad someone else is looking after you now you don't have a prefect supervising your every move." He sounded so cocky, that prefect status had really given him a boost of confidence. Good, if there was anyone that deserved to have a little more belief in himself it was him.

I went to ask him how that was going, I'd been curious to hear it from him rather than just Joshua, but in that moment Alex and Cassidy bound back through my door, excitedly, with three large pizza boxes and some sides in their hands.

I shushed them quickly and motioned to the phone in my hand and thankfully they got the message and grew silent, almost, Cassidy still mouthed to me to ask who was on the phone. I mouthed back that it was Logan and her eyes lit up excitedly and she snatched the phone out of my hand.

"Hey Logan," she said sweetly. "It's Cassidy, Isaacs flat mate. He's a little too drunk to be talking to you right now, so we are going to feed him some pizza and sober him up. Please call him back soon, I've not seen him smile this much in the two months I've known him."

She paused to hear his reply and then grinned wider herself. "Good night to you too, Logan," she chirped, before she hung up and chucked the phone back at me.

"Logan said he believes in you and he also said sleep well, but you are not going to sleep until you tell us why you thought calling your cute little ex was a good idea."

"Did you just drunk call your ex?" Alex said as he looked down on me from where he'd perched on my bed frame, three empty cans now on the floor next to me. That was gross and definitely not the answer.

"Don't look at me like that." I grabbed at a slice of pizza and chowed it down quickly. I'd never eaten my feelings before, but it was probably going to be better than drowning them in alcohol.

"Logan didn't seem to mind," Cassidy shrugged as she plonked herself down in the middle of my bed, a slice of pizza in each hand. "You can tell he cares about you, he sounded concerned when you vanished off the phone."

"After you snatched it away from me," I corrected. "We were having a lovely conversation, I'll have you know." I replied between mouthfuls of pizza. Damn this stuff was good.

"To save you from yourself," Cassidy nestled herself in between Alex's legs and handed him up a slice of the pizza.

"You two are gross. Why am I friends with you?" This single life sucked, good thing they'd brought a large pizza each, I could eat my feelings for days at this rate.

"Why aren't you doing anything about your situation?" Cassidy stretched her legs out to the point they were resting across my shins, she really knew how to take liberties.

"What do you mean?" Which situation was she talking about? My failing academic career, my failed relationship? Everything in between?

"With Logan. You know, love of your life? Probably the cutest ginger I've ever had the luxury of viewing pictures of." Alex elbowed her in the back. "Hey, I said ginger, not *guy*, you're the hottest *guy* I've ever seen."

"After Wyatt?" I suggested with a smirk and if I'd have been close enough, Alex probably would have elbowed me as well.

"Touché." She leant forward and slapped my knees before she helped herself to another couple of slices of pizza. "But seriously. Time to wife him up, before someone else does."

"Look, I need to sort this shit out with my grade first," I sighed, the pizza hadn't helped as much as I needed it to. I was not a comfort eater at all. "Then I'll figure him out." Whatever happened, I'd figure it out. I had to, I would not give McGill up, I couldn't. With his belief, I knew I could fix it all. He may not have been there with me physically, but with him by my side metaphorically I knew anything was possible.

"Well, if you aren't gonna make a move on him any time soon, we need to find you another man or woman? That's still an option, right?" I nodded, reluctantly, I guess it was.

"I don't need another person, Cassidy," I gritted my teeth together. When I'd been her wing man she'd kind of laid off of her attempts to find me someone, but now she was back in full force as Alex wrapped his arms around her.

"We'll see." Her eyes glinted mischievously as she bit into her pizza. What had I started?

~ Chapter Eighteen ~
Logan

Even though my time in the hospital had been almost a complete blur to me, the thing that stuck out like a clear summers day in the middle of winter was October and her visit to see me. I was still shocked to this moment that when she left it had felt like our feud was over, like the anger had drained from her and she'd forgiven me.

Today would be the test of that today. Our biweekly prefect meeting and this one was going to be a big one. I planned to make an announcement that could start a huge project for us that would need a quick turnover. I could not wait to get started.

That did not stop me perpetually biting at my lips, Noah had already swatted at me a number of times, but I continued to do so as my leg jigged up and down in my seat as we waited for October and Ameliah to show up in the grand hall. With every passed minute, my feet only tapped more irritably against the tiled floor.

"Can you stop?" Noah demanded as he pushed my feet onto the solid ground. "It's going to be fine, they'll be here soon, they'll get a strike against them from their head of house if they don't. Plus, you said October left things on a good note, right?" I nodded. "Then stop worrying."

It will be fine, I repeated over and over in my head, it had to be. "What if that was just because I was in hospital? People being hurt makes you do crazy things," I replied, my internal chanting hadn't managed to settle my heart as it raced above tempo.

The door to the main hall opened and two girls, still dressed in their cheer costumes, dripped in sweat and panting like they'd just ran a marathon, entered. They were here and in that moment that was all that mattered.

"I'm so sorry we are late," October gasped out. "With Beth as our actual coach now, rather than prefect we get drilled like marines in practice now and she wasn't happy with our basket tosses today, so she made us run laps until she was. She's a monster." They both collapsed into the seats opposite us, Amelilah's forehead rested against Octobers shoulder as she tried to catch her breath.

"No worries." Noah handed October and Ameliah the bottles of water I'd bought for all of us. Being the good host that I was I'd bought water and donuts for all of us, if this went well I had no clue when this meeting was going to end, so best to keep us all fuelled up and maybe a little bribed too.

"Why are we in here by the way?" Ameliah asked after she gulped down half the bottle of water, the rouge tint to her face began to fade and as she dabbed at her forehead with a napkin it was like you could hardly tell they'd just had to train for the last two hours.

"Well, if you don't mind turning your attention the screen for a moment, all will be revealed." I pressed the button on the control in my hand and the huge screen lowered itself down in front of us. I'd been up all night, three nights running to make this presentation, for it to work it needed to be perfect.

"Well this is taking preparation to the next level," Noah muttered as the screen turned on. I had not even shown it to him yet or even let him in on my idea. I wanted to make sure it was completely doable in just a few weeks, before I exposed the craziness of it to anyone else, especially Noah, he was a lot more rational than I was.

I opened up the presentation and icy blue letters that read *Cherrington Academy's Winter Ball* and a photo of the Yule Ball scene from Harry Potter that I'd stolen from Google, appeared on the screen. Wow, maybe I had taken this too far, amongst the lack of sleep I'd forgotten I'd themed all of the text and images around my idea and the season it fell under.

Everyone looked confused, "Okay, okay, before you all judge this, please just hear me out. I know you're all about to think I've been watching way too many American Rom-Com films and TV series, but I actually think this is a really good idea and one that all the students will love at this school."

As I flipped to the next slide it was pictures of differently decorated halls for other winter balls that had been hosted before. "What I'm thinking is that we do white and gold as the predominant theme and then we'll integrate the colours of Victoria and Edwards in different ways, table decorations, plates and cups for the buffet food that would be provided." When I'd searched up winter balls a lot of it had been *Frozen* parties, so I'd been left with a limited amount to choose from.

The next slides were full of ideas for bands to play, I'd obviously made the suggestion that my choir would sing a number or two, it would make great practice for the competition season next semester. I'd thought of everything, the checklist for the presentation alone had been two A4 pages long. From food, to timings, to music, to colour themes, to whether we should have a dress code or not and all the logistical things in between like hiring a tech company to do lights and music when the band wasn't playing.

To the final thing on my list. Proposals. Like how people would invite their date to the ball. It had been something that Dean Withers had said about how he'd asked his girlfriend to their ball that had triggered this thought. I'd even talked it through with him and he'd agreed that the winners would win a scholarship towards their tuition at the school and a winter themed hamper, but the way this school was the hamper would probably be worth like a thousand bucks. Go big or go home may as well have been this schools motto. The basketball team got a god damn party bus to celebrate when they won a national competition last year.

I finished the presentation with an overview of everything and asked if anyone had any questions or concerns. If this meeting went well it'd be easier to put it to the school council, I just needed the other three of them behind me.

"I'm in, a chance to buy a new dress, find a date, get all dolled up? Yes please. Plus me and Libby could put our MUA business to good use and offer deals on hair and make up for the night. It's going to be incredible," October said as she opened her phone and started to text, most likely Libby so they could be prepared for all of this.

The other pair still looked sceptical. "You want to put this all together in a month? Have you even cleared it with the Dean yet?" Noah asked, and I nodded. Dean Withers had been my first point of call, he'd approved it quicker than I thought he would, said something about reminding him of when he'd been here. I'd looked back through the yearbooks for his time here and realised that at the end of every school year back then they'd throw a Summer Ball and it was a lot larger affair than what I had planned. Theirs came with circus tents and fairground rides, I just wanted a dance in the Grand Hall, a band and maybe a snow machine.

"What about a budget?" Ameliah had written a list of things she clearly wanted to question whilst she'd been watching my presentation, so I grabbed at it and reviewed them all.

"A basic budget is written, I didn't want to make all the decisions on my own, but Dean Withers and the events team gave me a figure of how much we could spend and it would be easy to do all of this within that price range. I have bands in mind and as I already mentioned the choir. I'm obviously not going to put gender limits on what students can wear, if the boys wanna come in skirts and the girls in suits then good on them." I felt like I should say *anything else?* but for now this list was enough. "Look, I've really thought this through, you know me, I've calculated every cost, navigated every risk, even made a complete breakdown of a timetable that would allow us to do this all in a month. Come on guys."

"I think it's a great idea." Ameliah finally smiled and I exhaled, she was a tough nut to crack some of the time, but her concerns were valid, this was a small amount of time to produce such a big thing. Especially for the whole school, it wasn't like I planned to limit it to just the eleventh and twelfth graders.

Noah still looked reluctant, he had not said a word for a while and his eyes still flickered over the handouts I'd given them with every bit of information that was on the PowerPoint. "What's the problem Noah?" I asked through gritted teeth, I had not expected him to be the problem here, I thought he'd have my back straight away.

"I just don't really get it. Like what the big dance and those cheesy American prom proposals," Noah groaned. "You want us to go around doing those and have it be a competition, are you serious?"

"They are just a bit of fun, Noah, if you don't wanna win you don't have to try that hard, just ask someone to be your date. I just thought they would be a bit of a stress relief for the next few weeks in between exams and the end of the semester happening." It was easy for me to say, I was not worried about either having to plan a proposal or being proposed to. Although Noah was still single as well, to my knowledge at least, so I wasn't sure why we he was kicking up such a fuss, at least this way we could go stag together.

"Whatever you say, Shields. You know that isn't going to be the case for all the competitive people, it's going to be chaos, if you had a boyfriend you'd probably be plotting some elaborate plan right now." Well *that* stung like a bee, I flinched a little and turned to pull out my USB from the screen. This meeting was over.

"I'm sorry man," he said, then Ameliah elbowed him in the stomach to get up to come over and talk to me, before I darted out of the hall. "I didn't mean it like that, I just want us to be sure that this will work and not end up being an epic fail. I can see you've done all the work for it, I just don't want it to snowball into this chaotic amount of work and it'll be too much for you. You're still recovering. Pun intended," he said with a chuckle and I couldn't help but laugh as well, he was such an idiot.

"It's fine, you're right. If I weren't single I'd be planning a proposal, but I'm not, so I won't be. I'll be able to put all my time into this so you guys can get dates and do all the proposal stuff and revise for your exams. I just need a little bit of help here and there with the practicalities and logistics. I know this just adds to what we are already doing with the prefect stuff, but I just think it would be something really fun to finish the semester of with and something we could leave as part of our prefect legacy for other years to do."

"I'm in, we'll support you in pitching it to the school council, but I'm sure they will love it," he smiled as he wrapped his arm around my shoulder.

"Group hug?" October suggested as she wrapped herself around us before she squeezed Ameliah into the mix.

"Hey guys," I squealed from the middle of the circle. "Broken arm here," I reminded and they all backed off quickly. With the sling off it was easy to forget there was a huge cast under my blazer, a blazer that was three sizes bigger than what I'd normally have to wear so I could get it over the chunky cast. The pain had died down a lot and the tonne of painkillers I took every day helped. It hadn't prevented me really doing anything, clearly considering I'd worked relentlessly at this idea.

"You guys can go though, I'll clear all of this up," I said as I watched October give Noah and Ameliah a side glance before they both dashed off, a quick goodbye thrown behind them for me. The pit of my stomach felt cold as I wondered why she'd wanted to get rid of them so quickly, the meeting had been so good and she'd been the first to jump at my idea, I thought things were finally back to normal.

"So I saw you followed Isaac back on Instagram again," she said as she tossed the empty confectionery package into the bin and swept the food crumbs off the table and on to the floor.

Damn it. I'd forgotten that would probably come up on her activity page, especially after I'd been through and liked a bunch of his newer photos from his time at McGill. It had just felt like the right thing to do after the phone call we'd shared a few days before. Things had felt okay between us, I'd realised I was ready to forgive him, maybe I'd even been ready for a while. Turned out that almost dying in a car crash made you really think about everything. I hadn't yelled at him the day I got into the crash because of what happened after graduation, but because I was hurt he had moved on, because part of me ached for him not to do so. This was always going to happen and I could either choose to be mad at him for the rest of my life and continue to hurt him, or I could try to be nice to him, be civil for the sake of all our friends. Truth be told I wanted to be nice, it's why I'd called him when he said he was a failure; I couldn't stand to hear him talk about himself like that.

"Yeah, I'm sorry, I really don't want things to be awkward again, but we've been texting and I've spoken to him on the phone and well, nothing's going on between us, but I think we might be able to become friends again, eventually." Although even I wasn't sure about that completely. It might take a decent amount of time to get to that point.

"What I said at the hospital was the truth, Lo. The thought of you two together isn't my ideal, but I wouldn't stand in the way of it. I know once upon a time you two made each other happy, you deserve to be happy, Lo." Without hesitance I threw my good arm around her and the trash she carried, it was all I needed to hear, I wasn't sure I could be with him again, but her approval meant everything.

"Does this mean we can start going shopping together again?" I asked with a cheeky grin. "Noah won't let me go into Sephora and look at the skincare."

She pulled me back into a hug and whispered. "Of course, ASAP please I feel like I have no idea what toner and moisturiser combination I'm supposed to be wearing right now." We both looked at each other with wet, glossy eyes, before we burst into laughter.

"I have some recommendations don't you worry," I

grinned as a single tear fell. This was one less thing for me to worry about, a huge thing crossed off of my worry list.

~ Chapter Nineteen ~
Isaac

"I know I said I was going to write a lot about University life, but I'd really like to write a piece on academic stress. I have a really good idea that involves comparing academic living and normal residential living and the different stresses and strains that comes with both of them and how to handle them," I suggested as the floor was opened up to other editors, after Jayne, the lead editor and creative director of the *Bull and Bear* discussed this month's issue.

"Well, get me a draft of it on my desk ASAP, Isaac and I might consider publishing it." That was probably one of the nicest things she'd said to me all semester. She'd called one of my pieces sub-par, even though she did go on to publish it, but it only got a half page feature. This I wanted to be bigger and better, maybe even a double page spread. If I wrote it right it could be helpful for so many people.

I left the meeting with an urge to write until my heart was content, until my fingers ached from typing. I'd felt the stress just as much when I'd been at Cherrington Academy, I thought that was what had contributed a lot to me having caused so much trouble whilst I was there. It was an easy outlet to sneak out to get drunk or to release frustration as I dumped boxes of condoms over the top floor banister. I enjoyed it to an extent, for a second I wasn't worried about my parents getting on my back if my grades ever slipped, but it could not have been healthy for me, or for anyone around me really. It had driven in part Charlie to fail twelfth grade, another guilt I had to live with.

So I'd resigned myself to my desk, turned my phone to 'do not disturb', slipped in my comfiest sweats and with a blank page open I jotted down any and every idea I had that surrounded this topic. Everything I'd felt, all the mechanisms I'd used to cope, how to satisfy parents that demanded the world of you without destroying your own soul.

The hours at my desk turned to days, I slept in intermissions, that was one of the good things about being pressured academically, my body had learned how to function pretty well on just three or four hours sleep. I hadn't completely lost my mind though, I'd showered and bought a tonne of food and snacks from the canteen, that was an improvement on stealing Logan's protein bars to fuel my way through a paper.

With a knock on the door, it slowly parted open and let more light in than I wished to see right now, my eyes were tired from the screen and my hand sort of ached from all the editing I'd done in the past couple of hours.

"You've been in here for days," Cassidy said. Her head popped through the gap of the pushed open door.

That must have sucked for her, Alex and Lizzy had both gone home for the weekend to see their families, she'd have probably been going mad on her own. But once I'd gotten the bit between my teeth I was determined to get it written. The topic was so personal the words had just flown freely on to the page, I'd tidy them up later when I edited the article. It had felt so good to get down all of the emotions, the stress, the pressure, the worry, the lengths you'd go for relief, how it could make you act out of character, do things you'd come to regret. It had been cathartic enough to only leave my room to eat and piss, I'd even passed up on a major party with the soccer guys at some sorority. It was an exclusive invite, but I was in the middle of the section about how to progress out of the guilt phase and I wasn't moving from it.

I held up the finished article, now covered in a mixture of neon highlights and mini post it notes. "I've been busy," I sighed. I needed to read over it a couple more times, type up all the edits I'd made and then send it to Lizzy she could give it a good once over before I submitted it to Jayne. But it was finished. It was so different to the area she wanted me to write, it had to be perfect, spotless of any errors.

"Yeah and now we need to get busy elsewhere."

I swivelled round on my desk chair and looked at her with half parted eyes. "Alex has only been gone for thirty-six hours and you already trying to jump my bones. I'm gonna have to say no, sorry." Her face look unamused and I decided I should probably shut my mouth before she shut it for me.

"I'm hungry, I've eaten in the canteen on my own for the last few days and I want to go out and eat nice food with someone, not on my own. So please, get dressed, do your hair and lets go, I spotted an amazing restaurant when I was out shopping the other day and now I want to check it out." It was exactly like I'd just written in this article, you had to make time for yourself and your own wants and needs.

"Okay, I'm sorry. I'm getting dressed. Give me five minutes." The second she shut the door I stripped down to my boxers, chucked on a short-sleeved shirt and the nicest jeans that I owned, pushed my hair back out of my face with some gel and met her in the corridor.

We walked up the hill and into the town centre, she directed me to what looked like an expensive steakhouse and grill, the huge glass doors showcased tables with polished wine glasses and multiples of knives and forks. I knew Cassidy wanted to get away from the canteen food, but fine dining really? That was not very us.

"Come on, it's going to be great, I read the TripAdvisor reviews and they were all amazing." She linked her arm in mine and escorted me in, turns out she'd already booked a table and a waitress led us to a two-person table in the back that was lit with an arched candle stick.

"Wow," I said as I shrugged my jacket on to the back of my seat. I was severely under dressed, I'd seen a guy in a suit and a woman in a cocktail dress on the way in. I looked down at my jeans and Vans, why had they even let us in? At least Cassidy looked somewhat more presentable for a place like this, but then again her make up always looked incredible and she was never not in one dress or another. The little red number she had on today was perfect for this kind of environment. Well she had read the reviews.

"Can you get a picture of me?" she asked after the waiter filled our glasses with a bottle of white wine she had apparently pre-ordered for us. She held the glass up in front of her, her lips formed into a pout that she did in almost every photo she took, the light hit her glittery face in the most perfect way as I captured the shot. "On Instagram please so it's already in the square."

I opened up the app on my phone and hovered it in multiple angles to get the best shot, I saved each draft and even applied her favourite filter to some of them so she would not even have to do her own edits later on. I was such a good friend.

As I went to close the app, his face caught my eye. I'd muted his profile from my home page for a while, but when he'd requested to follow me again after our phone call the other night, I thought it'd do me no harm to see his posts again. I wanted to see his gorgeous blue eyes more often. Just not in this context, not in a photo like that, one that cut deeper than any knife could.

"What is it?" she asked, before she impatiently snatched the phone out of my hand, her fingers played with the screen as she zoomed in on the picture to get a better look. "She's stunning," she commented, before she audibly gasped. "Oh wow, that's your ex and your other ex, he looks so hot in this photo, Issy." She traced her finger over the outline of his face, he looked older for some reason, more grown up, his jaw looked sharper, wow I'd really missed out there. "Wait, is this recent?" She scrolled down to see it had been posted less than an hour ago. "Are they hanging out?"

"I guess so," I shrugged. I attempted to grab the phone from her, but it was too late, she'd already began to scroll through Logan's profile, there were none of me or us anymore, except a couple of us all in the group, either just the boys or when things had been good with the girls. He'd deleted all our cute couple photos, I'd checked they were up for a while after I'd left Cherrington and then one day they hadn't been there anymore.

"Wow, if my exes started to hang out I don't know how I'd feel." she sipped her drink loudly.

"They don't have a room big enough for all your exes," I retorted. "Now give me my phone back."

"Oh shit, have you seen this?" she asked, as she thrust the phone in front of my face, she was now on Rafael's profile so I most definitely hadn't, our paths had not really crossed when we were both at Cherrington, being in different grades, different sports teams and the fact he'd never lived near me in the dorm meant I had no reason to follow any of his social media. She clicked on a specific picture and my stomach churned as I took the phone from her to get a better look.

They were stood next to DeCew Falls, cups of some kind of cold Timmy's beverage in hand, Rafael had his arm wrapped around Logan's shoulder, but worst of all, Logan had *his* arms wrapped around Rafael's naked chest, hand splayed out across his toned abs. Both of their hair was wet and matted, they'd clearly been for a swim together, Logan's shirt wasn't saturated, so he'd obviously been shirtless in the water with Rafael. The scene played in my mind, them as they splashed around in the water with each other, before they kissed up against the rocks under the falls, maybe more, that area could be super secluded at some points of the day. Logan was cast-less so this was clearly before the crash, how long had they actually been seeing each other?

I stopped myself from gagging at the thought, my spine curled at the image of Rafael's hands all over Logan's body. I wished I'd have taken him there, maybe if I hadn't have been such a coward about him and our relationship we'd have more memories than just make out sessions in his room and the hidden dates where we'd scrambled behind pillars not to be seen, even when we were officially together. We did this so we didn't cause any more upset.

"Earth to Isaac." she waved in front of my face. "You okay, hun?"

"I wish you hadn't showed me that," I said honestly, as I exited the app and locked my phone, I'd seen enough for a millennium. "I get it you know? Rafael's not a bad looking guy. When he was a huge basketball star at the school, before he came out, girls would fawn over him, literally pose with the posters put up around the campus of him in his basketball jersey. But, I didn't think that was what Logan would want," I shrugged hard, frustratedly.

"You wanted his type to be tall, lean and grey-eyed forever, am I right?" She partly was, if we couldn't be together I didn't want him to be alone, but I just wished we were still together.

"Whatever, it is whatever, it has to be. Eurghhh." I flung my head back and stared up at the high ceiling. "Can we just stop talking about him please?"

"What were you writing back there?" she asked, as her eyes scanned over the menu, I was still trying to work out why she thought we, as two poor University students, should be sat in an expensive steakhouse, but thus this is where she'd dragged me so I could have a break from my sweatpants and laptop.

"A piece for the Bull and Bear, a good piece actually, finally one of the first things that I've written for it that I actually love. I know they've published my pieces about the clubs and how to run the best pre's on campus. Oh and that piece me and Lizzy co-wrote on all the best restaurants nearby, but this is something different, personal. It's about my academic experience."

"This coming from your post-breakdown attitude after you got that bad grade?"

I nodded. "Yep, putting all of that to good use, maybe it'll prevent me from reacting like that again in the future. I told you my Prof said I could rewrite it thought, right?" That had been a blessing, I'd gone in and spoken to her just like Logan had recommended, told her about his accident and the stress I put myself under and she was actually really sympathetic.

The waiter appeared again, this time to take our food orders, his notebook flipped open and ready. I'd hardly even had a chance to scan the menu, but I spotted many dishes that sounded great, so this would be a pretty easy choice.

"I'll get the chimichurri ribeye please, with sour cream and bacon topped fries please." It sounded like a heart attack waiting to happen, but I'd shovelled a tonne of fruit and salad into my gob whilst I'd been writing. Those kind of things were the easiest and quickest things that I could get to take away from the canteen, as they were pre-packaged.

"How would you like that cooked?" The waiter asked, before he bit his lip and looked me up and down, that was all I needed right now with my highlighter-stained hands and a brain full of thoughts about my ex that I just couldn't turn off. A decent looking waiter checking me out. Plus did I really want to be that stereotype that got hit on by a waiter, I had no desire to be that sad sap right now. So I just muttered medium rare and turned my head away from him, looked down at my phone and pulled up a game app whilst he asked Cassidy what she wanted.

"I'll get the steak, eggs and hash, plus me and my friend will get a couple of your jumbo shrimp skewers to split please, gorgeous." My neck cringed as she complimented him, I almost wanted to remind her about Alex, but I wanted more so for him to just walk away and leave us be. Hopefully, it would be someone else who delivered our food.

"He was flirting with you," she grinned as the dark-haired boy walked away from us and back behind the doors of the kitchen.

"No, he wasn't." I'd never worked in the service industry before, but I was fairly sure you had to treat all your customers like that if you wanted a tip or to avoid receiving a bad review.

"Yes he was, he looked at you like you were the steak you'd just ordered. He was literally drooling at you, I mean I don't blame him, but I'd never be that obvious about it."

"Don't let Alex hear you talking like that, he might think you're flirting with *me*." She just fake drooled at me and licked her lips repeatedly like a hungry dog. "Cas, the steaks here are forty bucks, if the waiters weren't nice like that they would never sell a near average steak at that price."

"Whatever you need to tell yourself to sleep at night, but I know when a guy is coming on to me and he was definitely trying to get in *your* pants, which are way too tight, where did you buy jeans like that?"

"Logan bought them for me." She rolled her eyes. "What? He has very good taste? He tailors all his own clothes and he knows how to spot vintage pieces in places like the Goodwill. I'm telling you, he's probably going to being working in Vogue before he's 25 or like with Versace." She faked a yawn and started to pick at her nails. "What?"

"You're never going to actually get over him if you don't even try. Burn any clothes he picked out with you, delete all the pictures you still have of him on your phone and social media and heaven forbid take the picture of the two of you off your wall, that's creepy you've been broken up for like almost 6 months now."

Maybe she was right, maybe it was time.

~ Chapter Twenty ~
Logan

Out of the corner of my eye I could see Noah as he slid towards me on his desk chair to the side of my bed. I pressed send on the group email that I'd just wrote for the whole of Edwards dormitory to announce the Winter Ball and about the prom proposals, before I looked up at his expectant eyes and waited for him to speak.

"I want to run some ideas by you for my winter ball proposal." I felt almost giddy as he said those words. Who was this Noah? Coming to me for advice on how to be romantic. I could get behind this.

"Okay. I'm listening…" I said as I shut my laptop lid and placed it on my bed side table.

"I have some ideas, but you're a lot better at this shit than me." I looked at him, with narrowed eyes, like *bitch please?*

"You do realise I've had two failed relationships in the last 12 months and you remember how fucked up they were, right?" I chuckled as I pushed my back up against my head board to get comfy.

"Whilst that may be the case, you're still much more of a romantic than me and I really want this to work. I don't wanna win the best proposal or whatever, but I still want it to be good." He climbed on to the edge of my bed and pulled out his phone. "So," he started as he scrolled through a few pictures on his phone, "I'm thinking of getting a big display of flowers like this and proposing to her in front of these. I feel like she'd love it, because then she can get some amazing pics in front of them."

"Hang on, who are you asking? You can't expect me to help if I don't know who you are trying to cater for, not every girl is going to say yes to you because you bought her some flowers."

He rolled his eyes and lent back on his elbows, his phone now on the bed beside him. "If I tell you, you're going to make it into this huge thing and it really isn't. I just need you to help me, you know as my best friend."

I groaned at him and pushed him backwards so he fell flat on his back, he knew I couldn't resist when he played the best friend card, it only got worse when he played the *you're like a brother to me* card, I'd always cave at that. No-one could deny how clever he was. "Look, I'm going to help you, try and stop me, but you need to at least tell me some things about her so I can design this proposal around her."

"Okay," he said as he smiled at me coyly. "She's a girl, she lives in Victoria, she goes to our school."

"Noah," I warned with a harsh stare.

"Eurgh, she's different, she likes cool bands that other people don't listen to, none of your show tunes or chart crap, she's into photography - she has this secret Instagram account that no-one else at this school follows and you should see the pictures, they are incredible. Which is why I was thinking that flower back drop would be perfect for her to get some shots in front of after the proposal. She's on the debate and look, we've been dating for almost a month, you know I've been seeing someone, I just don't wanna put a lot of pressure on this."

As he spoke I racked my brain for who he could be talking about, I'd been to several of the debate meets to support Ameliah and I could picture most of the girls on the team, mainly because ninety percent of the team was female. I'd never met Jessie and I'd only ever seen a handful of photos of her, so I wasn't really aware of what his type was - which didn't really help me to narrow down the choices.

A couple of the girls in debate were also in the choir and they loved the show tunes we sang, so I could at least rule out Savannah and Rebecca. Some of the Debate team were also ninth and tenth graders, I really could not see Noah going out with a girl a lot younger than him.

That left, of the girls I could think of off the top of my head, either Margot, Lara or Kiera. They were all cute and pretty nice, so I could work basing it on either of them. I only really knew Margot, out of the three, on a more friendly basis as we had English together, so I prayed it was her.

"Okay. I can work with that. What bands does she like?" I asked curiously as I pulled open the drawer of my side table where I kept a multitude of journals, coloured pens and notebooks.

"No," he said firmly and I looked up at him from where my arm was reached into the drawer, like I didn't have a clue what he was on about. "No songs. You and your little show choir are not going to woo her into saying yes with a song. Don't even think about it." It was too late, I'd already opened my note page and wrote *song?* at the top of the list of ideas, he should at least consider it.

He was having none of it as he slid his phone across the bed to me, it showed me the list of ideas he had already had.

Wall of flowers in the backdrop - perfect for photos afterwards.
Dinner at Rise Above and special proposal there.
Invasion of the debate club meeting with the proposal to be debated

by the club (tell everyone else what is going on, except her.)

The first two were good ideas, the flowers would be cute and from what I could remember about going to Rise Above with the girls last year, the vegan food had been pretty great. "The last idea sounds amazing. I feel like it's creative, different and a lot more personal. You could always get her a bouquet of the purple flowers you were going to use as a back drop and give them to her after the proposal.

"You think? It all seems a bit crazy though, like to disrupt a whole meeting? I think she may actually kill me."

"Trust me, I'm tempted to do that every day, but I've restrained myself so far. Mainly because I know nine times out of ten you have good intentions, I'm sure she will too." I chuckled sarcastically, sometimes he really did my head in. "But, seriously," I said as I wrote out the idea at the top of a new page in my notebook, "We can go and talk to Ameliah about it, she'd be able to get the whole team on board without letting your girl in on the secret. It'll be perfect." I began to write *talk to Ameliah* below the title when all of a sudden he started to protest, waved his hands around frantically to stop me.

"No. You can't tell her." He all but yelled at me, I hadn't heard him shout like that since the eleventh grade and it shook me to my core a little. I had to take a deep breath and regain my composure to remember that we weren't in that place anymore.

"But, she's the captain and the best person to talk to?" I argued.

"I know, but…" He paused for a second, clearly to search for a contradiction to my argument, but when he couldn't he just closed his eyes and resigned, reached out to clutch at the cushion in front of him as he sighed in defeat. When he opened his eyes he said. "Okay, look, don't freak out okay? I swear if you do I won't let you help and I definitely won't help you with whoever you're going to propose to."

"Which is going to be no-one," I added, I was going stag.

"Irrelevant." He waved me off, before he looked up at me and stared me dead in the eyes, to the point adrenaline shot down my spine as my nerves were piqued by his intense stare. "It's Ameliah I'm going to ask, we're dating."

I scrambled to push away the comforter that surrounded my legs and leapt on top of him, I engulfed him in the tightest of hugs my broken arm and shoulder would allow and squeezed like I was trying to let out all the air in a balloon. "Oh my god." I chattered into his ear, I grabbed at his shoulders as I pulled away. "You and Ameliah? Really? You aren't fucking with me?" I clapped excitedly as he nodded in reply, a grin stretched across his face that he just couldn't contain. "Why didn't you just tell me when you went on that date?"

"Logan, I was in a serious relationship for the last five years of my teenage life, I've never done this whole dating thing. Me and Jessie met in middle school, before she moved to Hamilton for High School, we just held hands at recess one day and became a couple. I didn't want to announce something, especially to someone who was friends with both of us, if I wasn't sure it was going to get serious. But I really like her, Logan. I never thought I'd start to feel this way about anyone else again, after Jessie." He let out a deep, shaky breath and I pulled him to another hug.

"I'm just so happy for you man. Like you have no idea. I can't wait to tease her about this." I'd already started to plot how I could mock her about this, I'd have to wait till after the proposal, but it'd be worth it to take some more time to come up with something good.

He pushed me away and grabbed the notebook. "So we are going with this plan?" He turned the page round to me and I nodded, my head bobbed at a ridiculous rate and he shook his head and stood up off my bed. "I'm going to go to lacrosse practice and then we can prep." He placed the book down on his desk and grabbed at his lacrosse bag. "See you later." The door shut behind him and I grabbed my phone. It was only 5PM, Lacrosse practice wasn't till seven.

I fired a text to Charlie and told him to meet me outside my room right now. I jumped out of bed with a bang to the floorboards and swiftly pulled on a sweat jacket Before I knew it I was outside my room and the sound of footsteps thundered above me as Charlie flew down the stairs.

"Where's the fire?" He was out of breath and a bead of sweat dribbled down his forehead. I had told him to come right away.

"Come with me," I replied and grabbed his hand. I pulled him down the stairs and out into the courtyard just in time to see them sneak out of the gates. The heat hit me, it was that gross kind of humidity that slapped you in the face the moment you stepped outside, but I did not let it stop me as we chased after the pair of them. "Look." I pointed towards the swarm of trees that covered the driveway like a forest arch.

"What am I looking at," he asked as he squinted into the distance. I gripped the side of his head and turned it in the direction of Noah as he walked hand in hand with Ameliah.

"Is that?" He turned to look at me as he pointed at the couple as they got further and further away from us.

I nodded, my grin only grew wider, I was at the point where I wanted to wave my arms around and jump up and down.

"Oh my god." He panted as he clutched at my arm and we both jumped up and down on the spot like maniacs.

"They're dating," I confirmed and then squealed in unison with him.

Luckily, there was no one around us as 5PM was when the dining hall opened to serve the evening meal so most of the students were in there, because no-one should have to see us dance around like loonies, because two of our best friends were together, the two most unlikely people that I could even think of.

"How long?"

"Just over a month apparently. I told you something was going on with him when he got all dressed up that night and wouldn't tell me where he was going." I'd literally harped on about it for days as I tried to work out why he'd created so much mystery around that date he'd been on.

"Well I did not see *that* one coming." Neither did I. Their figures faded into the distance as the sun began to set around the forest that surrounded the driveway of Cherrington Academy. It was kind of beautiful really, both the orange sky as it blended into the deep purple and the newly found couple.

"I think they will be good for each other," I said as we walked back up to the dormitory and into the foyer. "This is good right? Why do I still feel a little worried even though I love Ameliah, and I know she'll be great for him and he looks so happy." There was still a cold tingle at the base of my spine that only reared its ugly head when worry was about to eat away at me.

166

"Because the girl he loved died just nine months ago and they are both two of your closest friends, you don't wanna see either of them get hurt." Charlie wrapped his arm around my shoulder as we headed back up the stairs and stopped outside my door.

"Why do I have this funny feeling you are not on this floor for me right now," I chuckled as I side eyed the door just down from mine. In that second Rafael stuck his head out at us and grinned, coyly at the pair of us. I raised my eyebrows at him and bit my lip in amusement.

"I'd say you were correct," Charlie replied as he sauntered towards Rafael, not even giving me a second glance.

"Curfew is at 10." I reminded them as I shut the door behind me and searched for my headphones. I loved the pair of them, but I'd use this time to catch up on missed episodes of Arrow, rather than have to hear whatever was about to happen in there.

~ Chapter Twenty-One ~
Isaac

I'd been sat, alone, for almost twenty minutes when I really started to feel annoyed. I'd twirled my straw in the same glass of Disaronno and Coke for the whole time, taking small sips every few minutes to keep myself occupied and to lower my annoyance to the fact that Cassidy was so late and I'd cancelled a study session with Lizzy for this because she told me it was important.

I checked the time on my phone once more, 8:21PM. I'd give her nine more minutes and then I'd leave and try to make the last hour of the study session, it was not like first semester finals were next week or anything. Fuck it. I decided as I scrolled through my contacts to her name and pressed dial, I planned to give her an earful before she even had the chance to show up.

"Cassidy," I said as she answered the phone. "Where are you?" I asked, I could hear a tonne of hustle and bustle around her, so maybe she was just on her way.

"I'm sorry I'm late, the subway sucks and I got trapped in a broken-down cart. I'm running down the street as we speak, I'll be there in literally a minute," she replied, but she sounded distant, there was no way that girl would run anywhere.

"Okay, well I'm here, I'll see you in a moment." I went to hang up.

"Look up," she said before I could cut the call. So I did, my eyes directly on the door as I waited for her to strut in wearing one of her signature tight black dresses like she was always ready to hit the club, but she didn't appear.

"I'm looking," I replied, as I scanned for a potential other entrance to the bar, although we'd been here so many times before and I'd never once seen one.

"Right there," she said and like clockwork she still wasn't there, her superpower would be being late if she had one. "I'm right beside you, turn to your left."

I couldn't hear her beside me, but as I turned to my left I was met with the face of the slightly attractive waiter we'd been served by in the restaurant the other night.

"I'm going to kill you," I muttered into the phone, but all I heard was her cackle as she hung up. She must have been nearby if she could see exactly what had gone down with him as he walked in, I'd wring her neck when I next saw her for this.

"You weren't expecting me?" He sat down hesitantly in the bar stool next to me and as I ignored what he said I signalled for the bartender to come back over, I could really use another double right now, maybe even a triple.

"I'm sorry, when Cassidy sets her mind to something, she executes it, regardless of what anyone else thinks."

"This doesn't have to be anything serious, I just thought you were gorgeous and then when Cassidy slipped what I thought was *your* number, I thought maybe you felt the same. When you suggested we meet here for a drink, it pretty much confirmed that." He slumped over the bar and his casted his eyes downward. I should never have joked with Cassidy about moving on, because I did not want to have to be an asshole to this guy.

As the bartender asked what he could get us, I ordered another double and a shot, just so I could get through the next few moments of being sat next to a guy who thought I was interested in him. I'd force Cassidy to reimburse me for this later. I downed the shot without a second thought and then realised I'd not ordered my 'date' a drink. Who I was sure wasn't a bad guy, so I should have probably got him a drink.

"What can I get you?" I asked and he looked up at me from where he'd rested his head on his folded arms on top of the bar. His grass green eyes brightened and I regretted asking, I did not want to give him false hope, that wasn't fair on him.

"A Jack Daniels and Coke, please, double," he replied to the bartender and I nodded in approval.

"Good choice," I replied. My old drink of choice, before the almond liquor had become my thing, in more ways than one. Maybe I should give this a chance. It didn't mean I'd given up on Logan at all, but if he'd moved on from me, I should at least give Luke a shot. There was nothing wrong with that. "Shall we take these to a booth?" There was a free one in the far corner which would probably be a bit more secluded than sat at the bar, easier for us to get to know each other.

He led the way and we both slid into the booth, him a little too close for comfort. We got settled under the dimmed lighting and then I spotted the single flower and the lit candle in the middle of the table. It was the same for all the booths that surrounded us, but still it was just a bit too romantic for the first time we'd ever been out. We should have stayed at the bar.

"Are you a student here?" he asked, a great first date topic.

"Yeah, first year English Major. What about yourself? I know you work in that restaurant, is that your full-time job?" I took a long sip, I'd need another one of these soon if this was how the conversations would be going all evening. Small talk grated on me.

"Part time, I'm a model in my day job and hopefully soon I won't need to work at Reuben's. I had a few shoots with some proper agencies a couple of weeks ago, just waiting to hear back from them." He swiped open his phone bringing up a whole folder of head shots and photos that had taken in front of a green screen. Very professional although I didn't care much for the vanity of it all. I couldn't, however, deny he was stunning. He had a very model like face, perfect chiselled cheeks, bold green eyes and hair that you could probably style any way you wanted, it was so thick and luscious. Good for him, I'm sure with a face like that he could go far in the industry.

"You look great." He continued to swipe through the pictures. There were hundreds, maybe even thousands all in variations of the same poses. He literally had his whole portfolio in his phone, I guess that was good for if he wanted to book jobs on the go, just maybe not to whip out at the start of a first date.

"I actually got asked once in the street if I was a young Leonardo DiCaprio and I was honestly so flattered. Like he really is one of the best-looking men on the planet even now at forty-five, and I mean for her to say a young version of him like that? It was one of the best compliments I could ask for, you know." I bobbed my head and went to agree, but I swiftly realised it was a rhetorical question. He wasn't finished. "But then I've also been told I look like Brad Pitt as well." If he'd have asked me I'd have told him I didn't see it, he was a pretty guy, that was all. "That's the thing with modelling you know, you don't get many compliments. You walk in to their shoots they dress you, plaster make-up on you, take the photos with straight looks on their face and you leave with a 'thank you', just a 'we'll be in touch'. So I never feel weird asking people for compliments, it's like I've earned them you know as I stand in positions for hours, with nothing but people telling me to change positions or tilt my chin up or look to my right. It can be soul destroying you know?" Again, he didn't want my opinion, he wasn't even looking at me. He was talking wistfully to the rest of the bar, almost like I wasn't even there.

I fumbled with the almost empty glass in my hand. Did he actually want me to speak? "I'm sorry," I said as I pushed myself out the booth. "The alcohol has gone straight through me and I need to head to the restroom. I'll be right back."

I stepped into the bathroom, headed straight for a cubicle and locked the door behind me. I set the seat lid down and did something I really was not proud of. I had been there when Lizzy had done it to Cassidy a weeks ago and I'd laughed and mocked her when she gotten home, but now I saw the use for it.

I whipped out my phone and sent an SOS text to Joshua and Alex just to be safe, in case one of them was busy and asked them to call me within the next couple of minutes and then darted back to the table.

"You okay?" Luke asked, a fresh drink in his hand and one waiting in place of my empty glass. I'd literally been gone for thirty seconds and he'd already been to the bar and topped us up. Fantastic.

Now I really did feel bad, but I didn't want to stick this out for another drink or another second if I could help it. "All good," I smiled as I sat back down in the booth with him, impatiently waiting for my phone to ring.

"So where was I?" he asked and before I could even answer he'd continued his story. "Yeah so I walked into the agency and I told them straight up that I wasn't going to model for some unknown company whether they were up and coming or not. I'd literally put a list of my preferences in with my portfolio like…"

My ringtone blared over the list of his designer brands and it wasn't until I pulled the phone out of my pocket did he actually realise it was mine. "Sorry," I muttered quickly as I answered the call.

"Hey Alex, you okay?" He just laughed at me. I should have made sure it was Joshua that called, at least I was not going to have to go home to be mocked by him for a failed date.

"Cassidy really fucked you over there man." He sounded way too pleased with himself for my liking.

"Oh bro I'm so sorry to hear that, do you need me to come home? I'm like a five-minute walk away. Yeah don't even worry about it, I'll leave now." I hung up quickly and pocketed my phone.

"You have to leave?" He frowned as he picked up his drink that was still full to the brim.

"I'm so sorry, my friends grandma has just died and he's really upset, he needs me." I tied my jacket round my waist and stumbled out from the booth, as I attempted to race towards the door.

"Will you give your number so I can text you and we can rearrange?" he asked and it would have been rude of me to say no. I nodded and entered a completely random number to his phone, checked that it was 10 digits and handed it back to him.

"I'll speak to you later, bye." I darted towards the door, kept the pace all the way down the road until I was on to a side path where I stopped and grabbed my breath. I speed walked all of the rest of the way home just in case Luke had decided to follow after me to make sure everything was okay or to continue the failure of that date back at my place.

Thankfully as I twisted my key in the front door and entered the kitchen, he was nowhere to be seen behind me.

"Was it really that bad?" Alex asked from where he sat with his coffee in the love seat, whatever he'd been watching on Netflix paused as I came through the door.

"Worse. What was Cassidy thinking? Yes he was a little charming when he served us, but that was his job." I flopped onto the other sofa opposite him. "Turns out the charm was actually just a cover for how cocky he actually is, like overly cocky. That man really loves himself, thinks he's god's gift. You should have heard him talk about all the complements he deserves and how hard it is to be a model. So arrogant."

"Her heart was in the right place though, man. She said she thought you were gonna cry when you saw that picture of your ex with his new man, she just wanted to help you get over him. Maybe this guy wasn't the right guy, but there will be someone else, just takes time innit." I got what he said, but I didn't want someone else. I wanted Logan.

"I just want him, nobody else, no one else even compares. It's crazy, I thought I'd realised the extent of my feelings for him and then I sat through this date and I just kept thinking, this would never happen with Logan, he'd never sit here and only talk about himself, not a care for me. He was always interested in what I was doing, that's how ended up being the first person I showed my poetry to." I punched the cushion beside me, once, twice. "I'm such an idiot, literally the biggest fool for letting him get away from me."

"You're in love with him, aren't you?" Alex's eyes were wary, they always were when it came to Logan. For him he was never sure how far to push; it was completely the opposite with Cassidy, she'd push till I fell apart about it.

"So much, like I don't mean to sound crazy, like I'm only nineteen, but I'm fairly sure he's the one you know? Like *really* the one, my life partner or whatever." I stood up and paced around the room, from wall to wall. "What do I do? I have to get him back, if he's the one I can't let him slip away so easy. I can't let it end like this." I groaned as I rested my head up against the coolness of the wall as hot blood pumped around me way too fast to the point it made me a little light headed.

"I'm going to get you a glass of water and you're going to lay on that couch, because you look like you're about to lose your mind." He was behind me and I hadn't even realised his hand now rested on my shoulder. My head was spinning.

I span around so quickly I almost knocked him to the ground. "Nope, nope no lying down for me. I need a plan, I need to figure out how to get him back. I need to prove to him that I love him and that I was wrong to walk away from him last summer. There has to be something I can do." He pushed a glass of water into my hand and I took it only in the hopes that it would loosen up the dizziness in my head.

"First drink that, then we'll plan together." He grabbed my shoulder again and guided me back down to the sofa. "Sit there, I'll order us pizza and then we figure out what the hell we can do to get you out of this funk."

~ Chapter Twenty-Two ~
Logan

"I'm still not sure about this," he sighed from where he was slumped over in the booth, sunglasses shielded his hungover eyes from the bright lights of the coffee store.

"Look, we already got Brock on board and the talks with Waterloo are going well, so why not make this a provincial thing? Maybe even national," I replied as I slid the biggest cup of coffee I could get for him across the table. Rafael had been hesitant ever since we'd started contemplating writing a piece for the bigger newspapers about the work we were doing in connecting LGBTQ and sporting communities together. I could understand why, a lot of pressure fell on him, he was already widely recognised in said newspapers after the piece they did on him over summer. I just didn't want to let that ruin all the hard work we'd already put into this project. Between being a prefect, the ball, and classes I was already ran off my feet. I would not abandon this project, otherwise what would have all this stress been for?

The door chimed behind us and in walked Charlie, he looked to be in a similar sorry state to Rafael; hair un-gelled and a hoodie that I recognised from what he'd worn when things were bad last year and he wasn't talking to me. "You both look rough and whilst I'm very happy about whatever this is going on between the two of you, we have work to do."

Charlie's grey tinged skin flushed rouge and he glared

at me from where he was stood at the end of our booth. "Thanks for making this a hundred times more awkward, Lo. Love you too," Charlie said before he stomped off to grab himself a coffee.

"Seriously though, just make it official already," I said to Rafael. "You do know that me and Noah live next door to you and the wall between our rooms is literally paper thin," I commented with a playful smile.

Rafael groaned loudly. "I hate both of you. Just because you aren't getting any action doesn't mean you should be listening with your ear pressed up my wall to hear what's going on between me and Charlie."

"Oh please, all we can hear is what sounds like wet seals smushing together whenever you two are making out. Neither of us are getting turned on," I laughed, as I clapped like a seal. At this he pushed his sunglasses over his head to scrape back his hair out of his face. It was then I saw the blood shot eyes, the dark circles and the sagging below them. "Christ, you need some eye masks for those bags, I'll grab you a pack when we get back to campus."

"Or I just need some sleep."

"Well, maybe if you and Charlie hadn't snuck out last night to get wasted, you wouldn't have that problem." You're welcome by the way, I covered for both of you by staying up till 1AM to do the bed checks instead of Julian."

"And we are very grateful," Charlie replied as he returned with his coffee and took a seat in the booth next to Rafael. I was going to need new friend with the rate all my current friends were becoming coupled up with each other, if I wanted to avoid constantly being a third wheel.

"Not being a prefect has turned you into a real Isaac," I teased. I couldn't be too mad at them though, especially Charlie. I remembered all the stories Isaac had told me about the trouble they used to get up to as a threesome before Charlie became prefect. Plus, Charlie deserved to let his hair down and have some fun. It was just a bonus that in the process he was making Rafael happier.

"Well, as long as you aren't gonna try and kiss me, we are all good," he said with a wink and it hit me a little that this was one of the first nice and relaxed conversations we'd had about him in a while. At the start of the year we'd both been a bit scared to broach the topic of him for obvious reason, but now the tensions seemed to have settled a little.

"Touché," I smirked back at him.

"I've been speaking to him, you know?" Charlie said a bit more seriously, his eyes locked on mine as he nestled his chin into his palms, elbows rested on the table.

I didn't, but I had had a feeling and just hadn't wanted to ask. "How's that going?" I was curious to see what had been said. I knew Charlie had wanted to talk to him about his old feelings when I'd interrupted their conversation with my outburst about Wyatt, but I didn't think he'd want to do that over text.

"Good, I think. I haven't told him though, not yet, I'm going to do it face to face. You don't have to worry though I'm completely over him. Like a hundred percent, have been for months," he replied with a look that told me he was completely confident about that. A shot of panic sprinted up my spine and my head turned quickly to Rafael, surprisingly he didn't look as confused as I thought he was going to but was this really a conversation Charlie wanted to have in front of the guy he was dating?

"Relax, he knows," Charlie reassured me whilst Rafael nodded at me. I felt the tension ease in my back, that was a huge step for Charlie.

"Yeah, when we aren't making out like wet seals we actually talk to each other. I'm now pretty much caught up on everything that was unknown to me over the last four years of being at this school," he said, a mischievous grin stretched across his face before he mocked the motion of throwing up everywhere.

"You didn't," I said to Charlie as I covered my warm cheeks with my hands.

"Oh I did. The slipper story will live on here forever at Cherrington, maybe I'll even put it as my yearbook quote," Charlie smirked. "The point of me actually telling you about him wasn't to tease you about your messy drinking habits, but because it's time for you to talk to him to. We may actually need him," he added in between long sips of his coffee.

"What do you mean?" I asked, my arms crossed in front of my chest.

"Well, he's part of the journalism team at McGill, so he has access to all the fancy writing software and a team of people who work in publishing so he would be able to help us a lot with that. Plus, you know more than anyone that he's a great writer."

My heart crumpled a little. There was a poem he'd written for me, wedged in the back of my dresser. When he'd first broken things off with me I'd read it every day, sometimes more than once. The edges were a little torn now and some of the ink had smudged with the relentless tears that had stained the page. I couldn't bear to throw it away, it was one of the things that proved what we had was real. I nodded in reply, I didn't trust the lump that bobbed in my throat to create a verbal reply. They were right; he was an exceptional writer.

"Look, I know the last time you spoke things weren't exactly great."

"Understatement of the century," I chuckled and the

lump in my throat sank back down. "We have spoken though. Text mainly, I followed him back on social media again and we've spoken once on the phone, but this is a big ask."

"But, he's sorry, he's really sorry, Lo. I'm not saying you have to be best friends with him, but do you really want him completely out of your life? Because, I don't think you do." Charlie spoke so genuinely and I couldn't help but think how much our friendship had grown since the fallout twelve months ago. We'd not been able to have this sensible, grown up conversation about Isaac at all last year.

"Charlie's right," Rafael added. "We all know what happened at graduation, but it's been months. You miss him, I hear it in the stories you tell and I know for a fact that you hate going up to the top floor because it reminds you of him." That *was* true, just the other day when I couldn't get hold of Charlie by text, I'd sent Raf up to bring him to down me, played the broken bones card to convince him.

" I know he's sorry, part of me has always known. It just scares me you know?" I swallowed hard to prevent myself from getting tearful. "I'm not over him," I admitted, as if they didn't already know that.

"A blind person could see that," Rafael replied. "I mean you had a chance at the start of the year with this and you didn't even blink," he said as he gestured to his stupid, smug face.

"It doesn't matter though. I can't," I tried to protest. "He's him and he's four hundred miles away and he broke my heart. I *should* hate him." I sighed, before I chugged down the last bit of my lukewarm coffee and laid my head down on my closed laptop.

Charlie stood up and shuffled out of the booth. I

turned my head up from where I was laying my head on my laptop and asked, "Where are you going?"

"To get us a box of fifty mixed Timbits so you can eat your feeling and we can fuel our dying stomachs so we can actually have this article planning meeting." With that he left to the counter and I was left being looked down on by Rafael with a concerned look on his face, his forehead crinkled and his eyes narrowed in on me.

"What?" I asked pointedly at him, as I sat up properly in the booth.

"Nothing. I'm just worried about you. I hate how much this whole Isaac situation is still eating you up, but it does make me think that whatever went on between you guys just isn't over yet."

"It was over the moment he didn't say he loved me back, Raf. How do we go back from that?" I asked, almost rhetorically. The hardest part was that I was so sure he loved me on graduation day. I'd waited months to tell him just to be sure. I didn't want to say those three little words for the first time to someone and have it lead to heartbreak. How wrong had I been?

"I don't know. I've never been in love," Rafael replied with a shrug of his shoulders, but I couldn't help follow his eyes as they drifted to Charlie. There was so much potential between then. "What I do know is that you are still mad about him, even if you are still a little mad *at* him."

"Aren't I supposed to be the person who worries about everyone?" I laughed.

"As a prefect, yes, as one of my good friends, no. I heard you and Noah talking about it all the time, but you have to share the load, you can't stress over every single thing on your own and if you need someone to talk to about how you're feeling with Isaac, then hit me up or Charlie. He can take it, he's very much so over Isaac now." He grinned and my heart lurched in my chest a toothy smile on my face, Charlie and Raf were going to make each other so happy.

I pulled open my laptop and typed in 'McGill Journalism' to the search engine. I wanted to see what this club was all about. This was a huge project that we'd spent the last two months working hard on, I didn't want anything to screw that up. Even if it was Isaac. What appeared was something called 'The Bull and Bear.' It checked out, looked completely legit. The website had a years' worth of University magazines on it and as I clicked through them they looked incredible. Very professional.

"Updates on what has happened in the last few days. Brock want us to go and talk on a student panel about diversity within sport next week. Obviously, I won't be doing that, but either of you two could go or both I'm sure they'd be happy to have two more people on the panel."

"I'll do it," Rafael jumped straight in, he was feeling so much more confident about his speaking abilities following on from the whole school assembly talk he'd done. "I have the bio project that's due in at the end of that week done and Charlie doesn't, because he's a slacker." Charlie pinched the side of his hip, I watched, with a little envy as Charlie's hand remained on Rafael's thigh after that.

"Perfect, makes my life easier." I ticked that off the top of my check list. "Waterloo have gotten back to me and they are definitely interested in getting involved. I'm thinking this project needs a proper name though, just so I can file all correspondence under it in my emails and so we can use it's official title whenever we are talking about it."

They both looked at me like they were fish out of

water and that I was probably going a little over the top, but I'd got the bit between my teeth now and I was determined to get this project off the ground. Having it appropriately named wasn't much to ask.

"Hmmm," Charlie thought out loud. "Why not just LGBTQ Diversity in Sports?" he suggested.

"I'm not sure it has a catchy tone to it, it's just a bit bland," I replied, but I wrote the suggestion down in my open notepad anyway, we had to make a start,.

"What about Put the LGBTQ into Sports?" I grinned up at Rafael. That was it.

"That's perfect. See you guys *can* be useful," I replied as I jotted the name down and circled it with my red pen. I quickly created a folder within my emails and named it that, before I moved all of the emails I'd sent and received so far into the folder. Everything looked so much neater now.

When I looked up from behind the screen, the pair of them were looking at me with marvel in their eyes. "And this is why I was never worried about you being prefect, I didn't for a second doubt that with your way too organised brain that you were the right person for the job."

I locked eyes with him and the tears that glossed over them felt like little pin pricks. "I learnt from the best," I smiled, softly before I grabbed at a napkin and patted my eyes dry quickly before I turned into a tearful wreck. We still had work to do.

"Now we have a project name I feel like we can really start coming up with ideas for the article. I think we have to start reaching out to colleges and other universities, see if there any other LGBTQ stories within sports teams and what experiences they've had, the bigger the problem we can demonstrate this issue is, the further the impact this article will have."

Both of them nodded at me. "Okay, I'll start contacting people I know within sporting teams across Ontario and I'll let you know what I find," Rafael replied and I ticked another one of my meeting objectives off the list. This was all going to come together nicely I just knew it.

With a deep breath I added, "I'll call Isaac and ask him what he thinks and whether he can help. I'll get him on board and this whole thing will be perfect." It couldn't hurt to ask, the worst he could say was no.

"I'm really proud of you, Lo. To be honest my pride in you is pretty endless right now. You've done so many amazing things since you became prefect, I have no idea how you're coping with it all. Makes me feel like I did the bare minimum as prefect," Charlie said and I shook my head at him. My three months as prefect was nothing compared to his three years.

"Hey, you had to put up with Beth," I joked. "She demanded half your time. It's easy doing this out of a relationship, no one holding me back or taking me on dates or bringing me an Indian take out. Or you know just holding me whilst I slept." Both of them looked at me like I was crazy.

"Way to project, Lo." Charlie chuckled and I lobbed an apple fritter Timbit at his head. I was stupidly grateful for these two idiots.

~ Chapter Twenty-Three ~

Isaac

"Road trip!" Cassidy yelled through my door, as her fists pounded against it. I reached for my phone from my bedside table, my eyes hardly open as I squinted at the time. It was 5AM on a Friday morning. Who in their right mind thought it would be okay to wake someone up like this at the crack of dawn? Although, Cassidy was not in her right mind, she'd demonstrated that pretty well when she'd forced me and Luke together for that date at that bloody bar. And what did she mean by road trip? I had no plans to go anywhere at this time of the morning.

"I'm serious, Isaac." She pounded again, before my phone began to ring, her name flashing up on the screen in the caller ID. This girl wasn't lacking in the commitment department, I had to give her that.

"I'm not answering, Cas," I grumbled as I pulled the comforter over my head and prayed that the ringing would stop.

"I have coffee and a breakfast pizza out here, if you don't get up we are going to eat it all without you." We? Who else had she gotten up at this crazy hour? She'd probably managed to force Alex to be up as he'd most likely spent the night in her bed, that had become a regular thing. Lizzy would not have been stupid enough to fall for this though, surely?

The smell of sausage and bacon wafted under the

door, she really knew my weaknesses, if I knew her how I thought I did she'd probably got the box held up to the door just for full effect.

"Okay, okay." I chucked the pillow to the end of the bed, peeled back the comforter and hopped out. I scrambled for a pair of boxers and sweatpants, before Cassidy burst her way in here and got an eyeful, she'd love that. I forced a t-shirt over my head, rubbed blearily at my eyes and opened the door to a fully dolled up Cassidy, already dressed for the day and her face painted with brightly coloured make up, the pizza box held up in front of her.

"It's got a fried egg in the middle of it, it's divine." She grinned as she opened the box and presented a work of art; the all-night canteen was good for some things. I went to grab a slice, but she swatted at my hand, before slamming the lid closed. "Road trip?" she said again, like I hadn't heard her the first time when she screamed it through my door.

"What the hell is going on?" I asked after I'd devoured my first piece of the breakfast pizza. Cassidy had led me down the hall and into our floors communal area, where Alex and Lizzy sat - both of them looked as tired as I felt.

"One of you make him some coffee, if he is gonna drive us he needs to be alert." She may as well have snapped her fingers at the rate Alex had shot up and raced towards the kettle.

"I'm not driving anyone anywhere," I interjected. "Not until you tell me what is actually going on." I collapsed on to the sofa next where Lizzy was munching a waffle that Cassidy must have picked up for her. She'd really gone out of her way to bribe everyone out of their rooms at this dumb hour.

186

"Niagara Falls," Cassidy said, confirming my worst nightmare. I'd seen the sparkle in her eye when me and Alex had been talking about it last week, I should have known she'd been plotting something like this. "We all keep saying how we want to go there so badly and now classes are done and we've sat our final exams, I say let's go." She clapped excitedly, but nobody else moved, everyone remaining slumped on the sofa. "Pack your bags kids, we are going on a road trip." She waved her arms around to try and motivate us up out of our seats, but still nobody moved.

I almost wanted to laugh as she got excited about this trip. What she hadn't accounted for when she asked me to drive them there is that I'd grown up twenty minutes from the Falls, the 'we' she discussed was just the three of them, I'd already seen them a countless amount of times.

"If I drive you guys to Niagara you do realise I'm not bringing you back here, right? You'll have to get a bus back or something." Cassidy looked at me like I'd just kicked her puppy, but that would not work with me right now, not in my sleep filled haze. I was not going to drive all the way there and back, just have to go straight back for the Christmas break, she was having a laugh. I glared at her with stern eyes and eventually she caved.

"Fine, we'll get the bus back, but does that mean we can go? Because I've already packed my weekend bag and I'm ready to go!" Alex finally thrust a freshly brewed cup of coffee into my waiting hands and as waft of hazelnut syrup invaded my nostrils I decided to throw caution to the wind.

"Fuck it, road trip it is," I said with all the energy I could muster up at this ungodly hour.

"Yes!" Cassidy fist pumped the air. "I'll pack a snack bag for the drive, you guys go pack some clothes and we'll meet back here at half five to set off." She clapped her hands impatiently and waited for us all to move, but I had no plans to go anywhere until I had inhaled all the caffeine I could. Seemed like everyone else felt the same, Lizzy was still half-asleep on the couch, left over waffle rested on her chest, whilst Alex snuggled in the loveseat, a throw covered most of his body. "Move," Cassidy shouted which was followed by a tired chorus of excuses before she actually hauled a groggy Lizzy to her feet. "Guys, come on," she pleaded. "This is going to be the best weekend, I'll literally plan everything, I'll find us an Airbnb on the drive down and we can look at all the stuff there is to do down there. Maybe we'll even pop in and see Isaac's crazy boarding school."

This piqued Lizzy's interest and she shot off in the direction of her room as quick as her tired legs could carry her. Cassidy cheered and dragged Alex up from his seat back to his room, his eyes were still half closed. To be fair she'd probably just pack his bag for him anyway, he didn't really need to be awake.

I downed the rest of the cup of coffee, chucked a few pairs of jeans and some t-shirts into a duffel, alongside the essential toiletries and with a slow drag of our suitcases to my car, we hit the road.

Cassidy chatted aimlessly all the way to the gas station about the playlist for the journey she'd devised last night, whilst Alex and Lizzy slipped into slumber once more in the back. I envied them so much when Cassidy practically still hadn't stopped her relentless chatter as we pulled into St-Catharines. At this point she'd scrolled through every review of each attraction in Niagara, read me a tonne of reviews like I hadn't actually been there myself, and then booked us an Airbnb in downtown St-Catharines, that was so close to Cherrington we may as well have just inquired about my old room there.

"Okay, this place is so cute," Cassidy commented as I parked up the car in Carlisle street, just outside the Airbnb. "I've already seen so many little shops I want to go in." That was the best thing about Downtown St-Catharines, a lot of it was independently ran shops, bars and restaurants by the local community.

"So where are the Falls?" Alex asked as we traipsed our bags into the house and dumped them in the lounge area.

"About a fifteen-minute drive from here," I replied as I swiped through the messages on my phone. Just before we'd pulled out of the gas station I'd dropped Joshua and Charlie a text to warn them of our arrival, but now they demanded we meet up with them and go get dinner. "Anyone up for dinner at Kelsey's with my pals? It's at the top of Clifton Hill so we can walk down and see the Falls lit up at night after."

"Is Joshua going to be there?" Cassidy asked and Alex tutted behind her, Cassidy was still a little bit fascinated by the guy. Something about him really had her intrigued in a non-romantic way. To be fair they would make a really good pair of friends given the chance.

"Yep and you can finally meet Charlie as well." I slipped out of the hoodie I'd chosen to be comfortable in on the drive over and riffled around in my case for a nicer jumper to wear for dinner.

"What about Logan?" Lizzy piped up from where she lazed on the couch.

"Didn't want to push it. We had such a good conversation the other night and the texts since have been pretty cool. Don't wanna do anything to rock the boat like introduce him to you three idiots." That didn't stop the hope that had slowly started to build up inside of me. I'd do anything to see him whilst I was back for

Christmas. I had no idea what his plans for the break were, but Cherrington had another week of school before they broke up, so I hoped to at least catch up with him once or twice before he left. I had to put my plan to win him back into action, Well, first I actually had to derive said plan. It was a work in progress.

Everybody quickly showered and changed before the short drive out to Niagara; before I knew it we were all sat in a booth for six. "I have to warn you, before you find out yourself," Charlie started. "Raf, Logan and Noah are at some superhero comic event literally two minutes down the road, just in case we bump into them." Charlie started before we'd even had the chance to open our menus.

"Wonderful." I slammed open the menu, to the point it shook the table with its hard casing. Everyone at the table glared at me, but I waved them off. "Sorry, sorry. Drinks?" I suggested as I turned to the cocktail page, Kelsey's did the best jugs of Sangria I'd ever tasted, they came in the biggest mason jars, like you needed two hands to hold it. I could do with several of them if there was a chance I was going to run into my ex and his new man.

"Not for me, I have to drive back to Hamilton this evening, me and the folks are going for brunch in the morning as my sister is coming home tonight." Joshua's sister had gone to some fancy fashion school in New York for her degree, she was about to graduate.

"You know *I* never say no," Cassidy grinned as she examined the fishbowls you could get here, Alex peered over her shoulder as they debated how many they would need between themselves for the evening.

I closed my menu and placed it back in the centre of the table, the original three of us always got the same

190

thing when we came here, the huge platter of nachos to share and then I'd get the bacon mac and cheese. The waitress quickly took all of our orders and returned with our drinks, by then everyone was already so hyped up the table was alive with chatter. "I'm disturbed," Charlie whispered from beside me, his eyes narrowed in on Joshua and Lizzy as they chatted animatedly across the table to each other.

"Wow. Is our little Joshua actually managing to talk to a girl?" I teased, as Lizzy gestured wildly to him about something before she pulled out her phone to show him something else. Out of the corner of my eye I suddenly spotted auburn curly hair and piercing blue eyes.

They entered the restaurant arm in arm, Noah trailing behind them as he carried a huge bag with some comic symbols on. Logan had that beautiful bright smile on his face that I treasured every time he allowed me to see it. The smile quickly turned to laughter at whatever it was that Rafael had just said. Everyone else must have heard his high-pitched laugh as they turned their heads to where I'd spotted him. The movement was rapid as my McGill friends turned quickly back at me to check that I was okay.

"Oh man. I'm sorry," Alex said across the table quietly across the table to me, I didn't take my eyes off the curly haired boy, it was the first time I'd seen him in person since the hospital, his arm was out of the sling, but still in a cast, but his bruises and cuts had heeled up nicely, there was barely a scar on his face. The waitress led them to a table in a corner on the other side of the restaurant and I finally turned my head back to look at the group.

"He's okay, you know?" Charlie rubbed at my shoulder, but I just reached for another sip of my sangria. "The cast comes off next week and his collarbone and ribs are fine, the doctors have all said he's recovered nicely."

Whilst that was part of my concern, it was not the main reason I felt so distraught. I really had lost him and all the hope in the world would not get him back if he'd moved on with someone else, someone who had not already hurt him beyond belief.

"I know, I know. Tonight isn't about him anyway." I replied as I raised my glass, well jug. "To new friends and old, it's good to be back for Christmas and to be able to show these losers our life here." I cheered and we all clinked our glasses together. I'd push any thoughts of him to the back of my mind, tonight was about everyone at the table, a night to enjoy, not drown in my own self-pity.

The food went down a treat, the drinks had flowed like a stream. With all of that consumed, we started the walk down the hill to the Falls, me and Charlie lingered at the back as Alex and Cassidy strode miles ahead of us hand in hand. They were much more excited than the rest of us. It was Lizzy and Joshua, however, that had us dragging our feet. They were stood so close together as they walked that their fingers had brushed together multiple times.

"They would be so cute," Charlie cooed, he'd kept just as much of an eye on them as I did. Joshua definitely deserved someone like Lizzy, she was thoughtful, caring and not one of those girls that would fuck a guy over. She was driven and outgoing, she'd put Joshua to shame with how much alcohol she could consume. She was just a little bit quiet sometimes, often retreated to her books when things got hard, Joshua could use some of that in his life.

"Well if something good like that could come of this trip, I won't regret being woken up at five AM to drive

192

down here today." Thank god for the alcohol in my system, because after that early start I'd probably be exhausted.

"I like your new friends, I'm glad you've found such a good bunch at uni. Less worry for me, especially Alex, he seems to keep you all in line." There was good old prefect Charlie, even when he was a sophomore in the role he still worried about the seniors that went off to college. He'd said once, being a prefect, some of the boys became like his kids, which back then sounded super messed up, but now I could see his point.

"You've got a nice little friendship group going at Cherrington now though, I saw a photo you posted of you, Lo, Noah and Rafael. Very boy band esque." I chuckled, but with every post I saw like that I felt more and more like I really had left the school behind, left a brotherhood behind, like I'd lost a limb.

"Yeah, friends," he laughed with me, but there was more there, his cheeks tinged pink and I was sure I did not want to hear whatever he was about to tell me.

"Please don't say it. When it's just in my head it isn't real." I picked up my pace so I could get away from him, but he only gripped on to my arm and stopped me in my tracks.

"What are you talking about?" he asked, his hand still wrapped around my arm, as he squinted at me.

"Logan and Rafael," I replied simply and he shook his head, a look of delight spread across his face.

"There is no Logan and Rafael," he said like I was being absolutely ridiculous. I tried to shake him off but then a coy smile spread across his face. "But, there is a *me* and Rafael," he smirked, a blush as red as a tomato radiated from his cheeks.

I was literally an idiot. "Wow," I said. "Wowwwwwww." I could have almost face palmed.

Suddenly the sentiment was echoed in front of us, as the view of the Falls came into sight for the rest of the group. Cassidy had already whipped out her phone to take as many pictures as possible. When I caught my first glimpse it hit me that I'd actually missed the sight, the gush of the water and the way the multi-coloured lights lit up the streams really made me feel like I was coming home.

"We'll talk later," Charlie said, as we caught up with the rest of them, they wanted to grab a big group photo in front of the view. I'd heard all I'd needed. I still had a chance here, I just needed a plan. As we grinned for the stranger we'd found to take the photo, I knew I was in the right place, with the right people, to make this plan. There was still a chance.

~ Chapter Twenty-Four ~
Logan

"Logan?" He answered almost as soon as the dialling tone had begun. I jumped back a little bit as I hadn't prepared for him to be so fast, I wanted to get comfy on my bed before we had this conversation.

"Hey, yeah sorry it's me. Are you free? Can you talk right now?" I asked as I attempted to pull off my jeans one handed, before I slid under my comforter and into bed.

"Give me literally five seconds. I'm just in the lounge," he replied before I heard him scramble around in the background. All the faded chatter I could hear as he answered the phone disappeared until I could just hear him breathing as he moved to his bedroom. "You still there?" he asked a little breathlessly into the phone.

I stifled a laugh at the almost panic in his voice about me being gone. This wasn't the time. "Yeah, I'm still here," I said as I pulled the comforter up to my chin and checked one more time that the door was in the locked position. For some reason, I'd felt the need to lock the door for this, I didn't know if it was because I didn't want Noah hearing this conversation with Isaac or that I just wanted us to be alone whilst we talked, just me and him. Like it had always been before. I didn't want to believe it was the latter. I had moved past that. For good measure I'd sent Noah on a prefect task this evening, that would keep him away for a good few hours. It wasn't like he didn't have his key to get back in anyway.

"Are you okay?" he asked and I had to suck in a sharp breath to keep my heart from getting broken all over again. There was a compassion in his voice that seemed to only be reserved for me. It was the softness I'd gotten from him when he first helped me unpack, it gave him a humanity that some people failed to see through his sarcasm and his wit.

"Getting there, you know? Thank god it wasn't my right arm that got broken, I'd probably have fallen so far behind in classes otherwise," I said light-heartedly. I knew that wasn't what he'd meant though, he wanted to know why I was calling.

The line went silent for a few beats, I probably should have taken more time to think this through and plan how I was going to approach him about this. Maybe I should have wrote a script? I now didn't feel prepared enough to ask or to really have this conversation with him. But, I couldn't hang up now, that would have just been plain cruel.

"Okay, so you know Rafael?" I started and I heard him let out a shaky exhale before I could even move past my opening sentence.

"I do," he replied half-heartedly, before he laughed almost too hard. It was kind of weird.

"Did Charlie already talk to you?" I asked. Damn, I'd really wanted to be the one to reach out. I'd kill him when I saw him later, I'd made it so clear to him that I needed to do this, that I had to take this step with him so we could work past everything that had happened between us. Maybe even be friends one day or at least civil.

"He did, I'm not going to lie, for a while I really thought you two were together," he sounded somewhat sad about that, his voice incredibly monotone as he spoke into the phone.

"I'm so confused. I literally have no idea what you're talking about?" I replied.

"You and Rafael," he replied simply.

"Together? What the hell are you on about?" I really was confused.

"I thought you two were dating, but now I know better. Charlie told me about them."

Wow, he *was* an idiot. Is that why he'd been so weird with Rafael at the hospital? I laughed, hysterically into the microphone and had to put him on to speaker so I could put the phone down on my bed before it flew out of my hand as my whole body shook with laughter. He really thought I'd called him to say I was in another relationship.

"Are you laughing at me?" I heard him quip as another round of laughter erupted through me. Once I started, I couldn't stop and there was something so cathartic about laughing with him that I'd loved from the very beginning. Even if I was currently laughing *at* him rather than with.

"No," I managed to gasp out in between belly laughs. "Well, actually yes," I confessed. "At the fact that you thought I'd be calling to tell you I'm in a relationship with Rafael. Wow, how did you get into university with a brain like that?"

"I don't understand?" he replied and it was like he was laid next to me. I could almost see him with his crinkled line in his forehead, as he screwed up his face enough to crush all of his freckles up together.

"Me and Rafael definitely aren't together, you idiot. Just friends and it won't be anything more, as now you know he's dating Charlie," I replied, a grin spread across my face. It was finally official. I didn't want to be the guy to jinx it, but they seemed kind of perfect together. Thank god for Charlie, he was such a star, like all of the time. He had been exactly the right person to help Raf deal with everything that had happened post him coming out. I'd done as much as I possibly could, but I hadn't been looking for a relationship, not with him anyway.

"I just assumed when I saw him looking so distraught in that waiting room and the fact that Noah had told me you'd been on your way to meet him for dinner when you crashed. I guess I just put two and two together and came up with this humiliation. Trust me, Charlie put me in my place and stopped me fretting," he replied and there was that tug in my chest again. He sounded almost as relieved as I felt that he was so bothered about me potentially seeing someone else.

"Relax," I said and something fluttered within me as I heard him audibly breath out.

"Hang on? So, what about you and Rafael then? Why the hell did you open with that," he asked.

"Well, ever since he came out, and everything happened with his sports scholarships and the press around it, me and him have been working on a project to raise more awareness for LGBTQ communities within sport. Hopefully, we can make some kind of difference. Like starting up some bursaries for people from LGBTQ communities so they can still get sports scholarships, rather than having to rely on homophobic sports scouts."

I was so proud of how far we'd come, especially with the relationships we'd started to build with some of the nearby Universities like Brock and Waterloo. They were on board with encouraging more diversity in sports and we were even in talks about getting some donations and funding for the scholarships we wanted to start. "Charlie said you've been working with the journalist team at McGill, so we were wondering if you would be able to write us a killer article that we could get published locally or maybe even nationally to hopefully get some more recognition for this issue."

"I can do that," he agreed quickly. "I'd need to get some more information off the both of you, probably do some interviews with Raf and other guys like him, but it can definitely be done. Just get me whatever you guys have right now on the issue and I'll start writing."

"Seriously?" I replied, my hands clutched at the sheets to keep me from squealing or doing anything else just as embarrassing. "You're the best. Thank you so much."

"You don't have to thank me. I'd love to do it. I'll even talk to the team here and see if we can get it published in the Universities magazine and locally."

I grinned, over-excitedly. This had gone way better than I thought it would. "You have no idea how much this is going to mean to Rafael. I can't wait to tell him! When I first came up with this idea it all seemed like a bit of a pipe dream, but now, seeing it all come together, I just ahhhh!" I trailed off, it was so indescribable the difference that this project could make if it actually happened.

"You're incredible, you know that right?" There was an overwhelming amount of pride in his voice and it almost pushed me to tears, because we hadn't had a happy conversation like this in over six months. And god I missed this. There was something about making him proud that I almost strived for. It was like when I'd come out to the group, there'd been such a warmth in his voice and a caress of honey in those grey eyes as he sat across from me at that table in Denny's over a year ago. Christ, I loved him for that. "You've achieved so much as a prefect so far, I've literally been getting weekly updates from Joshua about what's been going on over there.

Sounds like you've got everything completely under control. You and Noah, the dream team, who'd have thought it?"

"He's been amazing. So, so proud of him. He's like a different person, but with all the best elements of last year Noah." No matter how much he moaned about having to do some of the tasks, I knew he was glad I'd asked him to be my deputy.

"Not as bad as we all thought he was, huh?"

"I think he was just hurting," I murmured back as I turned on to my good side and curled myself into the comforter. There was an ache in my chest that wished he were here beside me, his arms wrapped around my waist and me tucked up under his chin.

"Hey, Lo?" I nodded like he could see me. "I'm really glad you called."

"Me too," I whispered back, as I nestled the phone between my ear and the pillow. "Tell me about McGill and Montreal." My body relaxed into the mattress and I couldn't help but feel just that little bit less anxious. My anxiety had been so much better recently, I'd kept up going to see Dr Meredith and I'd been proactive about self-care, no matter how hard it had been in between my final year of high school and being prefect and being President of Show Choir. But, this had been the first time in a couple of months I could just feel my muscles at ease.

"I love it, Lo. Turns out I actually made a good choice for once in my life." I bet in that moment he had a small, charming smirk on his face. I could practically hear it in his voice. "I wasn't cut out for the academic living halls though. I dipped out of there within the first two weeks." He laughed and I laughed too, it was like we were in sync again.

"Why does that not surprise me?"

"Hey, you didn't have to try living there. Picture your room, but in like every room of my dorm and on steroids. The guy I was sharing with had a wall tapestry with the periodic table on it and he'd colour coded slots on his timetable for when he could shower."

I laughed harder than I had in months and it soothed me even more into the comfort of my bed, this was exactly what I needed to ease all the tension that twelfth grade had thrown into my back and neck muscles. If I tried hard enough his voice would be all I need to imagine him here with me.

"Well I'll have you know that me and Noah now share a calendar for prefect duties and he actually appreciates it," I grinned, that had taken a lot of convincing for Noah and a good amount of time for him to come round to him using it again.

"I bet he regrets asking you to live together for another year," he teased and something squeezed again in my chest. I spooned my comforter in the hope it would magically transform into Isaac as I tried to imagine what would living with him be like?

"Don't be jealous," I shot back, two could play at that game.

"Whatever you say, babe," he drawled out and I could so easily allow myself to get caught up in this game. Part of me wanted to; I missed his snark so much. The other screamed at me. It reminded me how much he'd broken my heart just six months ago and that I'd be crazy to fall back into this and let him do it again.

"Well, I guess if I get into McGill you wouldn't want to be roomies then?" I twirled a loose thread that had escaped from my sheets between my fingers. This was a fantasy I'd allowed myself to indulge in way too many times. Except we weren't roommates, we were partners that lived together.

"I didn't even realised you'd applied here?" he asked, the shock evident in his voice.

"Yeah, it's not my first choice as I'm leaning more towards Ottawa, but it's amongst the schools that I applied for." When it had come down to it, me and Noah had chosen a lot of the same schools; Ottawa, McGill - Noah more reluctantly so than me, Waterloo. The only differences being that I'd also applied for Toronto and Brock and he'd just applied for Trent.

"Hey, we are a good school. It offends me that it's not your first choice," he joked and then I heard him yawn. I pulled the phone away from my ear and realised it was almost ten PM, we'd been on the phone for over an hour.

I was tired too, I'd stifled back a good couple of yawns whilst be we'd been on the phone to not be rude, but also because I didn't want to have to cut the call. I'd enjoyed talking to him far too much and I wasn't ready for it to be over just yet.

Screw it. I could either allow this to really hurt me right now, or I could just engage in it and allow myself to really enjoy whatever moments we could get. Because, no matter which way I looked at it or how I felt about him, he was always going to be my first love and that wasn't going to go away. He still erupted a swarm of butterflies from inside me and made me smile like nobody else ever had. Just for tonight I'd allow myself to indulge in what my body and my heart craved.

"Isaac?" I murmured.

"Hmm?" he replied, wearily. He sounded like he could hardly keep his eyes open too.

"Will you stay with me on the phone till I fall asleep?"

"Of course," he whispered back.

That was all it took, the hushed tones of his voice and the levelness of his breathing, the white noise of my fan. I was content and no-one could take this away from me or criticise me because I talked to him. Even if I was being a complete sad sack by asking my ex-boyfriend to help me get a decent night's sleep for the first time in ages.

As silenced engulfed me, I drifted off peacefully, but as my eyes closed tight and my breath evened out I swore I heard him say he missed me.

~ Chapter Twenty-Five ~
Isaac

"I've missed this," Charlie grinned as we sprawled out across his large 'prefect bed', Joshua found himself reclined in the arm chair we'd bought in tenth grade so all three of us could sit comfortably in here to watch movies on the old pull down screen we used to have hung on the far wall.

"Me too," I replied, as I made myself comfy at the head of the bed, Charlie always had one too many pillows for my liking.

"Me three," Joshua added and we all burst into laughter. There was so much familiarity in this room, none of the bad had ever happened in here, we'd always fought in my room or in the corridors or in Julian's office. There was always too much warmth in here to allow us to be mad at each other. That was just Charlie through and through really. I always used to think it was because it was his job as prefect, to give a friendly, approachable atmosphere to his room so the students would feel comfortable to come and talk to him, but even as when he wasn't it still remained. It really was just Charlie.

"I swear though, you two have spent more time in St-Catharines than you have in classes this semester. Just can't keep away?" he added with what Charlie thought he was a smirk, but actually it was still just his regular smile, just a little more lop-sided.

"Did you bring us here to reprimand us for our bad

university habits or are we actually going to catch up and then put on that new Spiderman film you keep telling us we have to watch," I said as I finally made myself comfy against the headrest, Charlie just a metre away from me at the top of the bed.

"I can actually summarise both our first semesters for you Charlie, don't you worry bro. I spent the semester getting seventies, because I'm so average, in all my bio med classes. Me and Callum have trained more than ever to make the lacrosse first team and Callum forced me to join some weird coding club, that turns out isn't so bad. Isaac, even though he goes to way less classes than I do is still getting above eighty in everything, he got four articles published last term in his university paper, but he did sleep with Wyatt and that severely brings down how good his semester was."

"Hey, we said we weren't going to mention that again," I interjected.

"I definitely didn't agree to that," Charlie replied.

"And I lied. Plus, you can't talk Charlie, you kissed him," Joshua laughed

"I was fifteen and naive."

"I was drunk," we said at the same time.

"Shut up, I hadn't finished," Joshua shushed us and fell silent so he could continue. "Isaac also made the soccer team, found three new friends that aren't better than us, but oh wait, he also pined over Logan the whole of the semester. Literally still text me all the time for updates even though I was over an hour away at a different school not stalking his every move in St-Catharines." Joshua looked oh so smug, as he crossed his arms across his chest like he'd just revealed my most embarrassing secret. Which he pretty much had, but I wasn't going to give him that.

"Really?" Charlie asked. "What is actually wrong with

you?"

"Hey. We are friends now again. You can't be angry with me for this still?"

"No, I mean, you literally have been infatuated with him for over a year, and you still haven't done *anything* about it except be a twat and break his heart and then ignore him when he needed you the most. Then break his heart all over again just as he started to sort out his mental health and thought he had a good thing going with you."

"What Isaac is worried about is that Logan now fancies Rafael and is over Isaac." I swotted at him to try and get him to shut up. I hadn't had the chance to tell him about the revelation Charlie had made to me a few nights ago and clearly Charlie had not told him either.

"Well, actually," Charlie interrupted a coy smile on his face, "Me and Rafael are kind of seeing each other."

"Hang on, what?" Joshua cried. "You didn't tell me this. When? Where? Wow."

"Still the same over-excited puppy," I remarked, as Joshua bounced on the spot in his armchair, at least being at university hadn't destroyed his spirit just yet.

"We've literally been on like ten dates, it isn't serious yet, we are just seeing how things go. It's been a tough few months for him, I don't wanna put too much pressure on labelling our relationship or whatever as he's been through a lot. I really like him though and I think he feels the same. Although, I am thinking about proposing to him."

"Excuse me?" Joshua screeched, he could hardly keep his arms under control as they practically flapped around his head before he fist pumped the air. "When?"

"Charlie, you do just realise you said no pressure and then proposing in one breath? I don't think you quite understand what no pressure entails," I drawled out.

"You idiots, prom proposal - for the winter ball, not for marriage - get a grip."

"We have a winter ball now? Why didn't you organise these kind of things when you were prefect, Char?" I asked. "So many missed opportunities to sneak alcohol into punch just like all those awful rom-com teen films you made us watch."

"Shut up," he shot back and pulled out a notebook from the side of his drawer and tossed it down on the bed. "Logan's got me looking over all these crazy plans for the night. I'm talking colour themes, food platters, bands that he wants to play."

I picked it up and scanned the jam-packed book full of pictures of different venue lay outs, menus from different caterers and at the back, his ideas for his suit. I flipped slowly through the pages and let out a shallow sigh as I came across *that* picture., I slouched against the headboard and stroked tenderly over the picture glued to the back page. It was him in that suit we'd searched high and low for when we'd been in Toronto. I'd never actually go to see it on him before he customised it, but he looked incredible. It was perfectly tailored to his body and the colour complemented his hair and his eyes just like he'd told the shop assistant when we'd bought it.

"You can't torture yourself like this forever, you know?" Joshua said as he peered over my shoulder at where my focus had landed on the back page.

"The way I see it, you have two options; either stop moping over him and move on, or man the fuck up and do something about it," Charlie said, as he pried the book out of my grip and placed it back down on the bed.

"Like what?" I asked, exasperated. "We've just got to the point where we can actually talk to each other on the phone, after months of not speaking, I can't expect him to just want to get things back to how they were last year, not after everything that happened."

"You have to start somewhere, anywhere would be better than the position you two are in right now. You're miserable, he's literally become Charlie and just thrown himself completely into being a good prefect. It's not a bad thing, it's just he's become a bit of a robot. No offense, man," Joshua said pointedly at Charlie.

"What about a prom proposal? Go big or go home is what I'm thinking right now. This is your chance to salvage something really good. Something you both ruined out of fear, guilt, something that caused so much pain, to way too many people, for you two to just give up on it like this," Charlie spieled, but everything he said was right, it hit home. Everything reminded me of him, even five hundred miles from him I saw him everywhere, in that stupid guy I had to share with in the first week, in the choir that more often than not performed at the half time shows of our games, in every single shopping centre Cassidy kept forcing me to go to.

"Are you serious? So we plan a proposal, then what? We have absolutely no idea if he'd say yes or not," I shrugged and heaved out a sigh. "What would this prom proposal even consist of? What are you doing for Rafael?" I asked Charlie. I'd never asked anyone to a dance before, I didn't even go to the twelfth-grade prom.

"I'm not telling you that so you can copy me, it's supposed to be personal, something that represents you and him. Noah did something really cool with the help of the debate club for Ameliah."

"I feel like I've walked into some alternative universe where you're actually going after what you want for once in your life and Noah and Ameliah are together. Where am I? Because this isn't Cherrington Academy."

Charlie and Joshua shared a look and Charlie shook his head as if to dismiss Joshua from saying anything. My eyes narrowed in on their interaction, but I didn't say anything. Partly because I feared what they would say in reply and partly because I already knew and had done for years. When they broke out of their little communication bubble they caught how I stared at them.

Charlie drew his brows together and a look of realisation flashed across his eyes. "You knew?" he all but stuttered out, the smile that had been on his face vanished.

"Hang on, hold the fuck up. You knew? Since when?" Joshua asked as he flew to his feet abruptly and paced towards the bed to sit on the end of it.

I nodded. "I've known since like November of ninth grade," I replied with a shrug. "Look, I never said anything, because I had no proof to say you did like me and I could have just imagined it. How awkward would it have been if I'd have just outrightly asked you if you fancied me, what if I had misread the signs, I'd have been humiliated. So, I just left it because I was so happy to be friends with you guys. I didn't want to ruin that. Plus, just a few weeks after I realised you and Beth started dating, so I just let it be."

"Wow," Charlie said bluntly as he chewed on his bottom lip. "Wowww, I never realised I'd been *that* obvious."

"You were very obvious, I caught you staring all the time, when I'd just gotten out the shower, when I got changed, when you thought I was asleep. If it were anyone else you'd have creeped them out enough for them to move rooms. I just thought it was endearing, plus you kept up with my games and all the fun we had. It didn't help that I was so great to look at, I couldn't blame you for staring," I wiggled my eyebrows and Charlie snorted out a laugh. We all cackled loudly together and Joshua both pulled us into a group hug.

"Well," Charlie said as he pulled away from the hug. "Now that's out in the open, we have a prom proposal to sort out," his eyes now lit with this inner glow and I couldn't help but think maybe I should have brought this up last year, so we could have duked it out then and maybe we wouldn't have lost touch for so long. Although, we'd both grown so much in the last five months, maybe that time apart had been necessary for us to come back together like this.

I flopped back, flat out on the bed and stared at 'Dear Evan Hansen' poster Charlie must have stuck up on the ceiling at the start of this academic year. Every year there were more theatre posters, more books, more vinyl records stacked in alphabetical order in his display cabinet above the light blue, vintage record player. "What about a song?" I suggested. Both of them turned to look at me with condescending smiles and Joshua tilted his head as if to say *again?*

"But you can't sing," Joshua said with a laugh, before he was hit on the side of his head with Charlie's decorative cushion for his witty commentary.

"Way to state the obvious, idiot. Beyond the point. Last year for Christmas I bought him some sheet music and for him it was like I'd figured out how to end climate change," I recalled. He'd literally sent me multiple selfies of him as he posed with the sheet music and well how he'd expressed his gratitude for them after we returned to school from Christmas break. I'd literally scoured the web for weeks for some of those pieces, a couple of them were limited edition and first copies from Broadway performances. It'd been worth it to make him happy. That should have been all the clues I'd needed to realise that I actually cared about him way more than I'd realised at the time. I guess that's why I'd chosen then to break up with October. I should not have done that on Christmas day, though.

"I remember that, he text me photos of them just before we came back to Cherrington from Christmas break. I didn't know that was you?" Charlie said, his jaw set as he looked at me with confused eyes. "You got him the mug for his birthday as well right?"

"Full of surprises me. I got pretty good at gift giving to be honest, like I feel bad that I was doing it behind everyone's back, especially Octobers. But it was undeniable I did a good job. And it wasn't just a mug, it was a hamper. It contained all his favourite things, a gift voucher to his favourite Indian restaurant, a signed limited-edition play book for Wicked when those two famous women were in it and some vintage cuff links I'd found on-line."

"You got him a playbook with Kristen Chenoweth and Idina Menzal's signatures on it?" Charlie's jaw dropped as if I'd just told him I was about to become Prime Minister.

"Forget all of that. We have to plan and for that we are going to need a little bit of extra help. A certain someone's roommate, maybe?" Charlie suggested as he waved his hand in front of him as if to remind himself to move on from the playbook.

"Noah hates me, he won't help."

"He doesn't hate *us* though," Joshua responded and before I could even ask what he was up to on his phone, the sound of a text being sent bleeped out of his phone. Charlie's phone also went off and I looked at him with a raised brow.

"You two have a group chat with him?"

"And Raf," Charlie added.

"We also have a separate chat with Logan in it as well, don't be jealous," Joshua stuck his tongue out as his phone went off with a reply. "He's coming up here now, be nice." He shot me a glare that warned me to be on my best behaviour, it was so hard to subordinate to Joshua when his warning glare still came with his chocolate brown puppy dog eyes.

"What's going on?" Noah asked as he entered the room, his head flinched back slightly as he spotted me sat at the head of Charlie's bed. "Why is he here?" He trailed off as he pointed at me, his other hand rubbed at his forehead. "It's almost curfew and Logan will have a fit if he comes in and sees *him* in here."

"That's where you're wrong, Castle, because me and him, we've talked and things are actually okay between the pair of us." The look on Noah's face was all the satisfaction I needed as he scowled at me. "Why did you guys think this was a good idea again?" I asked as I turned to Joshua and Charlie once more. "He isn't going to help us."

"Help with what?" Noah slid himself on to Charlie's desk comfortably; he'd definitely been in here before, and that made me green with envy.

"Isaac is going to propose to Logan for winter ball," Charlie replied and Noah stood up immediately.

"Over my dead body is he," he waved his arms in front of him in a cross motion before he strode up beside me on the bed. "You do *not* get to walk in here and hurt him again, was the first time not enough?"

"I love him and I don't want to be apart from him anymore." I pushed myself up off the bed and squared up to him, my shoulders back and arms crossed in front of my chest. "You know if we were together, properly this time, we'd be happy, he'd be happy. Doesn't he deserve that?" Noah's glare broke as he realised I was right, he stared down at his feet as he shuffled from heal to heal. "You guys all get to be happy, you and Ameliah, him and Rafael, Joshua and well, he's still working on that. I just want one last chance to be happy with him, please?" I reached out and placed my arm on Noah's. "Noah, I'm begging you, this is so embarrassing, but I desperately want the chance to make things right."

He shrugged my hand off him, but regardless he nodded. "What are you thinking?" If I hadn't already embarrassed myself enough with the begging, I'd have hugged him. Instead it was time to get down to business.

~ Chapter Twenty-Six ~
Logan

"Rafael may actually kill you for this," I chuckled as we finished colouring in the large bold letters we'd spent hours sketching out. Turns out we weren't very artistic at all, the bin full of crumpled bits of sketch paper could tell you that. Charlie had suggested we buy a laminator earlier to make the art look glossy, if we couldn't even sketch basic letters I couldn't imagine how we'd have used a laminator to make them better. I was glad we'd left it in the store.

"It'll be worth it. I freaking hope it'll be worth it. It *will* be worth it right?" Charlie presented me with the final letter he'd just coloured like he was showing me a masterpiece. It was two in the morning and we were a bit buzzed off the lack of sleep and the adrenaline that came from being up so late, they had both hit us in the weirdest ways. For Charlie, he'd really began to lose his mind, it was like a five-year-old on a sugar rush.

"You do realise he is one hundred percent going to say yes anyway, right?" There was absolutely no doubt about that in my mind. The way Rafael looked at Charlie, well, it was the way Isaac looked at me when we were first together; when he gave me the Christmas gift, when we ate curled up in bed together, heck even when we made up after we fought. I wished them a lot more success than we had. It was Charlie and Rafael though, there was nothing that could go wrong there. Charlie cared too

214

much and Rafael had been so hesitant about going out with anyone, Charlie had broken that down. I knew they both loved each other, even if it was super early on in their relationship for those three words.

"I don't know that," he said as he hung the last letter on the crazy washing line that Charlie had erected across his room with multiple pieces of rope. I surveyed the whole line and it actually looked ridiculous, all the letters painted in Toronto Raptors colours. At 8PM we'd raced across St Catharines to Michael, where we'd bought way more paint, paper, brushes and all the other random arts and crafts shit we spent over a hundred bucks between us on. "Should we have put glitter on them or something?" he asked as he stood next to me and stared like a mad man at the washing line.

"No, definitely not." I was putting my foot down there, I was desperate for sleep. "This is a crazy enough stunt already, we don't need glitter flying around the dining hall that would cause even more chaos than this is already going to." I'd already seen a guy get glitter bombed as his girlfriend dumped two buckets of glitter that she'd wrapped in a ten-foot scroll and released over the second-floor banister of Edwards to invite him to the ball. That glitter had been an absolute pain to clear up. Julian had been no help at all, he just took one look at the mess and said to me in his best head of house voice, 'the ball was your idea, so this is your mess to clear up'.

"Should I tone it down?" he asked as he began to re-organise the dried letters into the order they were supposed to be in. I was so glad I did not have to sleep in this room tonight, if I'd have woken up to those dangling over me in the night I'd have probably had a heart attack. No ball proposal was worth that. Although considering the frantic look on Charlie's face as his eyes darted around way too quickly, maybe this one was.

"Okay we're done for the night," I said taking control of what was a spiralling situation. "You need to sleep, I need to go and make sure the house is still standing after I left Noah in charge for the evening, knowing him he's probably snuck off campus with my keys and Ameliah, so good luck to whatever I'm about to sleep walk out to. I'll see you in the morning. Do not touch the letters anymore," I said as I stood at the door, my gaze on his bed as I waited for him to catch on. He looked up at me with the best puppy dog eyes he could, but he was too tired for them to be effective and he knew it was time to concede.

I averted my eyes as he stripped down to his boxers, but when I heard his mattress dip, I turned back round to check he was there for the long haul.

"What you not going to come tuck me in as well?" I switched off his light switch, which left him only lit up by the warm glow of his bedside lamp.

"Good night, Charlie," I said as I carefully shut the door behind him and then almost shit myself when I saw a light switch on downstairs. For a moment I'd forgotten about the hundreds of students that slept around us. I hurried quickly down the stairs and threw my door open before anyone of them could bring trouble to me, or worse report me for being out of bed.

"You've got paint on your face," Noah said as I slipped into the room, the overhead light still on and him sat up in bed with his laptop open in front of him.

"And when did miss Ameliah leave?" I stepped into the bathroom and grabbed my flannel so I could wipe off the paint and change into the pyjama's I'd grabbed from the end of my bed along the way.

He just chuckled in reply which told me everything that I needed to know, giving Noah free reign as deputy prefect was like taking an alcoholic to a free bar. With my pyjamas on and my face clean it was finally time for me to descend to bed. "Any huge problems I should know about tonight?"

"None. Nobody even knocked the door, me and Ameliah did bed checks by the way which kept Julian from finding out that you were up in Charlie's room to this hour." He closed the lid of his laptop and slid it into the bottom drawer of his bedside table. "Everything ready for tomorrow?" he asked.

"Just about," I sighed, as I dabbed a night oil into my skin. "Rafael is not going to know what hit him, trust me." With a spritz of toner I could feel sleep as it tried to take me. "You ready for me to turn out the light?"

No reply, just darkness. "Thank you for taking over tonight, you're the best," I murmured into the pitch-black room and he hummed in reply.

"Good night, Logan."

I'd slept like a baby, whereas Charlie definitely hadn't. He'd thickened up the black outline on all the letters and took the laminator he'd apparently found in the common room to every sheet of paper on his own once they were dry. I'd reprimanded him, but I couldn't be angry at him; I couldn't wait to see two of my closest friends be happy because of this. Between classes we'd polished off the proposal and consumed a lot of coffee to get us through the day, we'd only parted ways properly after the final class, me to do prefect duties and Charlie to stress over whatever else he felt the need to stress over. Which led to a text about forty-five minutes later that had our gangs food requests for dinner on, apparently so they could all be seated ready for the proposal.

"I have one chicken, one steak and one pulled pork burrito," I shouted like a food street clerk as I handed them out between the three of them already sat at the table.

"What did you get?" Noah gestured to the container tucked under my arm, as he peeled back the grey foil.

"Burrito salad," I replied as I dropped on the bench next to him. "Cutting back on the carbs before winter ball, I actually want to be able to fit into the suit I bought last year, whether I'm going stag or not." Damn all the pizza and pasta I had consumed post break up with Isaac, it had done nothing for my previously trim waistline.

"Oh please, you look great," Rafael shot me a wink and Charlie smacked his shoulder, but Rafael only laughed harder and winked at me again.

I waved him off. "Regardless. I'll be tucking into this, so please stop being ungrateful and chow down the food that I just fetched for all of you lazy sods." In all fairness, Noah and Raf had just finished at their retrospective sports practices and Charlie had ran around like a headless chicken from the moment classes finished.

I'd seen him rushing around in the dorms after class as he transported all the letters we'd made in a box to hide in the changing rooms for after basketball practice was over.

"How is this semester almost over?" Charlie asked, as he pulled out his phone, it was so close to go time.

"Please don't start getting all sentimental on us, Montgomery. I've already seen Logan compiling photos from this semester into a scrap book, talking about the fact that we are all so close to graduating and leaving this place will probably reduce him to tears."

"Accurate," I replied as I scooped up some chicken and beans with my fork, this salad sucked. Not enough sour cream or hot sauce or anything else that made a burrito so good.

A horn honked throughout the hall and I clasped at

my ears, as did many people around us, others searched frantically for where the noise had come from. We probably should have thought about the panic that noise could probably cause, but too late to go back now, it was all about to begin.

Bailey jumped on to the table first, the trays that were placed on it clattered around him, but that didn't stop him, or anyone else as he reached out a helping hand to Kelvin to join him up on the table. "Attention please," they called out with the megaphones they clutched before hauling the rest of the team up there with them. Luckily, me and Charlie had, had a spare few minutes in their hour-long practice to push together as many tables as possible, because there was no way that whole team would have gotten on to one singular table.

This had all been crazy rushed, so the boys were all still in there kits, hadn't even had the chance to shower yet. But they'd all been under strict instruction to wear their team jackets, otherwise this would not work at all. The poor guys, Charlie had drilled them so hard over this. If I hadn't been completely scared of him when he'd been yelling his instructions, I'd have been really proud of his meticulous organisation and timings.

"What the fuck are they doing?" Rafael asked around a mouthful of burrito. Slowly his team mates began to unzip their jackets, each to reveal a laminated placard with a letter on draped around their necks like a huge necklace. Thankfully, for Charlie's blood pressure, they were all stood in the correct order and with each letter Raf became a little more clued in on what the hell was happening.

As the final letter that spelled out *winter ball, Raf?*, was revealed, Charlie leapt to his feet and joined the basketball team on top of the table. "Oh shit, this is actually happening." Rafael pinched himself and I couldn't help but giggle; I was completely astounded that Charlie had managed to convince the whole team to get up and embarrass not only themselves, but also their captain who would definitely kick their asses later.

"Fraid so," I replied as me and Noah turned back around to face the action. It was going to be truly unmissable.

"Sorry to disrupt dinner, but really with all the crazy proposals that have been going on over the last couple of days are any of you really surprised to see this right now?" The crowd of diners laughed in reply, most of them looked up in delight at the ex-prefect, others confused as they tried to work out who he was about to propose to.

That had become to be a game we'd all had to play over the course of the last few weeks, especially some of the crazier proposals that didn't specify names, like when Oscar had written a poem for his girlfriend and highjacked the PA system in the school, read it out loud through every class room and then realised he had not once mentioned the name of his girlfriend.

"If you'd have asked me three months ago if I thought I'd be doing this, I'd have told you 'hell no.'" The crowd only laughed harder and I could see Charlie relax a little from up high, the cheers only motivated him to speak on. "I'd written off getting into another relationship anytime soon after last year, but then I was reintroduced to a guy who I'd known of for the last three years, but just hadn't met all of." This was the only part of the proposal that I had not been privy to, maybe if I had I would not have welled up like a baby with every word Charlie spoke. "Then he went through hell when he came out and the way he handled it, fought all the injustice that came with it, I couldn't help but find him more attractive. Then my best friend practically forced us together, but I could not be more thankful for him as I knew I'd found a good egg. Which is why I'm up here, humiliating the both of us in the hopes that he'll be my date for the ball. So, Rafael Danetele, will you go to the ball with me?"

All eyes were on Rafael, there was a singular moment of silence before Rafael stood up, strode over to the table and pulled Charlie off it, straight into a kiss. Everyone around them took it as a yes and applauded wildly. Me and Noah jumped to our feet and cheered for the pair that had come so far in just one semester.

As it sunk in around us what had just happened more people clambered to their feet and clapped for the couple, Raf had become the poster child for inclusivity in sports over the last month and he'd become more recognised around the school, even more so than what he was when he'd been the huge basketball star. The diners went wild for the pair, but they were way too busy to see.

I marvelled in the fact that people cheered for the gay couple, that would not have happened at my old school and woah I was not about to let my mind wander there, not in this really happy moment.

As the hysteria died down and Charlie and Rafael finally broke away from their kiss, Noah leaned in and said, "Don't you feel like you've missed out now?" I desperately wished I didn't, but there was nothing I could do about that. So I just shook my head.

"Nope, I got to help with this and with yours and Amelilah's, I think I've had my fill of proposals for one semester. Plus, I always knew I wasn't going to get asked, so I never expected it, that way there's no disappointment when my imaginary boyfriend doesn't show up to ask me," I chuckled as I stabbed my fork into what remained of my burrito salad.

"Tell that to the poor lettuce leaf you just impaled." I stared down at the container, my fork had sliced through the polystyrene bottom and the sauce had leaked out on to the table below.

"Fuck off," I grunted as he peeled back the foil a little more on his burrito and took another bite, damn I regretted not getting a proper burrito.

~ Chapter Twenty-Seven ~
Logan

"You look miserable," October commented as I slid onto the bench, my pasta salad in one hand and my open laptop in the other.

"Don't start this again. You know I'm absolutely fine, just busy with the ball and choreographing the show choir to perform at our local competition and again for the ball.

"You *really* do look miserable. You've planned this whole winter ball, but you don't even seem to be that excited for it," Noah commented as we sat at dinner with Ameliah and October. We'd been calling these dinners unofficial prefect meetings, but what they actually were was us just eating food together as friends. It was all still a little bit foreign for us, we'd all sorted out our differences, but the path below us still felt a little bit rocky sometimes. These dinners were progress, if we had to label them prefect meetings for now I would.

"It's because he doesn't have anyone to go with," October replied around a mouthful of her veggie burrito.

"And you do?" I replied, from where I typed behind my laptop, different coloured table cloths filled my screens. I knew when we started planning this winter ball that it would be a lot of work, somehow I'd ended up taking on most of the responsibility. Not really a surprise when you thought about it. I just wanted the perfect coloured table cloth to fit our blue, red, white and gold theme. I was thinking gold, but all this stupid site seemed to have was bronze or copper coloured cloths. Not good enough.

"Well, that's where you're wrong. I'm going with Eric Carson," she bragged, of course she was going with someone who couldn't stay out of trouble. He was one of the brothers who'd caused carnage this semester. He'd beaten Isaac's record number of pranks for a year, in just one semester. Him and his brother were tenth and eleventh grade pains in my ass.

"That disturbs me, you really have a type for trouble makers don't you?" I commented, as I googled yet another party store website. I'd gotten streamers in every different colour of our theme, the banner had letters in the alternating blue/white and red/white themes of the Edwards and Victoria houses. Gold table cloths would be a perfect fit to complement all of this. Especially with the white chairs that had the gold legs that we'd sourced.

"Are you not even planning on asking anyone?" Ameliah asked, as she pushed down my laptop lid shut and gestured for me to eat the still full bowl of pasta in front of me that was probably cold by now.

"Who do you want me to ask? Charlie and Rafael are going together and the only other openly gay guys I know are ninth or tenth graders, I'm not that desperate, yet," I replied as I picked at the spinach of my side salad.

That shut them up. They all just looked at me a little blankly. "Look. I'm glad you guys are going with people and I'm sure you'll have a great night. But, I just want to have all the plans done and if we aren't actually going to have a planning meeting then I'm gonna spend my evening in my room finalising catering numbers and trying to find a snow machine that isn't already booked for the middle of December." I gathered up my laptop and notebook and shoved them in my satchel. I pushed my plate of food towards Noah as he'd been eying it up since I got it. "Eat this," I said and he grabbed at the bowl, forking the left overs into his mouth. He was a real glutton.

"Come on, Lo. It's not going to be any fun if you aren't enjoying all the hard work you've put into this," Ameliah replied as she clasped my hand and attempted to pull me back down onto bench.

I went to protest, but a loud blare of high-pitched white noise rang through the speakers in the dining room. "What the fuck?" I said as the lights dimmed and students filtered into the dining hall through the many entrances, they clutched at guitars and a guy I recognized to be Chris dragged a portable keyboard into the hall. Weird things like this had been happening for the last couple of weeks, prom proposals had seemed like a good idea on paper, in reality they'd caused chaos. People pulled the fire alarms to get their dates outside for plane fly overs of *will you go to winter-ball with me?*, the other Carson brother had climbed onto the roof of Victoria to ask his date to the ball.

At least Charlie's proposal had been controlled. No wreckage, no loud noise except the foghorn, not too much destruction.

I'd seen enough of these this week to not want to sit through another. "I'll see you guys later," I said as I grabbed my now empty bowl of pasta and headed for the waste bin. I scraped the food remnant's into the bin and stacked my tray, just as the opening bars of Wicked's *As Long as You're Mine* started out. Now I definitely needed to leave, I couldn't see a proposal to my favourite song.

Crowds had gathered at the sound of the music, which made it even harder to navigate a clear route out of the dining hall than usual. I sighed as I pushed my way through the overwhelming amount of people that blocked all of the pathways out of the hall. I sighed as I stood at the back of a small crowd that had formed.

"Hang on, didn't he graduate last year?" someone murmured in front of me, I tried to peer over the crowd, but I was pretty sure I was surrounded by the whole of the basketball team.

"Yeah, he did," another one of the maybe basketball players replied.

How sad did that make me; someone's partner had come back to ask them after they'd graduated and I couldn't even find someone in the school to go with. I resigned myself to leaning against a nearby table and decided to wait until the performance was over before I attempted to leave. If I pushed through this swarm of people I'd become trapped in, I'd end up in the middle of the performance and I definitely didn't need that kind of embarrassment right now. I was already going to be the Edwards prefect who attended his own winter ball single.

The first vocal bars rang out and my head shot up at the male voice taking lead of the song. I needed to get a better look what was going on right now. I climbed up on to the table and dropped my messenger bag to the floor. As I hoisted myself up, I spotted him, microphone in hand looking like he was part of a boy band as Joshua, Charlie, Rafael and Noah swayed behind him. I stumbled a little as a sudden coldness hit my core and I struggled to recover from how disorientated I felt as I watched him slide round a microphone stand and perform my favourite song.

This wasn't happening.

I turned back to where I'd previously sat with everyone and spotted Ameliah and October as they nodded in time to the beat, Noah's seat next to Ameliah now vacant. I knew every single guy that surrounded him, members of the show choir *I'd* put together. Chris behind the keyboard, Oscar and Jess on the guitar, four of my favourite people on this Earth singing back-up to the man I loved more than anything on this earth. Had for a year, despite the mess of a year it had been.

Everyone's eyes were now on me as I stood like an absolute idiot on a table, for a split second my breath caught in my throat as Isaac pointed at me and sang, awfully, "I'll make every last moment last, as long as you're mine." He was headed towards me, performed elaborate twists and turns to reach me at the edge of the table, a hand outstretched as Noah and Charlie's more capable voices took over the lyrics.

"You always wanted a duet," he grinned re-bumptiously. This was it, the situations of flight or fight I'd been working so hard to tackle with Dr Meredith over the last six months. I could either take his hand or push him away and clamber over these tables as fast as possible to get out of here.

No time like the present. I slid my hand into his and allowed him to tug me down from the table and into the centre of the crowd. I wasn't even scared as his warm hand closed around mine, it didn't tremble once, he just pulled me closer and our bodies fit together like missing pieces of a jigsaw.

"It's now or never," he whispered as he offered me the second microphone. I took a deep breath as I gathered myself, before turning back to the people watching us and took over the second verse. The crowd cheered and hollered as Isaac held me in his arms as we sang the words together, my microphone thankfully turned up a lot louder than his.

I clung to his arm as we finished up the last line of the song. He span me out in an almost slow-motion fashion and allowed me to bow in front of the crowd before he got down on one knee in front of me.

"I'm literally the world's biggest idiot. I let go of you way too easily and that was the most stupid thing I could have ever done. You know, I suck at this emotional shit, but I know, now, that we were meant to be together, you were brought to this school to be mine. Sometimes I thank the lord that you transferred here, because I'm not sure where I'd be without you. Like seriously, I'd have probably been expelled, I wouldn't have graduated or gone to McGill. I wouldn't have dealt with some of my anger or have fallen in love properly for the first time."

Tears dripped down my face and I watched his glossy eyes so intently, because if I'd have broken eye contact I'd have probably collapsed, overwhelmed with emotion.

"This doesn't make up for how much I hurt you or what I've put you through in the last year, but I'd really like to start making up for all of that. And that starts with this ridiculous prom proposal. So, Logan Miles Shield, will you go to the winter ball with me?" he asked elaborately, as he pulled out the most ridiculous ring with a snowflake on it.

I let him flounder for a moment, after everything he deserved to squirm for just a few seconds longer. The time didn't change how I felt though. This had been all I'd ever wanted. Some may think I'd been stupid to hold out hope it would come, to not move on and find someone that would give it to me from the off, not take a year to finally make his mind up. A lot of people were probably laughing at me right now for even contemplating saying yes. But, as I looked around the room, October smiled and nodded at me, Ameliah now wrapped up once more in Noah's arms held up her thumbs and Charlie, Rafael and Joshua were all stood behind Isaac like some ridiculous back up dancers. They were all that mattered, I didn't care what anyone else thought, except them. No other guy would have made me feel like my whole body was on fire after doing this, but him. There was no-one else in the world I'd have waited over a year to get this from. He was the one.

There was a pin drop silence around us and I realised I'd left him down on one knee for way too long, to the point people glared at me in anticipation of my answer. Even he looked worried as he scrubbed his free hand through his hair.

"Yes," I whispered to him and then again even louder this time for everyone to hear. "Yes, I'll go with you!" I pulled him up off the floor and into the tightest hug I could muster. It was perfect, his arms wrapped around me, me tucked up under his chin. It felt so right, like cocoa on a winters night and a breeze on a hot summers day. There was nowhere else in the world I wanted to be right now.

Especially when the cheers and applause pulled us out of our bubble, the most important people now surrounded us. October grinned and clapped with the crowd, a look on her face that told me she approved as she nodded her head slightly at us, that had me all choked up, we'd come such a long way. Noah and Ameliah stood behind us, hand in hand, with Charlie and Rafael next to them, Rafael's arm around Charlie's waist, they looked so cute together. And Joshua, well he just bounced on his heels in excitement for us, the first to run up and pull us both into a celebratory hug.

"Woah, careful," I croaked as he crashed into us. "Remember my broken bones that have only just healed," I said, before we burst into laughter.

"Sorry, sorry," he replied, before he clapped his hands-on Isaac's shoulders. "I can't believe we actually pulled that off." He pulled Isaac into another tight hug.

"None of you thought to give Isaac some singing lessons first though?" I chuckled, as I slid my hand into Isaacs and squeezed it hard. This was it, I was never going to let go again.

~ Chapter Twenty-Eight ~
Logan

"It's perfect." I surveyed the decorated grand hall. We'd done an incredible job, everything looked amazing. Everything I thought about my prefect team had been true, we worked together perfectly. We'd spent eight hours last night until almost one AM in the hall, hung every banner, positioned every balloon and made sure that every table looked immaculate with the correct shade of gold table cloth and the Victoria/Edwards table decorations in the centre of the table.

We'd coated every single chair with a satin white cover, a huge gold bow attached to the back of each chair. The stage was decorated with a gold foil background that would look great as a back drop when the band and choir played every song. I'd even had some of our volunteers mop the dance floor till it was spotless, even I was stunned at how sparkly clean it now looked.

As soon as we'd returned back to Edwards, me and Noah had collapsed in exhaustion, hardly even spoke a word to each other except to congratulate each other on what we'd achieved. It had been a blissful night's sleep and we both had woken up ready to take on any last-minute problems and then get ready for our winter ball.

"T minus two hours till the doors open to everyone else. I think we are ready," he agreed as he stood hand in hand with Ameliah.

"He's right you aren't touching a single decoration

now. It's perfect, your vision really came to life," October added as her arm draped around my shoulder. "Next year's prefects are going to struggle to top this." She smiled smugly, but she was right we'd pulled all of this off in just over a month and it really was incredible.

"Okay, let's have the media team come in and take some photographs for the Christmas article and then I'll have the band do a music run through so I know the staging is going to work and that the tech isn't going to fail us." I surveyed the checklist in front of me, there was still a tonne of things I hadn't crossed off, I could do them on my own though.

Noah pried the list out of my hand. "That is what our ninth and tenth grade volunteers are for, hand that list over to Chris and Kirstie and lets go get ready. This is our last chance at this winter ball thing and we deserve to enjoy it. Now come on, you've got a skincare routine to do, hair to style and that ridiculously overpriced suit to put on." He handed the list over to our wonderful volunteers and I thanked them endlessly before I'd been dragged back to Edwards.

"It's going to be fine, what are you always telling me about worry lines? You need to stop otherwise your face is going to stay that way," Noah said as he poked at my forehead on our walk back.

I knew he was right, but I still didn't want anything to go wrong. We'd hyped this ball up so much, I wanted it to live up to everyone's expectations, exceed them. Not have it flop. At the start of the year I'd said as prefect that I wanted to make a difference, make a change. This was one of those things, I wanted to give every student here a chance to make amazing memories and for them to walk away having had the best time at this school they could possibly have had. Like I had had in just my two short years here.

The whole time I was getting ready I could feel my anxiety eating away at me, with every swoop of gel through my curls and every squirt of moisturiser to my face I could feel it bubble away inside of me, niggling at the lining of my stomach, caused acid to rush up into my throat. As I stared in the mirror one last time to check how I looked, I remembered what Dr Meridith had said in our first session - *We still have work to do, Logan,* and I did. So much more work, whether that was here at this school or elsewhere at university or in my job. It didn't end after this ball, after tonight. I'd put a lot of my worth on the line tonight, it dependent upon how well tonight went and that hadn't been fair on my mind. Tonight was going to be incredible no matter what, I had to give myself a break and congratulate both me and Noah, and Ameliah and October on what we'd achieved.

"I'm ready," I said as I appeared out of the bathroom and twirled in-front of Noah in my suit. I looked fantastic, even if I did say so myself.

"You look good," he replied as he pulled on his own suit jacket and straightened out his bow tie. "I know this is all a bit American," he pulled out a large white box and opened it to display the prettiest pink and purple flowered wrist corsage, "but I bought this for Ameliah, do you think I did okay? Her dress is like an ombre of these two colours, well at least that's how October described it to me."

Tears welled in my eyes, at the boy, no man, that stood in front of me and the stunning corsage he'd presented to me. I choked down a gulp and breathed in deeply to keep the tears from falling. "You did wonderfully," I commented as my fingers stroked the flower. "Not bad for someone who couldn't even tux shop on his own," I grinned as I pulled his collar into

233

place, his midnight purple suit looked incredible with the dusky pink, floral bow tie we'd picked. I'd already seen Amelilah's dress and I'd orientated him to something that would complement it but wouldn't be too matchy matchy.

He placed the box down on his dresser and pulled me into a tight hug. This wasn't something we did very often, but when we did, god it overwhelmed me. Noah wasn't the most affectionate boy, so I treasured every moment of it. "Love you man," he whispered into my ear and I just squeezed tighter.

I'd seen him this morning, as he looked at the picture of Jessie that he kept tucked in his bedside table. This would have been a momentous night for both of them, he'd have taken her as one more celebration closer to them graduating high school and starting their lives together. I hurt for him, that type of loss, at this age or any age was hard to get over. I was just glad he had Ameliah to dance with tonight, someone he could sway to the slow songs with and not feel alone at all.

"Love you too," I whispered back as I clapped his back. "Come on, we can't be late to our own ball," I chuckled and with one more once over we were out the door.

~Chapter Twenty-Nine ~
Isaac

It was almost laughable as I spotted him across the dance floor just as Selena Gomez's *Back to You* started to play. I'd challenge anyone in this life to find a more fitting song for our relationship. I smirked at him as I strode towards him, past Charlie and Rafael as they grabbed punch, and Ameliah and Noah who were squashed in a booth together. "You wanna dance?" I suggested as I held out my hand, I'd worked on my moves a little since the proposal, I had the basic steps now mastered.

"Well," he replied as he looked around us, his eyes scouted out the guys who wafted around us, "I'm not getting any other offers." He licked his bottom lip and clutched his hand in mine.

I led him out on to the dance floor and my mind flash backed to that night in the Moose and Goose, I was about to be heavily showed up, I'd forgotten exactly how good at this he actually was, a natural born performer. "Go easy on me okay? Remember I play soccer, I don't dance!" I said as he took his other hand and copied exactly what I'd watched on YouTube a dozen times, upbeat pop dancing, that's what the video was called. It was a whole lot of shimming, swinging my hips and moving my arms in every direction, just this time with a partner. I'd got it under control.

It was as he swayed his hips perfectly in time to the

beat I noticed what he was wearing, that suit he'd spent way too much money on when we'd been in Toronto. It looked incredible, exactly how he'd talked it up to be when he'd tried it on in the fitting room and had it tailored to his physique. He was right when he said the evening blue was in his colour palette, whatever that was, because it complimented all his features, his pale skin, auburn hair and those baby blues that still made my heart feel like a wave crashing against the rocks.

"You okay?" he asked and I realised I'd been stood still for way too long as the music played around us, staring at him like he was a dream come true. He was.

"How did I get so lucky?" I questioned. "You look absolutely incredible, like so good I can't believe we didn't book a hotel or something for after this ball ends."

"Good thing I've already had this thought then isn't it. Well, to be fair it was Noah's idea, I don't think either of us wanted to have to wrestle to have the room tonight, so we both booked rooms at the Four Seasons," he smirked. "Although, I think half of the twelfth grade did too, because the only rooms they had left were suites."

"You're amazing. This whole night is amazing, we've never done anything like this here, we have the twelfth-grade prom, but it's always faculty organised and lame. I didn't even go to mine, well you know, it wasn't really a good time." We both shared a look, eyes locked as he nervously played with his hands, I shook my head, not tonight. "What I'm trying to say is you've smashed it out of the park, look how much everyone's enjoying it." I watched him survey the room in anguish, he'd been nervous all evening texting me every ten minutes or so about something he was worried he'd forgotten to do. I couldn't see any of it when I arrived, just sheer perfection.

He let out a trembly breath into my shoulder. "You

have no idea how much I've needed to hear that right now. The planning squad have all kept saying it's awesome, but they had to, they didn't want to stress me out, this project kind of became my baby."

"I can see that. Plus, Charlie showed me the book." That was a planner gone into overdrive.

"What book?" Logan probably had not meant for me to see that book, but fuck it, Charlie had shown it to me, he could take the fall for this one.

"With all your ideas in, for decor and music and this gorgeous fucking suit, which let me just say looks incredible on you, the photos were one thing, but in person, well..." I bit my lip and pushed back any lustful thoughts right now, that could wait until the suite later.

"It does look pretty good, doesn't it?" He gave me a little twirl and I gaped at how good the fitted trousers made his ass look. My eyes must have lit up like casino slots because he gave a devilish grin, clearly he'd achieved the reaction he'd wanted.

The pianist on stage began to play the opening notes of Ed Sheeran's *Perfect* and some of the younger members of Logan's choir started their harmonies. He looked at me, hesitant eyes that wouldn't lock with mine, he didn't move towards me and I could tell he wasn't sure what to do in this situation. Neither was I, I'd never properly slow danced in my life, but I was willing to try, with him.

I placed my hand gently in his, my other arm wrapped around his waist and I tried to mimic the position I'd seen dancers go into on the YouTube videos I'd watched to prepare myself for this. His lips parted into a small smile and his head rested on my shoulder as we stepped slowly across the dance floor.

I watched in wonder as couples and friends swayed around us, everyone moved in and out of each other in a care free fashion, completely lost in the moment with their partners. I could see Charlie and Rafael across the floor and even Ameliah and Noah had emerged from the booth for this. The choir sounded incredible as they hit every note, I'm sure Logan had a hand in this arrangement as he hummed it softly in my ear.

"You not gonna get up there and give us a song?" I asked as the chorus kicked in and one of the boys took over all the lines, the other boys provided backing vocals.

"Not tonight, all twelfth graders have the night off so we can celebrate. I know this is the first time we've done one of these things, but it'll be one of our last dances and I hope for the other students only one of their first," he grinned as he switched his head to lean on my other shoulder.

"You'll have to give me my own private performance later on," I pressed a soft kiss to his head and leaned back in to him so we could finish our dance to this song.

We ended up in that position for the medley of slow songs before the choir handed back over to the DJ and his remix of the songs of the year. We slowly parted from each other, I felt reluctant to do so as I'd have loved to have stayed wrapped up in him forever.

Panic at the Disco played through the speakers and for a moment we just stared at each other as everyone bopped around us. "What?" He tilted his head to the side and I still couldn't take my eyes off him, he was stunning, even though his curls had now matted with sweat from the hot hall and the beads had rolled down his face and onto his cheeks. I swiped at the beads and he crinkled up his nose, I threatened to lick up the sweat, but he crinkled up his nose, so I just wiped it down the side of my slacks.

"You're just too gorgeous, you know?" His already flushed skin tinged to beetroot and I laughed hard as he tried to hide his face back in my neck. "I'm serious," I said as I tilted his chin up to look back at me. "I am crazy about you and I'm so ready to start our future together, wherever you end up next year it won't stop us. I don't want to be without you."

"Even if I moved to England for University?" he teased and I pushed him away from me, at this point I'd probably move continents for him.

"We can make this work right? I really mean it, I want to try, I want us to be together. I feel like we are so meant to be I can't even tell you." My eyes pleaded with him as I brushed my thumb across his cheek, our bodies swaying in time to the music, completely moulded together. There was a warmth in my stomach, a desire, not lustful, my heart just ached to be with him.

"We can," he grinned and leaned his cheek into my hand, I cupped his cheek and pressed a slow, long kiss to his lips, his arms threaded round my shoulders and it really was like we were one.

"I'm never going to fuck up again," I whispered against his lips, our foreheads resting together as he brushed his nose against mine. His blue eyes were glossy like the glimmer in the sea when the sun shone on it, and as I ran my tongue over my bottom lip he kissed me once more, eyes shut tight as he lost himself in our kiss. Was this what coming home felt like?

A throat cleared behind us, we broke apart sloppily to find we were no longer alone, Noah and Ameliah one side of us, Charlie and Rafael the other. The song before had faded out and an upbeat Rihanna song blared around us.

"PG please, Wells. You're at a school dance not in the middle of a club." We both glared at him and he retreated behind Ameliah, his arms wrapped around her waist. We did not need reminding of that photo right now.

"We should do something about that?" I whispered into his ear, my tongue grazed against the outer shell and Charlie gagged in disgust and covered Rafael's eyes with his hands.

"Please excuse my friends, they don't know how to act in normal human environments."

"I agree," Logan whispered back. "Well, enjoy the rest of the night, the band that are playing between ten and eleven before this thing ends were chosen by Noah, so if you don't like them blame him, because we are out of here." With a small wave to our friends, he took me out of the hall and led me to his car. I pushed him up against the passenger door and kissed him like it was the last chance we were going to get, my tongue desperate against his as I fumbled my hands around his waist.

He placed a steady palm on my chest to push me backwards a little his face now completely flushed. "What?" I asked, innocently.

"Hotel suite," he reminded me, as he opened the passenger door and stalked round to the other side, so he could drive like a mad man to the Four Seasons down the road and finish what I'd started.

EPILOGUE
Logan

The air was crisp around us as though we should have been in the middle of fall with crumpled leaves on the ground and Halloween just around the corner, not in the middle of a May summers day. It made me grateful to be nestled in between Charlie and Ameliah, as we stood on the side of the pitch to watch Noah do his thing in the soccer Championship game. It was cold for May, so cold I'd got a jumper on and the weather forecast had predicted snow for this week. Climate change at its finest.

"We definitely wouldn't have done this for him last year," I joked, to which Ameliah punched me in the arm in reply before she succeeded to laugh along with me.

"A lot has changed hasn't it?" Ameliah said, I couldn't help but nod in return, a small wave of emotion washed through me as I thought about everything that had happened in the two years that I'd been here. The group wasn't smaller or bigger, the people had just changed, others had come and gone. These were the right people to still have by my side though.

"I'm proud of him," I said, as I sniffled back a couple of tears. The two years I'd lived at Cherrington Academy well, they'd been an absolute ride, too many ups and downs to be considered a safe roller-coaster. But, being stood on the side of the pitch, to watch the Championship game, graduation just a few weeks away, it made all those highs and lows worth it.

"Me too," Charlie added, Ameliah nodded in agreement. I wrapped my arm around her and tucked her into my side. "He's grown up so much, I guess he's had to," he said with a resigned sigh. "But, part of it was your doing, Lo, you know."

"Mine?" I asked. "What do you mean?"

"The both of you have grown together, *because* of each other. It's crazy to think that you guys once upon a time didn't get along now. But you two fixed each other, you were there for him throughout him grieving for Jessie and he helped you through all that your mental health and this crazy house threw at you. You've been the best prefect pair that the students could have asked for this year. Plus, you made him your deputy, kept him on the straight and narrow and gave him something to do when he could have had other things on his mind."

"It's true. He talks about you a lot, he'd kill me for saying it, but you're his hero. I don't think he'd have gotten through the last year without you. He looks up to your strength and feeds off it," Ameliah grinned, soppily.

"You guys are going to make me cry." I palmed the best I could at my eyes to stop the tears from falling, but that was inevitable. "He's been like a brother to me, I'm so glad we still have another four years together, even though sometimes he does my absolute nut in. He's exactly who I needed to live with when I think about it. His brutal honesty, although sometimes can hurt, is what you need from a brother, he puts me in my place," I said as I smiled through the tears. "You picked a good one missy." I pulled her closer to me once more and kissed the side of her head. "I hope you two make each other incredibly happy. I mean with a body like that I'm sure he already does," I winked at her and she looked up at me with shocked, yet amused eyes.

"Hands off," she said as she elbowed me in the ribs, I pushed her away in return. "He's mine."

"Don't we know it. Don't think I haven't noticed those bruises on his neck. We've been sharing the concealer you lent me last year."

She rolled her eyes. "I always wondered where I'd lost it. That was thirty bucks I'll have you know."

"It's almost all gone," I chuckled. I wasn't surprised with the rate I'd had to paste it on Noah's neck and mine on occasions.

"You and Isaac are both vampires," Charlie said to Ameliah. "It's gross."

"Who's a vampire?" Isaac asked as he approached us, two hot drinks clutched in his hands from the food truck.

"Why are we talking about vampires?" Rafael trailed just behind Isaac and slid his way in between me and Charlie.

I looked at Ameliah and Charlie and we shared a knowing smirk before I shook my head at the other two. "No reason," I replied as Isaac wrapped his arms around my waist, I leaned into his touch and whispered. "I'm really glad you're here." I grinned like an absolute loony as he placed kisses down the side of my neck. Vampire. I swatted his hand away and reminded him we were in public, but to me it really didn't matter. I'd become so intoxicated by his scent, that cedar wood musk and his favourite mango shower gel had been something I'd missed immensely when we were broken up.

"I wouldn't be anywhere else." He ruffled my curls softly, before his hands wound around my waist once more. "Just two more exams babe and you're out of here."

"Is it weird that, that actually makes me quite sad? I'm not sure I'm ready to leave, this place is my home," I said and that same lump, the one that came about every time I thought about leaving Cherrington Academy, bobbed to the top of my throat. It pushed tears into the pools of my eyes that I'd tried to cling to. It was such a bittersweet feeling, I'd found such a safe haven here when I'd needed it the most. The next steps at university were so unknown.

"Not at all," he said as he pulled away from me and took my hand in his. "I miss this place all the time, probably why I've spent so many of my breaks here. But, you aren't going to be alone. You and Noah are both headed to Ottawa, plus I'm just going to be two hours away in Montreal, I'll be there every other weekend - you'll be begging me to leave."

"Plus, you'll have me and Jay in Toronto," Charlie interrupted. "We will literally be just a few hours' drive away. There will be no separating us," Charlie said as he shovelled the fries he was sharing with Rafael into his gob.

They'd gotten grossly cute over the last couple of months, practically inseparable. Good thing Charlie hadn't been prefect this year, who knows when any of that work would have gotten done. I had to look away as Rafael started to feed Charlie the fries, it was enough PDA to churn anyone's stomach.

"Why are we best friends with him again?" I muttered for only Isaac to hear. It felt good to be able to say that again, about all of us. The road had been rocky, but we were all on solid ground now and it was incredible to know that in just a few weeks I'd be on that Graduation stage with my best friends. My boyfriend and Jay in the crowd as well to share in the experience we didn't get to enjoy last year. A shot at redemption.

"You made a choice about your major?" Isaac asked. I'd been going back and forth for months over what to choose. I'd contemplated heavily about Gender Studies, but realised it involved way too much Sociology for my liking. I just wanted to do something that would make a change, being a prefect for the last year had really lit a rocket inside me to want to help people, make real change for them.

"I'm going to major in Public Administration, being in Ottawa I'll hopefully get some hands-on work with politicians, learn about policy and how it all works from the inside. I want to be writing those bills that change everything."

"You're going to be incredible. I'm so proud of you," he beamed down at me and tipped up my chin to capture my lips.

We'd become so caught up in each other, we hadn't even realised that our coffees had gone cold on the ground. "Well, it's not like I've been cold with you glued to me." I giggled, as he pinched at my sides. "Although, I do feel bad that I currently have no clue what the score is."

"It's 3-2 to us," Ameliah commented, her eyes glued to her man on the field.

"Do you think you could sneak me in tonight?" he asked, that mischievous grin he'd harboured all of that first year I knew him, spread across his face once more.

"And what do you suggest I do with my roommate? He loves me, but there's no way in hell he'd let you stay whilst he's still in the room. He knows how handsy you are."

"I'll be good," he whined.

"I'm not going to lie, but I'd find it really hard having you in my bed and not even getting to kiss you," I groaned.

"Now who's handsy?" he retorted.

"You're both gross," Ameliah chuckled. "You

literally can't keep your hands off each other for more than two seconds."

"Can Noah not just stay in your room for a night? You're the deputy prefect, you don't have a roommate, that must grant you some kind of leniency?" Isaac all but begged.

"Fine, fine, I'll have him at mine. Don't say I don't do anything for you Edwards boys." She shook her head, but I could see that cheeky grin on her face. She'd never say no to having Noah in her bed. Nobody would.

"Well then. I know what we'll be doing tonight then," I said as I ground my hips against Isaac a little suggestively.

"What's that then?" he asked, his eyebrow raised.

"Studying for my biology exam."

We'd studied for about ten minutes before we'd wound up back in bed and distracted for the rest of the night.

It didn't matter though. I'd breezed through my exams. The many timetables I'd planned for me and Noah, so we could combine our prefect duties with all the prep and revision we needed for our exams, had worked like a dream. That's something that Joshua said had been Charlie's downfall as a prefect, he hadn't shared the load enough with his deputy. Me and Noah had got that down to a tee.

That didn't take away from the stress of the final exams though, everything rode on them, but we'd made it out the other side with no sign of a breakdown in sight.

It made standing on that graduation stage together so much more satisfying. We stood next to each other as they announced Rafael to be valedictorian, no poem this year, but there was a little shout out to the both of us, alongside Charlie and Isaac for all we'd helped him achieve in bringing together the LGBTQ community and the world of sports. The project had only just properly begun, but universities and schools across Ontario were starting to take on our initiative. Pride shone in my smile as he walked away from the podium and kissed Charlie on the lips. We'd come so far from the boy who wouldn't pull down his hood at the start of the year in classes or corridors.

I was so excited and overwhelmed as I shared the stage with my classmates, choir colleagues and my best friends, I hadn't even batted too much of an eyelid when Wyatt and his parents sat next to Isaac in the crowd.

My parents had showed up too, which actually shocked me. Mainly because I hadn't really gone out of my way to let them know when Graduation was. I'd just dropped it in the very rare passing conversations we'd had. They didn't cry throughout the ceremony or beam proudly and whoop and holler for their child like Eliza and Freddie Castle had when Noah was called to the stage. They hadn't even approached me when I left the stage, it had been the Castle family who'd swooped straight in and hugged me and Noah tightly. They'd congratulated me like I was one of their own. Even Wyatt, who had slowly grown on me, gave me a big brotherly hug.

I'd come to terms with the fact that, that was never going to be how my parents were. They weren't bad people, they just didn't want to be parents. They were to career focused, they never neglected me, I'd never gone without, but their heart and emotions just hadn't been in our relationship. As I turned eighteen, I realised it didn't hurt me as much anymore. I had my own family now. They surrounded me on the stage and they beamed at me from the crowd.

I locked eyes with him as I pulled away from Eliza's

grip once more, nodded at my parents from where they clapped along with crowd, but it wasn't them I was headed towards. It was him. He was who I needed to be with, the person who's eyes I could feel on me the whole time I'd been on stage. He carried a ridiculous bouquet of flowers, which he dumped in my arms as he kissed my lips softly, they were moist from the few tears I'd seen him shed as my name was called.

"Congratulations Mr High School graduate, how does it feel?" he asked.

"Good, it feels really good. I can't believe I made it, there were way too many points along the way where I was just ready to drop out." He swooped some curls out of my face and kissed my cheek. "Next stop Ottawa, hey? I know I made the right choice there." I gazed towards the Castle family, where Wyatt had Noah in a headlock and Eliza and Freddie were reprimanding their boys with the proudest of smiles.

"I'm glad you're going to have them so close by, even Wyatt. Turns out he's actually a good guy, even if he is a bit of a man whore."

"Don't remind me," I said, rolling my eyes playfully. Wyatt wasn't a threat; he never had been.

"I love you, you know," he said, as I stared him straight in those big, beautiful gunmetal grey eyes that were still as hypnotic as they were on the first day I met him. Every fibre of my being vibrated as he moved closer to me and took my hands in his. "I really freaking love you and god I wish I'd said it this last year, but I need you to know now that I'm so madly in love with you."

And I did. I knew.

I am beyond thankful for everyone who bought and supported book one of the Cherrington duology as it made publishing Coming Home possible!

To my family, who continue to be beyond supportive towards my dreams of being an author and love me regardless of how many books I write or sell.

To Ella, Paige and Liv, who are honestly the best friends I could ever ask for. I love that you're now so interested in my writing and I love sharing it with you. Thank you for everything and for just always being here for me, I love you guys so much!

Finally to my best writing pals: Han, Lou, Alicja and Leanne, damn I adore you. Not only are you always motivating me and cheering me on, but you're my biggest inspiration when I'm writing away because y'all are thriving! Not only that, but you are ALWAYS there whenever I need you. We bonded over our love of writing and books and somewhere along the way you all became super close friends to me and now I just can't imagine you lot not being in my life. Thank you for all your support of writing this book – Leanne and Alicja when I was writing it in July 2019 and Han and Lou for being my publishing pals, I couldn't be happier to share a publisher with you and be on this journey with you two! Love you lot!

Also, big thanks to Hayley for designing such a beautiful cover, I freaking love it and to SRL for taking a chance on the sequel to Cherrington Academy and giving me the duology I've always dreamed about.

ABOUT THE AUTHOR

Rebecca Caffery is a BA Politics graduate and enthusiast, who can always be found curled up reading somewhere when she isn't working on a new novel idea. She grew up in Birmingham, UK, where she's been writing since the age of fourteen. It wasn't, however, until she moved to Canada for a year that she found her voice and passion writing again and was inspired to write Cherrington Academy.

Outside of the writing and reading world she is a Netflix addict and loves to watch anything with a heart wrenching romance plot, just like the books she writes.

Where else to find her?

Twitter - @BeckaWrites

Book Blog – www.rebeccajcaffery.com

CPSIA information can be obtained
at www.ICGtesting.com
Printed in the USA
LVHW042055270421
685730LV00007B/7

9 781916 337398